His Missing Wife

Jaime Lynn Hendricks is an author with nearly 20 years' experience in print media and marketing. *His Missing Wife* is her first novel. She lives with her husband in New Jersey.

Jaime Lynn Hendricks

HIS MISSING WIFE

CANELO

First published in the USA in 2021 by Scarlet, an imprint of Penzler

This edition published in the United Kingdom in 2022 by

Canelo
Unit 9, 5th Floor
Cargo Works, 1-2 Hatfields
London, SE1 9PG
United Kingdom

A CIP catalogue record for this book is available from the British Library.

Print ISBN 978 1 80436 108 5
Ebook ISBN 978 1 80032 553 1

Originally published as *Finding Tessa* in the USA and Canada

Look for more great books at www.canelo.co

Printed and bound in Great Britain by Clays Ltd, Elcograf S.p.A.

1

For my parents, Hank and Geri

1

James

Flashing blue and red lights late into the night always spelled trouble. James's neighbors may have had their fill in the past, but that wasn't his fault. Tessa was the one with a flair for dramatics—a fallen branch meant calling a landscaper before the tree collapsed onto the roof. Grab a bat when the dog barked, in case someone was breaking in. Rush the plumber over for a leaky faucet before the flood destroyed their new home.

This time, it was James who had made the emergency call—to the cops. Because Tessa was nowhere to be found.

Three taps. A nightstick on the front door. Candy, their cattle dog, shot up and barked.

"No, girl!" James pointed, disciplining her. She took two steps backward before she turned and went obediently to her bed in the corner of the kitchen and slumped down with a sigh. James rose from the silver paisley-patterned chair that Tessa always called "fancy" and answered the door.

"Officer Cannon, sir. You the one that called?"

Officer Cannon stood at least six-foot-five, and even James had to crane his head north to look him in the eye. The man was mammoth. "Yes, I'm James Montgomery. Come in."

The screen door squeaked as James opened it for the cop, who revealed a typical officer crew cut under the hat he removed before stepping into the foyer.

"Great entryway," Cannon said.

As an interior designer, Tessa had taken advantage of the lofted ceiling. The walls were painted a faint silver, almost white, and so anyone could detect the slight metallic tint, especially now with the moonlight bouncing in from the front bay window. All the fixtures that held candles and pictures were chrome, and large crystals hung from the overhead chandelier. Tessa always said first impressions mattered.

"Thanks. My wife designed it," James said, wincing at her mention, and wanting to get on with it. The reason for the officer's presence wasn't to discuss home furnishings. "I think something happened to her. She's missing. Look over here."

James walked the officer to the back of the house and pointed to the window next to the kitchen table. It was his favorite part of the house. Five big windows in a semicircle surrounded their breakfast nook and had an unfettered view to the lake in the yard. It was a decent sized body of water for suburban New Jersey, and they were lucky enough to be at the end of the cul-de-sac. Private. Water on one side, woods on the other.

Now, one of the windows was broken. Shattered glass on the ceramic tile floor. A sideways chair. Strands of Tessa's dark hair, more than usual, in a clump on the ground. There were a few drops of blood. More than a few, actually. Splatters.

Just like the splatters on his shirt, which he'd already changed out of.

"Did you touch anything over here?" Cannon asked.

"No. Well, the back doorknob, which was unlocked, and I thought that was weird. We always lock it after we come in or let the dog in. I opened it when I couldn't find Tessa inside. I thought maybe she was having a glass of wine in the yard."

Cannon's eyebrow rose. "At nine at night? On a Thursday?"

James hesitated. "It wouldn't be the first time. But she wasn't feeling well. She said she didn't work today. I mean, she works from home, but said she was going to have soup and lie in bed. She texted me this morning. It was the last time I heard from her."

Cannon wrote in a pad. "Anything else?"

"It was late when I got home from work. Candy greeted me at the door and—"

"Candy?"

"The dog." He pointed to the now curled-up ball of fur breathing steadily on her bed. "She's usually upstairs in bed with Tessa when I get home late. Anyway, the house was dark, so I went right upstairs, thinking Tessa was sleeping. Her side of the bed was pulled back, but didn't look slept in. I checked the bathrooms, and she wasn't there. God forbid she had to go to a walk-in clinic or the emergency room if she was *really* sick, but I didn't get any Uber receipts to my email."

Officer Cannon looked at him with doubt.

"Tessa doesn't drive. She either walks or Ubers everywhere. So, I came into the kitchen."

Cannon took dictation like a pro, never asking for clarification, jotting down quick notes. "And that's when you found the broken window and the blood?"

"Yes. And her purse is over there on the counter." He pointed to the beige Michael Kors bag that he bought

3

her. "Her phone is plugged into the charger. That's when I knew she couldn't have left on her own. Women don't leave the house without their purse and phone." His hand went to his head. "The blood, officer. Do you think it's hers?"

Cannon pressed a button on the radio on his shoulder. "Can you get a forensics team and Detective Solomon down to 32 Lovett Road in Valley Lake?"

"Forensics?" James leaned his arm against the wall to steady himself.

Cannon's eyebrows rose and he pressed his lips together. "It doesn't look good." He stared pointedly at James, his eyes accusatory. "You always get home past nine?"

"No, not always. I—I had a meeting that ran late."

"And where do you work, Mr. Montgomery?"

"I'm the branch manager at Valley Lake Bank. We're trying—we, as in me, my boss, and my coworker—we're trying to secure the financing for the new shopping center that's going up off Main Street."

Officer Cannon shook his head and curled his lip. "All of those big stores are going to put our mom-and-pops out of business. We like our two-block Main Street. We don't need a Big Lots or a TGI Fridays in Valley Lake."

Neither of those were contracted with the builder as far as James knew, but it wasn't the first time he'd heard pushback from the locals who wanted to preserve their Norman Rockwell painting.

Since the local officer wasn't on board with the Town Center plans—most weren't—it was about twenty *you're-the-reason-this-town-is-going-to-shit* minutes later until the rest of the team showed up. A man and a woman, both with forensics, wore hip length coats emblazoned with the letters "CSI" on the back and dusted for fingerprints. Their long Q-tips swiped the blood drops on the window and the floor. The hair, Tessa's hair, was placed into clear evidence bags.

A man whom James assumed was Detective Solomon entered after forensics, and he looked right out of a true crime movie from the fifties. His beige trench coat hung to his knees and he wore a fedora tilted to the right. He was short and round, with a bulbous red nose and wire-rimmed glasses that attempted to distract from his lazy left eye that James noticed regardless. He reeked of cigarette smoke.

Detective Solomon approached James and shook his hand. "Mr. Montgomery."

"Hello, Detective," James said, shaking firmly. Solomon's hand was damp.

"It seems we have a bit of a problem?"

James repeated the story he told Officer Cannon, right to the last detail.

Solomon stood, deep in thought, and went into what was likely a prepared speech.

"Anything else missing?" he asked as he looked around, right into their living room where the sixty-inch television still hung on the wall, with speakers and other various electronics surrounding the space, not a rogue wire anywhere.

"No sir. Everything is here, as far as I can tell."

"Mmm. So, we have no reason to think this is a robbery gone wrong, then?"

"I really don't think so."

"Did you have any problems in your marriage?"

It's always the husband. "No, Detective. We're newly-weds. We got married on Memorial Day weekend, almost four months ago. Kind of a whirlwind romance. We eloped."

"I see." He, too, wrote down details in a pad. "How long were you dating?"

"About a month," James quickly lied. It was even less than that, and he suddenly felt stupid for rushing into something so huge. "It was fast. I know." He felt like he needed to defend his rash decisions to the detective.

"Mmm. And where did you meet?"

"In a bar." James paused, not wanting to give out all the real details of their initial meeting. Their situation back then was precarious at best. He'd lied to her in the beginning, but he didn't think those details were pertinent to the investigation.

"Aha." It was a statement. "Do you know if anyone wanted to hurt her?"

Yes, James knew of her past relationships. One in particular. But there were many bad situations from her past, even if she kept the details close to the vest. "She had some pretty terrible luck with men, from what I understand. A couple of abusive boyfriends. An abusive ex-husband too. She said she always jumped from relationship to relationship. She said didn't like to be alone, and I guess she made some mistakes."

Solomon looked up from his notepad. His eyes stared from above his glasses, which were now at the tip of his nose. "His name? The ex-husband?"

James shrugged. "I don't know. She refers to all her exes only as 'Asshole.' She's never given me any of their names. I don't think she wanted to be reminded of them." He shook his head slowly. "I've never pushed her for details. Maybe a mistake. It all just happened so fast, and I wanted to protect her. To show her that all men weren't like that."

Even if he'd heard they were.

"Mmm." The detective was a man of many words. "Is she originally from New Jersey? Age? Maiden name?"

"She's thirty-one." James thought back to one of their earlier conversations. "I don't know much about her upbringing except that it was bad. Foster homes and stuff. I never met her family. I think she has four siblings, but I don't know if they all have the same mom or dad. She said once that Tessa meant 'fifth child' so I just assumed. I don't know where she was from." He paused for a beat, then continued. "Her maiden name is Smyth, with a Y; she hadn't changed her last name to Montgomery yet. She's still Tessa Smyth." James, realizing his stupidity, put his hand on his head. "I don't even know if Smyth was her ex-husband's name or her maiden name."

"Mmm."

"She had it rough growing up. Clammed up every time I tried to talk to her about it. I don't know shit, Detective. I'm sorry."

The detective blew out a puff of air. Scanned the kitchen again. Looked at Candy. "I think there's a good chance, whoever did this, your wife knew him. Or her."

"What makes you so sure?"

"The dog." Solomon nodded his chin toward Candy. "If a stranger breaks in, a dog will lose its mind. Most likely would've attacked, or at minimum warned your wife with excessive barking. Does your dog have any wounds on her?"

Glancing in her direction, James said, "I don't think so, but I didn't think to check." He waved her over. "Come here, girl," he said quietly.

Candy rose and walked toward him, her head low like she'd just destroyed another pillow. James pet her, from her black and gray head, down her brown spotted paws, and to her tail with the white tip, pressing insistently on her bones to see if she yelped from an unseen bruise. There were no visual cuts, nor any blood on her fur.

"No. She's okay," James said, and kissed her on the head. "Good girl, it's okay, girl. We'll find Mommy," he whispered in the dog's ear, and looked at her like he expected an answer. In English.

Solomon's notebook snapped shut and he asked for a recent picture.

James crept into their dining room to the sideboard where they kept their wedding pictures. They'd had someone snap them with his cell phone while they were at the courthouse at city hall, and then he had them printed from a photo app. He opened the drawer and they were still in a pile, unorganized.

His favorite picture had the two of them gazing into each other's eyes, but he realized that was a profile shot and would be of no help to the police. He placed it to the side in favor of one that had them both facing the camera. He was in a black suit with a white shirt and a yellow tie— yellow, her favorite color. Daffodil. She'd always called colors by what they represented. The designer in her and all. She wore a flowy off-white dress with lace sleeves and a sweetheart neckline, but not a proper wedding gown. Her dark hair cascaded in waves just past her shoulders, and her storm-colored eyes glowed with happiness.

Her expert makeup job covered the bruises.

James held on to it for a few seconds before handing it to Detective Solomon.

"She has bangs in this picture, but she's been growing them out. Tucks them behind her ears now," he said, making the same gesture she always did when she moved the hair out of her face. "Please find her, Detective," he said, and pushed out a tear.

James still wanted to keep their early life a secret. To be honest, he knew she'd lied about her past anyway, and with good reason. People lie all the time. But was she really Tessa Smyth? He still didn't know.

And he needed to make sure the detective didn't find out what really went on between them earlier that week.

Thankfully, he'd already destroyed the note he left her that morning.

2

Tessa

To say I'm a creature of habit is an understatement. I have a type, and I have a cycle with men that I'm unable to break, always overlooking their flaws. No matter how obvious they are—all my exes practically wore a flashing neon sign that said "Fix Me." Asshole One, Asshole Two, Asshole Three—I lost count. Eventually, I just called all of them Asshole. Asshole Number Whatever.

And now, here I am, running out after yet another man punched me. Again. And again. Then, he crossed a line, even for me. But this time, I thought ahead. This time, he'll pay.

After walking all night, I finally got to a bus station in a town twenty miles away. Yes, I walked twenty miles in the dark, following the side roads, careful not to be spotted by traffic cameras. It was warmer than it should've been this time of year. Even for nighttime, the heat bounced off the gravel and made my clothes stick to my body, but I had to get far, far away.

After purchasing my ticket with cash, I waited. The area around me smelled of homelessness and despair. The walls were piss yellow and reminded me of my first foster home when I was twelve. I've been separated from my half siblings and my full brother Kenny for a long time.

Unfortunately, my mother was a Monopoly board and the little silver penis game piece always trotted all over her, passed GO, and ironically never had two-hundred dollars. Last I heard, Kenny had a few kids with a few different women, half-brother Christopher was doing some hard time, and the half-sister twins, Sara and Tara, ran off. No one cared about the well-being of me, the youngest one. And thus began my cycle of LOVE ME.

I was giddy for the bus that would propel me away from yet another situation where I was in too deep. Married this one, too. I never learn. Get abused once, shame on you, get abused ten times, shame on me. This one, though, he was the best at hiding it. Not like the other Assholes. The first one I married—which wasn't even legal because I was underage and he, well, wasn't—was a tattoo artist. The one who threw boiling water on me and gave me the dimpled scar on my arm. The other men through the years varied from beer distributor to truck driver to landscaper. This last Asshole was legit nine-to-five, except when he had to work late, which was often. "Entertaining," he said. Because he had a stable job, I thought he was the ticket out of my hellish round-and-round of bad men. I thought I was finally going to be the lead in the rom-coms that raised me—girl gets cheated on, trusts no one, has hijinks with a new guy, falls in love despite their differences, and lives happily ever after.

Nope. Instead, he sniffed out the girl who needed to be rescued, and, pretending I was the heroine in said rom-com, I fell for it. He told me later that he saw my bruises when we met and knew I'd be a good little punching bag. Someone who wouldn't make waves. Someone who would let him do whatever the hell he wanted, because where was I going to go? Like I didn't know he was sleeping with his coworker too. The one with the Spanish name. Worst-kept secret in town.

Still in my hard plastic chair at the depot that makes my butt numb, I fiddle with my purse, where I have some newly purchased makeup. I open a compact. Peering into the mirror, I'm thankful the cut that probably needs stitches is hidden under my hair and you can't see the huge lump. The blue and purple around my left eye has slightly faded into a putrid yellowish green that is hard to cover with foundation. I press the foam pouf into the cream-to-powder mix and dab it under my eye, which cakes a bit under my not-enough-sleep wrinkles. Checking the clock on the wall, the one that looks like it belongs in a school classroom, I see I have enough time to check my bandage.

The bathroom in the public facility stinks like shit and bleach. I set my brand-spanking-new roller bag by the sink and place my purse on top, then remove the gauze on my upper arm. I cut myself on the glass that I staged in the kitchen. Which was good, actually. More blood than I intended to leave at the scene. The gauze doesn't stick to my lacerated skin as I peel it back—God knows I used enough ointment before I applied the dressing. The wound throbs and the covering with the dollop of bacitracin has given it a pus topping that begs for air, but experience tells me that I need to keep it hidden for now. A hefty pour of hydrogen peroxide and an airy, good night's sleep are at least a day away.

As I'm reapplying the ointment, the door creaks open and a woman, who could be sixteen or forty, drags herself in. She's carrying only a torn backpack and she gives me a half smile and a shrug when she notices our matching bruises before she disappears into the stall. I wash my hands and use the air dryer, which isn't one of the high-powered ones that are at all the restaurants now. This one spits out cool air that wouldn't move a feather. I pull back and wipe my hands on my clothes. I check again in my purse for two prepaid burner phones with all the bells and whistles—one for me to use at my leisure, and one for my contact to be able to get in touch with me. I'll need to assimilate into life, wherever I land.

North. I'm going north, just far enough away from the last mistake. He'll pretend to be worried, because who doesn't worry about their missing wife? Fuck him. Let him find someone else to abuse. Unless my plan works and they arrest him, of course. Although an arrest is hard without a body. Maybe it'll be *just* suspicious enough that it'll ruin his cushy life. Wearing two faces is not in his best interest, even if it's in mine.

Plus, I have help. Not *everyone* is on his side. I know some pretenders too, Asshole.

As I grab my bags to leave, I hear sniffing on the other side of the stall door. It's the teenage forty-year-old. Could be hushed cries, could be a coke habit.

I know better than to get involved in other people's problems. It never works out how you think it will.

Back in the waiting area, the muffled announcement comes out of the speaker. I'm sure it's advising us of a departure, but the way it sounds, he might as well be confirming an order from a clown face at a Burger King drive-thru. The number to my bus is flashing on the digital panel above my head and I follow the rest of the sad sacks who line up to board. Judgment weighs heavy when they see the covered bruise on my face and the bandage around my arm. They know I'm running away. But they won't ask. Maybe they know not to get involved in other people's problems too.

But of course, I am running—who gets on a bus from here to there at this ungodly hour? Everyone here must be leaving something, or someone, behind. The hippie in the hemp shirt with his pregnant girlfriend are probably escaping parents who think they're too young to marry and start a family. I happen to agree with them, but kids make mistakes.

Don't I know it.

Even the little old man in the little old man cap, wearing his proper sports jacket with the suede elbows and carrying the luggage without wheels is probably escaping life in a retirement home. He was probably told *We don't have the energy for you anymore, Dad. We have the kids and their homework and their extracurricular activities to think about.* His family probably gave up on him, and he's off to meet the new love of his life from the senior online dating site. I really hope that's the truth.

Some passengers are running away, and some are running toward something. I still don't know which I'm doing.

All I know is, I won't stop until Asshole Number Whatever pays for what he's done to me.

3

James

James couldn't sleep that night—why would he? The cops were just at his house. It was early, maybe seven A.M. when his cell beeped with a text from Rosita.

> A Detective Solomon left me a message.
> Said it was about you and Tessa. What
> happened?

He'd never called or texted Trey and Rosita last night—it was too late by the time the police left. He had enough other shit to deal with.

Rather than calling or texting her back, he ambled into the kitchen—the room that previously contained Tessa's blood and hair. Nothing like some evidence to go with your morning coffee. He decided to duct tape a garbage bag over the broken window to keep the air-conditioning contained. He'd have to make some calls over the weekend: one, to see if insurance covered it, and two, to get it replaced.

Candy followed his every move, as he went to the closet where they kept the extra garbage bags, and then into the garage, where he kept the duct tape on the second shelf. After retrieving it, he cut the bag into a square and secured it into place. He didn't know what else to do.

It was Friday morning. Was he supposed to go to work?

James looked at the leftovers—the leftovers from his wife. The stains on the tile, what was left after the swiping. The glass was cleaned up. Her hair was gone. After forensics left, well after midnight, he had gone to bed and forced himself to fall asleep, even though it was that horrific, broken sleep. Every sound woke him with a start. At least it was a nice departure from the nightmares. *It's all a misunderstanding*, he told himself. He decided to call his neighbor.

After starting the coffee, James strolled into their home office. He could call from the landline that Tessa insisted they have, but then went back into the kitchen and grabbed his cell. A clear record of what he was trying to do. *Looking for her* could be important, if it came up. The trilling of the phone line ate at him as he waited for an answer.

"Hello?" Nick said, his voice still scratchy with before-morning-coffee sound.

"Nick. Hi. It's James Montgomery."

"James," Nick said, then paused. "Did Candy get out again?"

Candy had gotten out of their yard three times in the last few months, always ending up at Nick and Gwen's, hovering at the open door of their pool house. She was the reason they'd met their neighbors to begin with. James had frantically run to each and every house that first time she'd gone missing, pounding on their doors, until Candy's wiggling butt came to the front with Nick. The faint smell of bacon wafted out of the entryway to the porch, where he saw a very satisfied Candy waiting, belly full of pig fat.

"Nah, nothing like that. How are you doing?" James decided to start. He didn't want to jump right into oh-my-God–Tessa-is-missing. A fact-finding mission seemed like a better idea.

Nick cleared his throat. "Woke up on the right side of the grass, so all is well. Is everything okay?"

"I was wondering if maybe Tessa contacted Gwen last night? For wine? Or anything else?"

There was a pause, then Nick answered. "Last night? Nope. Caleb has the flu. Gwen was taking care of him all night." He stopped, clearly not welcoming the intrusive early phone call. "Is there something I can help you with, or—?"

James sighed. "I don't know, Nick. Tessa disappeared last night. I got home late, and she was missing."

"Missing?" Doubt crept into his voice. "Are you sure she didn't—"

"I had the cops here. The kitchen window was broken. There was blood."

"Jesus!" There was a muffled sound, as if Nick cradled the phone to his shoulder, and he called for Gwen. When the voices came back into focus, James heard Gwen's voice as Nick told her what happened.

The percolator stopped with a glub, and the scent of Colombian beans filled the space around him. James opened the cabinet above the dishwasher and retrieved a mug and poured. He grabbed two small sugar packets that Tessa had swiped from Dunkin' Donuts and flicked them with his middle finger, then tore the paper and emptied them into his mug. Another text vibrated on his phone, which he ignored at first. "Her purse and phone are here. The cops suspect foul play. Did either of you happen to hear anything? See a parked car that didn't belong? Anything?"

James pressed his home button on his phone, and it was another text from Rosita.

> You have to call me before I call the detective back. I don't want any trouble.

James's face scrunched up. Rosita was pushy, she'd been gunning for his job when he was promoted right after he married Tessa. He tapped back.

> Gimme 5

Gwen came onto the line. "Oh my God, is everything okay? What happened to Tessa?"

Gwen and Tessa had struck up an unlikely friendship after the first time the neighbors rescued Candy. Gwen and Nick were about James's age and had a four-year-old son, Caleb. Gwen was obsessed with him, already a helicopter mom. She hovered over him at the playground, fought with strangers online about the necessity of vaccinations, checked all his food and clothing to make sure the materials were natural, and would drop everything just to get him a spoon. James wouldn't be surprised if she was still breastfeeding.

That's what made the friendship unlikely—Tessa had never shown interest in children. The contrary. She'd cover her ears whenever one cried in their vicinity, and she'd roll her eyes if there were children next to them in a restaurant, even if the kids were well-behaved. Yet she'd spent an awful lot of time down the block with Gwen during the day when she was supposed to be chasing clients.

"I don't know what to think. When was the last time you saw her?" James asked.

There was a pause on the line, and James could practically see Nick and Gwen whisper-fighting. The silence was deafening until he heard a wail from Caleb in the background. *Find Boo Bear, Mommy! Now!*

"I haven't seen her this week, but I gotta go. Here's Nick."

Just like that, she was gone, and Nick was back on the line. "Hey, man, if you need anything, call us, okay?" he said.

"Yeah, thanks. I'm going to stop into the police station before work. See if they've figured anything out yet. Let me know if you guys remember anything."

The line went dead, leaving Rosita's text staring up at him. He scrolled through his contacts and pressed her name.

It rang once. Twice. He pictured where she was in her condo, just five minutes away. Was she in the master bathroom, diligently applying her false eyelashes that she wore every day? Rolling her bleached-on-the-bottom hair into big curls, like she always wore it? Sitting on the bed, dressed, pressing her heel into one of the stilettos she always paired with her suits? Draping herself with a blazer, over a too-small tank top? Applying a pink metallic gloss on her plump lips? Lips that had—

"James!" she screeched into the phone, in a whisper, even though he knew she was alone. Probably. She was *probably* alone. She'd better be alone. "What the hell is going on? Why would a detective call me?"

"Tessa is missing. She disappeared last night. While we were out."

"*We* weren't out, James. It was a group thing." She said it with obvious contempt.

Originally, it was her idea to take VistaBuild out for drinks to try to win them over. Their corporate headquarters were in the DC area, although their direct contacts, Andy and Kyle, worked at satellite offices, and they'd already been approved for funding by James's bank and two others. Rosita wanted an edge. She'd mentioned to James, in a too-close whisper after VistaBuild left, that he should stay for a few more drinks with Trey and Aleesha. But really, with her. It turned into couples' night.

Only James and Rosita weren't a couple.

"Well, anyway, I told them we were all out with Vista," James said. "They probably just want to confirm that I was there all night."

She huffed. "I didn't see you *all* night."

"You know what I mean."

"Yes, I know what you mean, but you weren't there all night. You were gone for about a half hour. You told us you had a nosebleed. It was right before Trey came in."

Fuck, she'd heard him say that? He had to think of something to say when Andy noticed blood on his shirt. James paused. *Careful.* "I had to move my car. You know they ticket or boot or tow the cars in that vacant lot across the street after eight. I was trying to find a place to park on Main. It was packed, and yes, I had a nosebleed. I get them all the time. But I was just moving the car," he said again, to drive the point home. *See, I wasn't doing anything violent.* "I came right back in."

Her lips smacked together, finishing her gloss. He knew the sound well. "What am I supposed to say, James?

20

I don't want to lie, but I don't want you to get in trouble either."

"Just tell them the truth. We all went out for drinks after work. I left a little before nine. I mean, that *is* the truth."

It was the truth, and one more thought crept into his head.

Rosita was late. He'd met Andy and Kyle at the restaurant right after six, and she didn't get there till almost seven. They left the bank at the same time. Where was she?

"I'll be a little late this morning. I'm going to see if the cops have any new information. What time are Andy and Kyle coming back in?" The two men had been in and out of their office all week.

"Early. Before ten," she said. "Well. Anyway. Let's hope the cops find Tessa."

She hung up without uttering a *goodbye*, and James noticed the edge to her voice.

Yes, he'd stop at the station. Right after he dropped his shirt off at the dry cleaner's.

4

Tessa

Once I land at the bus depot, I grab my bag and head into the bathroom to brush my hair and teeth. It's early afternoon, and this station is filled with more people than the last one. These people look more like they are going on a trip rather than running away. There are parents with children clutching stuffed animals and even a few looking like they are headed to a business meeting, all dressed up, holding leather-bound cases.

In the bathroom, I lock myself in a stall and unzip my purse, fingering the little vinyl holder containing my cash—all nine thousand, one hundred forty-two dollars of it. Having been in this position before—leaving an abusive ex—that's goddamn lottery money. I can do anything. This time, I want to start over the right way. Every time I left an ex before, I'd jump right into something else, mostly because I had no money and nowhere to go. So I let men treat me however they wanted. I stunk of desperation, and I was always taken advantage of. Always.

There was no choice. Where was I supposed to go?

I finish freshening up, swipe on some extra deodorant, and walk back outside, a beautiful sunny day, still too hot for this time of year but with less humidity than my last living arrangement. There is a long cab line forming so I hurry to the back, not thrilled about my next destination.

On the bus ride, I had purposely researched areas on "that" side of town—the side with the million laundromats, the check cashing places, and the "WE BUY GOLD" signs in the window. Where people hang out on street corners to sell drugs or sell themselves.

In case my ex is watching me. He can't think I left and that I'm living high on the hog.

He'd rather have me killed.

When my turn in line arrives, the driver, Hobart, is an older Black man in his fifties with a potbelly and a stained yellow T-shirt that I know must've been born white. His hair, graying at the exposed sides, is under a beige-and-red plaid old-man hat. He looks adorable. Like a grandpa I've seen in movies. I don't know my grandparents other than what I've heard. If the stories are true, I'm better off without them. Not that I could ever believe a word out of my mother's mouth anyway.

He places my wheelie bag in the trunk and then plugs the address I give him into his GPS, and we are on our way to the no-tell-motel-type place I found. The pleather in the back seat is ripped and scratchy on my bare legs and the air is stuffy with a faint cigar smell. This cab clearly hasn't had a working air conditioner in years, and I can almost smell the last ten passengers.

When he pulls into the Empire Motel, Hobart slows the cab to a gentle sputter near the door to registration. The sign's neon is busted in half the spots and fluttering in the working spots. The outside is filthy and decaying. So filthy. Hobart turns to look at me in the back seat.

"You sure this is where you want to go, lady?" he asks with raised eyebrows, and his slight southern drawl and gravelly voice surprises me. He sounds like Ray Charles.

I press my lips together and smile a no-teeth smile. "I'm sure. What do I owe you?"

He tells me twelve dollars and twenty cents. I hand him fifteen and tell him to keep the change. I exit the vehicle at the same time he does, and he retrieves my bag from the trunk. He looks around, taking in the loitering men outside, ones with gang signs tattooed on their arms and faces. At the far end, there is a screaming baby in a carriage while the young mother ignores it and yells into a flip phone about child support. What can only be a prostitute comes out of one of the rooms and closes the door behind her, wriggling her skirt down as she leaves and then lights a cigarette. Marijuana is in the air as dollar bills trade hands in the form of a handshake.

I roll my eyes at how cliché the whole scene is. My guess is the cops don't even bother patrolling the area.

I'm not happy about needing to stay here for the night, but I need to be within walking distance to places where I'll be able to get my shady shit done. I don't drive and I'm not made of money so I can't cab it around all over the place until I find a job. I have to blend correctly in case I'm spotted. God knows the Asshole could have a tail on me. Controlling piece of shit.

This is all part of the bigger plan. I just have to survive the night. I've survived worse. I can do one night in the slum standing on my head.

"Hey, lady," Hobart says, then retrieves a card from the pocket over his heart on his T-shirt. He hands it to me with a grandfatherly look on his face. "If you ever need to go somewhere, you know, fast, call me. I'm usually around town. I can get here. Fast." He looks back at the grimy scene. "I don't want you standin' outside waitin' for no stranger. Not here."

"Thank you," I say, and I mean it. I slip his card into the front opening of my purse. "It was nice meeting you Hobart. Have a good day."

He shakes his head at me, still disapproving of my choice in sleeping arrangements, but gets back into the cab and drives off.

The wheels on my bag crunch over the paved lot and when I open the door to register, there is no relief from the outside heat. Yet another place with no working air conditioner. I hope the rooms are fitted at least with window units; I'll need the AC tickling my skin until the heat wave passes through and returns the weather to normal conditions. It should definitely be cooler this time of year than it currently is.

The man behind the bulletproof glass, Miguel according to his tag, is sweating profusely, making his dark hair stick to his head. He has a toothpick sticking out of his mouth, something another ex used to do. I hated it and still do. He scans my body up and down and curls his lip like a predator as I make my way toward him. I know his type—someone who sees a tiny, pretty little lady and thinks he can have his way with her. I've broken three noses in the last fifteen years and have no problem adding a fourth. My older brother Kenny taught me to push the bottom of my palm up from the nostrils to do the most damage. The instant blood, pain, and tears from the assailant give you ample time to run.

Confidently, I stride toward the glass and tap on it. Miguel doesn't take his eyes off me. My insides bounce around and I feel like a teenager running away from Jason

Voorhees at camp. "Hi. I need a room for the night." Never let them see you sweat.

The scene out front has left me shaking. If I wasn't so terrified of guns, I'd have one in my purse right now. I force myself not to look down and gaze with as much confidence as I can gather to meet Miguel's eye. Thank God the heat hides the real reason for my sweat.

Miguel slides a piece of paper into a drawer and pushes it my way, and it comes to the other side of the bulletproof glass. It wants all the regular information. Name, address, all of that. I pull the name Gloria Goldberg, address 250 Main Street, Apt. 12B, Phoenix, Arizona out of thin air. He won't ask for ID to prove it.

This is the type of place where cash is king, and I don't need a credit card on file for incidentals—it's not like I'm getting a steak with a 2005 Penfolds Shiraz delivered to my room from the kitchen. The "kitchen," from what I can see, is a dive bar across the lot with broken neon lights that probably only serves beer from a dirty tap. I don't even try to bargain the thirty-nine dollars a night even though I'm sure I can, and I take my key, an actual metal key on a yellowed plastic keychain, and go to my temporary Shangri-la on the second-floor corner.

Inside, the room looks like a casino and a garbage dump birthed a bedspread. It bothers me that it's so ugly because I've pretended to be an interior designer for years, when all I ever really did was look at Pinterest and shop the looks that I liked at Home Goods. None of which encompassed the mismatched mess in front of me. It was exhausting always telling the Assholes that I'd just moved to town and I was trying to build a client base. Like I went to college or something.

The bathroom smells of mildew but looks surprisingly fresh—looks can be deceiving—and has a small sink and stall shower. I have the sudden urge to scrub the place sparkling clean. Immediately, I remove the bedspread and swear that my next stop is Target or Walmart for a new, cheap pair of sheets and some rubber gloves and bleach. Even though I'll only be in this place for a night, I can't live in complete squalor. That was left behind with Foster Home Number Three, when I was fourteen and everything got bad. That was when I heard the twins took off from a different foster home, Kenny knocked someone up for the first time and left me, and Christopher did his premiere stint in juvie, which I know was just practice for the real thing.

All of them still had it better than I did there.

First things first: Time to blend.

The darker hair dye is hidden in my belongings, so I apply that, wait a half hour, and wash it out in the shower. The towel is slightly stiff, and I vow to add towels to my Target list. I certainly don't want "housekeeping" coming in and going through my shit. My skin crawls at the thought of them transferring one set of sheets to another room, unwashed, over and over. A black light in this room would probably make it glow like a Christmas tree.

After I dry my hair, I razor-cut three inches off, just because. It has a fun little uneven edge, just like me. I also give myself proper bangs again. It fits. Asshole didn't like the bangs and made me grow them out. Said I looked like a twelve-year-old.

I retrieve a pair of baggy jeans with holes in the knees and a ribbed tank from my suitcase and slip them on, and finish with foam flip flops that I got at the dollar store. My face is freshly washed from the shower, and I don't reapply my makeup. I need my bruise for Part Two.

Locking the door behind me, the stares at the fresh meat are obvious. Walking down the stairs, I get called vulgar names in Spanish as well as English, and I'm offered a "pick me up" from one of the men with cornrows who I saw making a deal earlier. I ignore them all, head up, crossbody bag strapped to my midsection, and set out on foot.

I know the ID place I'm looking for is less than a mile from here, a straight shot up the highway. It's still hot, still daytime although the sun is lower than it was when I arrived, and I curse the jeans that are sticking to my sweating legs, so I stop and roll up the baggy bottoms to let some air circulate. Just shy of a half hour later, I'm opening the door to the place and thankfully I see a young kid, twenty-one or so, at the register. He smiles at me.

"Hey, yo. Can I help you?"

"Hi." I smile, the really big *Yes You Can Help Me* smile, because it'll make him feel like my savior when I go into my sob story. He notices my black eye and I fake embarrassment and hold my hand over it, just for a second. "Yes, I'm really hoping you can help me."

"What do you need, honey?" He's chewing gum, his mouth wide open, and he has no game, yet he's trying to be sympathetic. It's what I'm counting on.

"Well. I—I just escaped a pretty bad situation a few days ago." I wince, like I've just been hit. I've certainly had practice perfecting the motion. He notices my fear as I dive headfirst into a speech I've given many times when I assumed half a new identity. "I need to get a job, and I need a picture ID. But the thing is, I left with nothing. I never had my birth certificate because I left home when I was sixteen, after my mother's boyfriend—never mind

28

that. I had to leave." The tears well up, as I let him believe I had a bad stepdaddy. The truth was worse, but he doesn't need to know that. The less detail the better. "The only thing I have is my Social Security card." My real one. Tessa Smith. Real number too. Go me.

The kid, Daniel, shifts uncomfortably, knowing he's being asked to make a fraudulent document. Not really *fraudulent*, but without the proper identification that the state requires to prove my identity. I need a head start on getting my life together. I *need* this ID. My stories have worked in the past.

"I know these IDs you make here have a state seal," I continue, "and I'll need that to prove my identity for when I finally get a license. It's all such a Catch-22. I need this ID to get a job so I can afford a place to live. I'll need proof of residence on a bill or something before I can even get a license. I just need a little bit of help." Puppy dog eyes. Even the bruised one. "I'm staying over at the Empire Motel right now. I don't want him to find me. I don't know where to go." If telling him about that shithole doesn't illicit a sympathetic response, nothing will.

He doesn't exactly say no, so I up the stakes. "I have a hundred dollars for you if you do this for me. Cash. I can give it to you right now. You can use my Social Security card, right?" I produce my authentic card and let it fall on the counter. It is really mine, but this kid knows I could've swiped it from any old granny's bag. "I'm just trying to stay alive. Get back on my feet the right way." For once, the truth. Mostly—it's hardly the "right" way.

He picks up the card and inspects it, probably used to seeing a hundred of these a day. His face is drawn, and I know I've won him over.

"Two fifty," he says.

Little shit. I try not to show excitement. "Oh my God, really?" The tears fall. Grateful tears, even if I fake them to make him feel like a hero.

Yes, I'm grateful. This ID card, with the state seal, is verifiable. It will have my full name, Social Security number, and picture, and works as a valid ID for pretty much anything. The best part is, my real Social Security number has three ones and two threes in it. That's always been helpful to me.

I fill out the form with the blue pen he provides, and he double-checks my card, again, then hands it back to me. Now is when I have to pray that he doesn't have the memory of an elephant, but something tells me he wasn't on the honor roll.

"I really can't thank you enough for this," I say, attempting to sign my name at the bottom. Then I shake the pen uncontrollably. "Crap. This one is out of ink. Can you grab another one for me?" I flash the million-dollar smile again.

"Sure," he says with a smirk and turns around.

It takes me literally two seconds to turn the ones on my Social Security number into sevens and the threes into eights. *Smith* quickly becomes *Smyth*. Not my first rodeo.

Daniel hands me a new pen, and I sign the form. He says he has to take my picture, and I ask him if I can use some makeup on the bruise, explaining that I don't want my permanent ID to remind me that I'm a punching bag. He obliges, and I dab concealer around it quickly. I wait five excruciating minutes for the photo to upload while he pecks my info, fake number and all, into the computer. He should've inspected my card closer and realized nothing matches anymore, but my guess is many people around here don't exactly graduate magna cum laude, if they

30

graduate at all. It prints out, and he laminates it. He hands it to me over the counter, then swiftly pulls it back from my open hand.

"Two fifty."

Little shit! But I smile as I peel back the bills, not letting him see the wad around it. "You saved my life."

He may not know he's been conned, but he really did save my life. Because now, I can try to have one again. This one better not include falling in love in 2.5 seconds. Better yet, this time I just want to know that *I* am loved.

I've been to plenty of battered women support groups. In secret, of course. Ninety-nine percent of the time, the women are afraid of men, afraid of relationships, and afraid to date again. Looking over their shoulders. Hiding. Scared. This is the only time of my life I'm ever in the one percent. Off the pharmaceutical smack for over a decade, bad men are still like a drug to me. I don't know if they sniff me out or if I sniff them out, but every relationship I've been in, one of us has been a goddamn hound dog.

That stops now.

I tug one of my burner phones out of my bag and send a text to someone who's going to help me make Asshole a suspect in my disappearance.

> Got the ID, all went as planned. Did you put that stuff in the house yet?

I wait. I get the answer in two minutes.

> Not yet, but I will. He hasn't told me you're gone yet.

5

James

James swerved right into the police station and parked his blue Altima in a spot close to the front, one of the ones reserved for people on official police business. Trying to locate his missing wife counted, as far as he was concerned.

The heavy glass doors slid open automatically as he approached and there was a woman at a counter in the front. Her name tag said Sally Rosen, and she looked like a Golden Girl, set hair and all. Her glasses hung around her neck from a tortoiseshell chain against her long-sleeve black sweater, which James didn't understand in the surprise end-of-September heat. She typed into a computer as she cradled a phone between her ear and her shoulder, giving out instructions to someone new to town, asking about holiday garbage pickup.

People bothered the cops with the stupidest things.

"Can I help you?" she asked as she hung up the phone.

"Yes. I'm James Montgomery. My wife disappeared last night. I was hoping to talk to—"

She held her index finger up to stop him, then pressed a button on that space-age-looking phone. He didn't know if it was a switchboard or the key to running the galaxy.

"Detective Solomon, a James Montgomery is here for you." She hung up and pointed to a fake leather sofa near the door. "Wait there."

So she'd heard of him already. In a small town like Valley Lake, a missing woman was probably taken very seriously. Especially one missing under these circumstances. A kidnapping or, God forbid, a *murder*, only happened in those small suburban towns in those damn Lifetime movies Tessa occasionally made him watch.

And in those movies it was always the husband.

James plopped onto the brown pleather couch, keeping a good distance between him and another woman about his age, who no doubt had been directed there as well. The woman held her purse on her lap and looked him up and down. He squirmed, thinking he was recognized, but earlier he'd checked the online police blotter and Tessa's disappearance hadn't been released yet.

Another male officer opened a door from behind the counter and whispered to Sally, then they both looked at James. Whispered again. Snickered.

"Mr. Montgomery?" he called from the other side of the room. "Can you come with me please?" He pointed to a door at the far end of the hall.

James stood, his tired legs wobbly, and walked to a door. He tried to turn the knob, but it was locked. Two seconds later there was a vibrating buzz and the door clicked and gave way. He opened it and the officer stood right in front of him.

"Mr. Montgomery. I'm Sergeant Lancaster. You saved us a phone call. Detective Solomon wanted to speak to you this morning."

Terrific. If he'd kidded himself for even a second that they didn't view him as a suspect, that idea was out the window.

He followed Lancaster down a long hall, narrow, with overhead fluorescent lights. The walls were light-gray or "ash" in Tessa lingo, and the doors on both sides were a faded blue, or "stormy sky." At the end of the hall on the left, Lancaster waved a key card over a small electronic box and the door opened. James's stomach tightened as he walked through the door.

Detective Solomon sat at a rectangular metal table and waved at a matching metal chair. James lowered himself into the cold, rock-hard chair, feeling like he was ten and had just got busted for nailing a classmate in the chops. Solomon had a stack of manila folders to his right and a single sheet of paper in front of him, which he stared at without making eye contact. He pushed the paper toward James.

"What am I looking at?" James asked.

"Tessa. We ran her current Social. And I say current, because it's not real. That number isn't even in existence."

James swallowed heavily, his Adam's apple bobbing up and down, which he realized too late made him look guilty. He knew the number on her ID card wasn't real.

"That's impossible. She has a state ID card." That was the truth. *Just the facts, ma'am.* "I gave it to you last night."

"Mmm. We can't find her in the DMV records. No license?" Solomon asked.

"No. She doesn't drive."

Was that even true? He'd bought her story about why she never got her license. Did she not bother to learn, or her foster parents, who were only in it for the money, wouldn't teach her? *Too many other kids,* they'd said. She was more comfortable walking anyway. That's why Valley Lake, where James worked, was such an attractive option when they decided to buy a house. Main Street, where all the town's industry was located, was less than two miles away. She welcomed the walks to get what she needed, and in this day and age, anything else they wanted could be delivered.

"A state ID can't be faked, Detective. Right?" James doubted his own statement, for *reasons*.

"Gone through the proper channels, no, it can't be faked, and her ID is real, which leads us to believe that she *hadn't* gone about getting it the right way. But as you said last night, you really didn't know much about her, did you?" He paused before he started with his real questioning. "Did Tessa come from money?" Solomon asked.

That question gobsmacked James, enough for him to chuckle audibly. "No."

"Something funny, Montgomery?"

James straightened. "She didn't have anything when we met. She'd just barely got her design business off the ground when... when this happened."

"So basically, you married a woman you didn't know much about, took her word for who she was, and now she's gone?" Solomon asked. "Gone, and left behind all that blood? Actually, come to think about it, we haven't even verified that it's her blood yet."

The accusation hung in the air around him, but James was undeterred. "I'm the one who called you, Detective. I gave you access to everything in the house. I let you collect DNA from the bathroom. I'm not hiding anything."

He was hiding a ton of shit, but he kept his expression neutral. Willed perspiration not to spring from his pores.

"Mmm," Detective Solomon said. "So, what brings you here this morning, then?"

James looked down. "I wanted to know if you found out anything. That's all."

"Nothing yet. It'll be another few days for that DNA you allowed us to gather. All we know is if she left on purpose, she might be pretty good at disappearing and becoming someone else."

"She didn't leave on purpose," James said, lifting his head.

"And you know this because?" Now Detective Solomon was interested, his eyebrows crawling toward his nonexistent hairline.

James chose his words deliberately. "Because we were in love."

"Mmm." He tapped a pen on the desk, the sound ricocheting in the sparsely decorated room. "Well, if you hear anything or think of anything that could help us identify who she was in the past, be sure to let us know."

"I will."

James stood and offered a hand, but Solomon didn't return the gesture, nor did he stand, or even look at him. He offered no parting words as James turned and left, navigating the narrow hallway himself. It was all he could do not to run out the front door.

Driving to work, he glanced at the clock. Just after eight A.M. The bank wasn't even open yet. The meeting with the detective didn't take as long as he'd thought. He was about to pull into the parking lot and noticed Rosita's red SUV was the only car there so far. Not wanting to be alone with her, he drove past the bank and down the block. Most nine-to-fivers weren't at their jobs yet and there was ample parking a mile past the bank on Main

Street. He guided his car into a spot and walked into Bean Addiction. The earlier coffee at his house wasn't enough to do the job on a morning like this one.

"Good morning, Mr. Montgomery!" Hannah, the barista, said. "The usual?"

Since he and Tessa had moved to town, no matter what time of day or day of the week he came in for his coffee, Hannah was there, and James wondered if she'd ever had a day off. She was probably twenty-five or so, and always wore her blond hair pulled back into a bun under her hat.

"Yes, please, and add a toasted bagel with cream cheese today."

"Rough night?" she asked with a chuckle.

Good Lord, how was he supposed to answer that question?

"You could say that."

He stepped away and gazed out the window, minimizing the possibility of being pressed further for details. Hannah took the hint as she focused on his order. Taking in the moment of normalcy, James spaced out, peering through the glass. A few old men sat on the benches that lined Main Street, probably up for hours already, reading newspapers, Bean Addiction cups in their hands. Were their lives going according to plan? Who were they? Widowers? Bachelors by choice? Or were their wives just missing?

Things weren't all roses with him and Tessa of late. It could be his fault. But the detective's discovery of who she was, or wasn't for that matter, rattled him.

"Here you go," Hannah called, and set his coffee and a small paper bag with their logo on the counter.

"Great. Keep the change," James said as he plunked down a ten.

He didn't usually leave double for a tip. He and Tessa weren't exactly flush with cash. If he was able to land VistaBuild, there'd be a sizable bump in his bonus come Christmas, but until then, they had to stay on budget.

They. Was that even real now? Or was it just him?

He careened his car onto Main Street and he made an illegal U-turn to go back to the bank. When he pulled into the lot, there were no other cars there. Where had Rosita gone?

Coffee in hand, he opened the front door with a passcode and secured it behind him—they didn't open for walk-ins for another forty minutes. He flipped on the lights with his free hand and the fluorescents overhead stuttered for a moment as the bank buzzed to life, room by room. He swiveled his head left to right—it was definitely empty, yet he felt like someone was here. Was he being watched? Of course he was. The bank cameras were always watching. But it was something else. What?

Tessa being gone was making him uneasy. That must be it. Settling into his office, a twelve-by-twelve space with a big window facing east, he set down his coffee and bagel and dropped his wallet and money clip into his center drawer, looking at the chairs on the other side of his desk, reserved for clients, with a wistful glance. Tessa had decorated his office. He told her what type of look he wanted, and he let her "vibe out," as she called it, in Home Goods. She'd returned with those two chairs, navy, sturdy, and comfortable, with rounded backs and black legs. The pictures on his wall were sloppy paint splatters in shades of blue, and he started to notice the little things. How the light-blue in the paint complemented the navy fabric on the chairs. How the penholder and his mainstay ceramic mug, both also blue, now fit the space. The fake palm tree in the corner of the room sat in a blue planter. Tessa's mark was everywhere.

Wait.

The blue leather picture frame that held their wedding photo on the desk was missing.

James ducked beneath the desk to search the floor. Nothing. Yanked open his drawers, his discomfort growing with each empty space. It was nowhere. A tear stung behind his eyelid, but he blinked it back. He felt like a shit—he'd only noticed it now because she was gone, but how long was the picture missing? It wasn't like he stared at it every day. And he knew it was there earlier in the week, because one of the guys from VistaBuild, Andy, commented on its simplicity when he was in the office earlier in the week and complained about how his wife forced him into all these elaborate shots.

But why would it disappear? Why now?

It was like Tessa was being erased from his life.

James turned on his computer and waited for Trey— he was going to have to tell him that he was taking a half day to try to sort this out, so he wanted to get a head start on his work.

Twenty minutes later, the door opened, and Rosita blew in wearing a fitted flower-patterned dress and another pair of what she privately called her "fuck me" pumps. Her huge emerald earrings didn't match her outfit, but she never took them off. He looked away, but she stopped at James's door.

"I thought you were coming in late?" she said. "Anything from the detectives?"

James looked up from the computer. "Nope." He wasn't going to divulge that they knew about Tessa's fake

Social Security number. How would that look for him? He knew it was fake too.

"That's a shame."

"Hey, were you here earlier? I passed to get coffee at Bean Addiction, and I swore I saw your car in the lot."

Her eyes popped for a half a second before she forced out an answer. "Nope. Must've been someone turning around. Or using the ATM."

He'd thought that for a minute too. "Did you speak to Solomon?"

"Left a message. Waiting for him to call me back."

"Good," James squared his shoulders toward the screen again.

Rosita hovered for a few beats, then turned to go to her smaller, windowless office.

That's when it hit him. The smell. Her perfume.

That's what was familiar to him in the entryway when he first got to the office. Rosita was there, and she lied.

"Hey, Rosita. Come back a second."

She turned toward him, her lips pursed seductively. "Yes?"

"My wedding picture is missing."

She shrugged. "And that has to do with me because... because why?"

His eyes narrowed. "No reason. I thought maybe you'd seen it. Are you sure you weren't here earlier?"

Her expression was of a six-year-old caught with her hand in the candy jar. "I said I wasn't. I—I have work to do." She turned and left. Quickly.

James smelled that perfume this morning. She lied. Why? He was going to find out.

6

Tessa

It's still light out after securing my ID card, so I walk to Walmart and buy a towel, a fitted sheet, a small pillow, and a large blanket. All together they cost less than forty bucks—gotta watch that bottom line—but I want to make sure I don't have to touch anything in that hotel room when I'm sleeping, and I need a nap before I figure out what to do with the rest of the night.

The rest of *my* night. My time. My *own* time.

A skinny white man-boy with a greasy ponytail who stinks like his last shower was four days ago offers to assist carrying my packages into my room. I decline, and he curses at me. He has meth mouth and the shakes, and probably wants to rob me for a fix. When I get inside, I lock the door and grab one of the burner phones and google my ex.

Nothing is out yet about him or me being missing. Maybe he didn't call the cops at all. I honestly never knew from one minute to the next how he'd react to any situation. Maybe he's glad I'm gone.

No. Too controlling. He'd never let me be the one to leave.

I strip the bed and lay out the sheet, then wrap myself in my new blanket and dream of my future. Of finally being loved.

When I wake, it's past dinnertime, even for me. My ex liked to eat early, as soon as he was home from work, and his dinner better have been ready, or else. I prefer my meals in the seven-thirty range, but who was I to argue with someone who controlled every last move I made? Now it's dark, and I remember that the only thing I've had all day was an energy bar I packed in my purse. I have two boxes of them with me. That's it. Energy bars and clothes. They're cheap and get the job done, and I learned as a preteen in Foster Home Number Whatever that sometimes, it was find yourself an energy bar or don't eat.

I've hoarded them my entire adult life. Asshole didn't try to starve me like Foster Mother Number Whatever, or that one ex-boyfriend from senior year of high school, before I ran off. (*Why are you so fat? I'm getting pizza, you ain't getting shit!*) That was said when I was a petite size four. The last Asshole and I ate quite well, actually. I mean, I could order the sixty-dollar New York strip, I just wasn't allowed to finish all of it, no matter how famished I was. There was something left in my subconscious that always needed a secret hiding place full of energy bars. Just in case. I'm like a dog with a bone, hiding the damn things in clandestine corners in case I never eat again. My favorite is strawberry granola, or chocolate with frosting if I'm feeling wicked.

This morning, I ate the chocolate one.

Looking out the window, the groups of people downstairs have doubled in size and male versus female ratio. Competing car stereos blast, one playing Jay-Z and another playing 50 Cent. Everyone talks above the sound, which makes everyone shout. It's like a garbage-people block party in the parking lot.

Thinking of the only person I trust right now, I take the card I got earlier and call Hobart, who agrees to pick me up in fifteen minutes. I spend the rest of the time covering my bruise and applying makeup that complements my bone structure. A contour brush can really go a long way. My eye makeup, overdone because of the bruise, looks harsh under the bathroom lighting, and I overcompensate with more eyeliner, which now that I step back and admire, looks good surrounding my gray eyes. Sultry. It should look better under the low lights of a bar.

I'm wearing jeans and a black silky tank and heels when Hobart texts me that he's waiting at the light right before the shithole and will be there in less than two minutes. He didn't want me waiting outside alone in the dark. Which is great really, because I'm used to feeling unsafe, but this situation outside right now is, in a word, hazardous. But it's only for tonight. Tomorrow, I'll find a place that's safer. I needed to be here, local to the shady places, until I secured my ID in case I was being watched as soon as I took off. I wouldn't want the ex to think I had money. *His* money. I've been swiping twenties off the grocery cash almost since the beginning.

This time around, I'm not going to hook up with the first loser I come across. Usually, I'll find someone who sweet talks me right out of my pants, and I'll believe that *this time it's different.*

It never is, though. My mother was a product of three straight generations of white trash, and it showed. She got pregnant with the twins at fourteen—by someone who worked construction with her father. A grown man. Gave birth when she was fifteen. Jumped from loser to loser, had babies with all of them—learned behavior from her own mother, who I don't even remember.

At least I did the right thing both times I got pregnant. My body, my choice. I really did try to break the cycle, and not popping out multiple children with no way to care for them was a start.

The TV was the unofficial babysitter in my house when I was little. The twins liked reality TV. Christopher and Kenny liked violent movies. I was raised by romantic comedies, and Reese Witherspoon was my favorite actress. I dreamed of being Elle Woods in *Legally Blonde* or Melanie in *Sweet Home Alabama*. Boss babes. Girls who get it done and are still able to find someone to love them, flaws and all.

A horn beeps. Hobart. I grab my denim jacket and open the door. Chants from the derelicts in the parking lot grow louder as I descend the stairs. Same vulgar shit as earlier in the day. One guy calls me *Mami* and says something about my *concha*. His girl slaps him across the face, then threatens to cut me, like it's my fault that her man is staring. Hobart's cab is just beyond her and she feels vindicated as I get into the back seat. Like her *Yeah, keep walking, ho* threat has anything to do with me leaving.

The cab still stinks, but I'm grateful for potbellied Hobart and his good sense.

"Thanks for coming," I say as he attempts to pull away from the melee.

"I knew you were gonna need me, in a place like this," he says as one of the men outside pounds his fist onto the trunk of the cab, prompting more *Ooohhhhh!* chants from everyone outside. "So, where you headed, lady?"

"Call me Tessa. We'll probably be great friends for a few weeks," I say with a laugh. "And where are we going?

I don't know, Hobart. I'm new to the area. I'm in the mood for a good meal. Take me someplace nice."

"There ain't nothing nice 'round here, but the next town over has a nice little area. Lotsa bars and restaurants. How far are you willing to go?"

"Well, how far is it? I don't want to be an hour away from my fantastic living situation. But take me anywhere that a girl can sit at the bar alone and have a nice meal with a glass of wine and not be considered a prostitute."

He chuckles. "Nah, not in that area. And you're lookin' at ten minutes. This side of town has the bus depot, so it gets the colorful people—I mean the *real* colorful people. The runaways, the whack jobs, the druggies—" He looks at me in his rearview mirror. "—the people hiding stuff."

Ahhhh, Hobart, you crafty devil, you. He knows I don't belong here. I'm quiet the rest of the ride, if only to appear mysterious now. Take that, Hobart.

Hobart assures me he'll be available for a ride later if I need one, my own personal Uber and bodyguard. The restaurant he recommends and drops me in front of looks like a classy wine bar from the outside. Asshole used to take me to a similar place in town. I open the door and survey the area as I step out of the cab. The place isn't very busy for a Friday night, which I welcome. Behind the bar, there are violet lights, amethyst if you will, uplighting the bottles against the mirrored wall, giving the place a jazzy vibe. I take my place on a leather bar stool, the kind that has a small spot you can lean back on, and I slip out of my denim jacket, laying it across the stool beside me.

I'm hungry. I'm thirsty. I'm in dire need of—

"Welcome to Wine Loft."

His tag says Damon, and he playfully slings a cardboard coaster with the restaurant's name and logo in front of me, then smiles when it lands *just so* at the tip of my fingers.

I've had bartenders before. Usually from the local watering holes that serve dollar beers and host dollar wing nights. Those from the past wore beer-logo T-shirts, cargo shorts, and flip-flops, and we'd do a shot or two, flirt, another shot, and I'd be counting ceiling tiles. Most of them were nice, until you did something without their permission, then the jealous rages always came out. Plus, they were alcoholics for the most part. Violent, small-town, trailer-living alcoholics.

Damon wears a long-sleeved black button down, with the wrists folded back, and I see the outline of a tattoo on his left arm peeking out of the cuff. His black pants and belt fit exactly right, and there's no ring on his finger. His dark hair is swooped off his forehead, making my stomach flutter. Dark hair is my thing. Every last Asshole had dark hair.

"What do you suggest, Damon?" I ask.

He looks at me funny, then at his own name tag. "Ahhh, yes. I'm Damon. You've robbed me of the opportunity to introduce myself." His smile is killer. Clean. Straight, white teeth. "What can I get for you?"

An open-ended question if I ever heard one.

7

James

James waited as Trey walked across the beige bank floor, past James's office where he tipped his head as a *good morning*, and headed into his own office. The best course of action was to get it over with. He waited until he heard the regular morning sounds—Trey's plastic coffee mug he came in with every morning hitting the desk, the squeak of the chair spinning, and a few buttons being tapped on the keyboard indicating Trey logging into the system. James stood and flattened his pants, then walked over.

Trey's door was open, and he had just taken his seat when James stood under the doorframe and knocked on the wall outside the entrance, even though his head was already poking in.

"Got a minute?"

Trey's dark eyes peered through his glasses. He looked the same as he always did—pants, collared shirt, sweater vest. Those damn sweater vests, even in the summer. Tall and dark-skinned, he gave off a Carlton Banks vibe. Probably danced the same too. His frown indicated frustration at James's presence. Things had been weird between them for the last couple of months. Since the *incident*.

He flung open a folder and scattered papers around, using the George Costanza method of look-annoyed-and-they'll-think-you're-busy, but Trey probably *was* annoyed.

"Right now?" he said, grabbing a pen.

"It's important."

James entered the office, bigger than his own and with two windows. A corner office, naturally. He shut the door behind him and took a seat on one of the big leather chairs in front of his desk. Trey's office was decorated differently than James's. He'd offered up Tessa's expertise, but Trey was clearly afraid of color. The beige surrounding didn't stand out from the rest of the bank. There were no plants, no knickknacks. One photo of him and his wife, Aleesha, and not even a wedding photo—one of them on a boat, on one of the annual vacations they took back to the Bahamas to visit her family. On one wall, he had an American flag, and on the other, a picture of the current president. Politics aside, he thought it was good for business to show unity.

"I need to talk to you about something," James said.

Trey took off his glasses and pinched the top of his nose. "This again?"

"No. Not that." James should've known it was going to be about Rosita and the—inappropriateness that went on. That had already been addressed, and even though it didn't stop, James knew better than to get Trey involved again. "Listen, I'm only going to be here for a few hours today. I have to get home. Tessa. She's—" She's what? James still struggled. "She's missing. She wasn't there when I got home last night after Jupiter's and there was broken glass and blood. I called the cops. They're looking into it."

"Missing?" Trey's eyebrow lines appeared, showing his midforties age even though he didn't normally look it. "Well, where the hell is she?"

"I don't know. The cops are suspicious. They took DNA and—"

48

"Whoa, whoa, whoa. Hold up, James. Is this a murder investigation?" His eyes went wide, and he gritted his teeth. "We're about to land the VistaBuild financing. If you're implicated in a missing-persons case, then—"

"Jesus, Trey. Stop." James huffed. "She wasn't murdered." He said it, but his voice wavered. "She's just—I don't know. I don't know what's going on. I stopped at the police station this morning and the detective in charge said the DNA will take a few days."

"Oh. Terrific. A 'detective' is involved now," he said, using air quotes. Then he looked at his watch, an expensive thing he liked to show off and called a *timepiece*. "Andy and Kyle from VistaBuild have been here all week getting liquored up on every bank's tab in the state and they're heading back later today. They're taking the weekend and planning for final financing by Monday. The last thing I need is this story hitting the wire."

The last thing *Trey* needs, even though this wasn't about him.

"Nice, Trey. Thanks."

His shoulders dropped. "You know what I mean. I'm sorry, man. I hope everything is okay with Tessa."

James pressed his lips together. There was other scandalous shit going on behind the walls of this bank. But no, nothing compared to a possible murder. And he knew that once the story broke Tessa's name would be leaked, and then of course James's name and his association with the bank would be too. And then the online comments on the article would follow, where everyone would say either that he was a heartless prick, partying it up at the bar while someone attacked his wife, or worse—that he was behind it.

He had to find a way to control the narrative. There was no way he'd come out of this as a grieving husband. Especially once it came out that he didn't even know his wife—literally and figuratively.

"Go home, James," Trey said, an edge to his voice. "Take a few days, next week too. Sort this out."

"But VistaBuild. They're coming back in today. What if they go with us on Monday?"

This was James's project—he'd groomed them from start to hopeful finish.

"We'll have Rosita do the heavy lifting. Andy was particularly impressed with her, so I feel comfortable with her handling everything if we get the call Monday."

Rosita must be happy as a clam that Tessa was missing. Boy, wasn't this all working out in her favor?

"So, I lose my wife, and now my job too?" James asked. "This is my responsibility."

"You didn't lose your job. But if this story gets out, I don't want you perp walking to your car when news vans and cameras show up later this afternoon. Because you know they will." He stopped talking for a few seconds, then slammed both hands on his desk. "Dammit!" he said, louder than James would've liked.

James looked behind him to see the curious faces peering at him through the glass, likely wondering what was making Trey so upset. Hailey, the twenty-three-year-old college kid who worked part-time as a teller while getting her MBA, had her hand over her open mouth in shock. Mickey and Carla, the full-time tellers, both quickly looked away when James made eye contact.

"Way to have my back, Trey," James said. "After everything I've done for you."

He stared at Trey hard, letting the statement hang in the air. The truth was, if James was a ruthless climber, he could've had Trey fired months ago, and slid not only into a promotion, but right into Trey's job as the boss.

People should be sympathetic. His wife was missing.

Trey softened for a hot second, realizing James held the cards. "Just take the rest of the day, James. It'll all work out."

Trey was still pissed, but James didn't have time for that. He got what he wanted, in theory—time today, to figure out things about Tessa. He hadn't expected to lose the project, though.

James turned and opened the door, and walked out while Trey called out "I hope they find her" behind him. He said it, but his words didn't ring sincere.

Like he was naked in a dream giving a speech, James felt his cheeks go hot as everyone around him avoided eye contact, likely wondering what pissed Trey off *this* time. Back in his office, he shut down his computer, grabbed his wallet, and walked toward the door. Rosita stopped him with a hiss from her own office, and when he looked at her, she waved him in. He sighed, not wanting to do this with her, now, here, but for some reason, he went in.

He knew why. Rosita was undeniably attractive, with a whole J-Lo thing going on. They'd worked together for just about a year, and each day since then she'd made sure that he knew she was available to him. Mistakes were made, even recently, but what could he really say? She was a climber. If it came out, she'd scream #MeToo and sexual harassment for having relations with someone who was her superior at work.

"Hey," she whispered, then motioned for him to close the door.

He did, only because she had a floor-to-ceiling glass panel next to her door, so anyone could see inside at any time. There was no way he'd be in a totally closed off room with her after the incident.

Her office was unabashedly Rosita. She couldn't break protocol and make it as wild as she wanted, but her touches were everywhere. Two leopard-print frames, one holding a picture of her and a bunch of girlfriends on the beach, fruity drinks in hand and wearing bikinis, naturally, and another of her with her two nephews. Her desk lamp was red and gold, and there were red-framed pictures of zebras and cheetahs on the walls. All her tchotchkes were either red or gold or leopard, from her pens and penholder to the small pillow on her chair that she used to support her back after sitting for most of the day.

She stared him up and down, tapping a pen against a notepad on her desk. "So, what happened? What did Trey say?" Her dark eyes glowed. Her perfume hung in the air like she'd just sprayed on a second coat.

James shrugged, deciding to play it off like it was his idea. "I asked for the rest of the day. He told me to go home now and sort it out. So that's what I'm doing." He purposely left out the part about how Rosita was suddenly in charge of *his* project, even though he was sure that it'd be discussed between the two of them the second he left.

Those lips pressed together, and she nodded, attempting to look sympathetic. "I'm sure everything will be fine, sweetie."

He hated when she called him that. It was beyond inappropriate, especially now. "I forgot my bagel."

Such a stupid thing to say, but he wanted to get out of there as soon as possible. He not only wanted to search online for the soon-to-be-released article, but he wanted to snoop in his house, in case there was something about Tessa that he'd missed. What he didn't want to do was stay in that office and ask what he'd been dying to know—why Rosita was at the bank early this morning, and why she'd lied to him about it. He didn't want to bully her—asked and answered twice already—but he was going to get to the bottom of it, one way or another.

He went back to his office and grabbed his cup, no doubt holding lukewarm coffee, took his bag with the bagel off his desk, and left. Like a heat-seeking missile, he sped out of the office with the intent to try to figure out who the fuck Tessa really was.

Of course, he was stopped in the parking lot.

"James? Where are you going?"

Fuck. It was Andy. James turned around.

"Hey, Andy. Where's Kyle?"

Andy pressed his lips together in disappointment. "Sick kid, he hit the road back home pretty early. His wife had a meeting she couldn't miss at work, so he has to deal with the doctor and all that stuff today. You have kids?"

"No, no kids." James began to perspire, and he knew he looked flushed, but he had to keep it together for his prospective client. "I'm sorry, man, but I'm not going to be in the meeting today either. My wife—she—something happened. I've really got to go."

Andy held onto his arm. "Is everything okay?"

What was James supposed to say? He went for sympathy. "I don't know. She's missing. She wasn't home when I got home last night. I have to work with the cops today."

"The cops? Jesus. Does this have anything to do with the blood I saw on your shirt last night?"

Andy's expression told James that he was already playing judge, jury, and executioner. *It's always the husband.* It took all of James's grit not to tell him to fuck off and mind his own business. "I told you I get nosebleeds."

"I see." He held out a hand for a shake and raised his eyebrows. "Well, I suppose I'll deal with Rosita. Kyle and I spoke at length last night after we left you guys at the bar. We're impressed with your terms. Maybe we'll see you next week, then?"

James shook his hand and nodded. "Great. You're in good hands with Rosita." He tried really hard to unclench his jaw. "I'll see you next week."

8

Tessa

Damon brings me a glass of Merlot, drops a menu, and then disappears in the back. It reminds me of that stupid, cliché phrase *I hate to see you go, but I love to watch you leave.*

I peruse the menu, wondering if I should try to get a job in a place like this. Waitressing or bartending for quick cash sure beats chasing realtors and builders to try to get them to use me to stage open houses. I never graduated from high school, and I lied in the past telling people I attended RISD for design. Still, I think I have a knack for decorating. Maybe I really *can* try to set something up here. Make up a business name, pay a fee, and advertise. Sweet talk my way into getting one client and use them as a reference to get more. I mean, really, how many people ask for school credentials? Sure, doctors and lawyers hang their diplomas on the wall, but how many diplomas does anyone see for a writer or a coffee shop owner or a personal trainer? I can just pay twenty bucks for business cards online and no one would be the wiser.

People always assume the best in others. I take this to another level.

When Foster Father Number Whatever, probably Three, favored me over the others, I assumed it was because he wanted to help me. I'd get the clean clothes while others had to trade to be seen in different outfits. I'd get the non-moldy parts of the bread. I got a fiver when he handed everyone else a single dollar. I got to get repeatedly raped while he left the others alone. He told me it was because I was his favorite. At fourteen, I was too young to know the scope of the abuse. At the time, I felt better knowing I was eating well while the others fought over a bag of cheesy poofs. Survival of the fittest. He abused me out of love.

Then Denise came into the house. She became his new favorite. Out of nowhere, my bread was green—when I was allowed to eat. One time, eating the leftover pieces of whatever they could find that they called dinner, when I asked for more, my foster dad hit me in front of everyone. No one said anything for fear of repercussions. Yet, the more he hit me, the more I sought his approval. I wanted to be the favorite again, so I kept going back. *I know he loves me.*

That's when it started for me. He hits because he cares.

Damon reappears from the swinging door that leads to the kitchen and stops in front of me. He takes two glasses out of the tub of rinse water by the sink under the bar and dries them with a rag, then flings it over his shoulder and smiles at me, that smile, which for some reason has the fairy tale in motion in my head. He'll be sweet and kind and rescue puppies, then he'll be jealous and controlling but that'll just show me how much he loves me, and how much he fears me leaving. That's love.

Stop, I tell myself. *Don't do it this time. Break the cycle.*

The Asshole is about to find out that even I have a breaking point. He may have put his hands on me often, which sometimes felt tender to me, even when it hurt. But the current bruise under my right eye is from a coffee mug. Came home early from entertaining clients, didn't like that I was eating ice cream (*"you're becoming a fat fucking bitch!"*) and whack, right across the right side of my face, and I faltered like a sack of potatoes. When I came to, he was gone, left a note that he was going back to the bar. That, a bunch of insults, and a warning about what would happen to me "next time."

Except there won't be a next time for him. The clues are there. The cops will find them.

I have help in ways he would never expect.

Patience, my love.

"So, have you decided on something to eat?" Damon asks.

I take a sip of my wine and place the glass back on the coaster, then fold my arms on the bar and look up at him. "What's the house special?"

He laughs. "We just use the menu. The chef is cranky."

I giggle like a schoolgirl. *Stop!* "Me too."

"Nah," he says with a smirk. "I can tell you've already got everything figured out."

Moron. "Oh yeah?"

"Yep." He removes the towel and wipes the bar in front of me, then puts a placemat and place settings on top. "Look at you—out-of-town girl, funky haircut, dressed nicely. And you're alone. Confident. Not glued to your phone. I like that."

Not a moron. "Well, how do you know I'm not meeting my date here?"

"Because this is a wine bar, I'm a bartender, and let's just say I've seen my share of Tinder hookups start this way. You don't always turn your head to the door when it opens. You don't give a shit who's walking in."

Observant. "And how do you know I'm from out of town?"

"I didn't. You just told me." He smiles again. "People here have a look. One that you don't fit." He makes a funny face and mocks someone texting on a phone, then brushes his hand against his shoulder and nods his head back, like he's flipping hair out of the way.

He's funny.

He's probably wonderful. *Stop!*

I grab the menu and scan for ten seconds while he waits.

"I'll have the organic roasted chicken, but instead of brussels sprouts can I replace that with literally anything else?"

He grabs a pen from behind his ear and jots it down in a pad. "We have asparagus or maple-roasted carrots."

"Surprise me."

Damon goes into the kitchen, and I purposely don't look at my phone, because I don't want to be like all the girls that he made fun of. I raise my head to the flat-screen television above the bar and there's a baseball game on. Yankees versus Red Sox. This will have to do for now, even though I'm not much into sports. I've heard everyone around here roots for that team. Rabid fan base, from what little I know.

Every so often I see Damon help other patrons, and I even get a little jealous as two girls hee-haw over everything he says. They're the girls that you hated in school. Primped to the nines, one with long blond hair and another with long dark hair. Both have their tits on display, wear too much makeup, and want to post everything on Instagram, which they scream about loudly every time they take a picture. Damon plays along, although he always comes back to me, and refills my wine without me asking. Barbie and Bitsy (that's what I'm calling them) at the other end of the bar don't like that, and loudly call him over to take pictures of them while they make kissy faces to the camera. He happily takes their iPhone and snaps away, then looks at me as he heads to the swinging door to the kitchen and makes fun of them by pretending to text and flipping his hair again, as he did earlier.

When he comes out, he places a perfectly roasted half chicken in front of me, one that has asparagus *and* carrots next to it, with a little dollop of mashed potatoes on the side.

"Everything look okay?" he asks.

"Scrumptious."

I learned that word from my mother, right before I was taken away. The first time I heard it, we all still lived together as a family. Well, me, my brother Kenny and all the half siblings, and whichever boyfriend my mother had at the time. She used the word to describe whatever was in the needle that her own Boyfriend Number Whatever brought home. After she passed out, I asked him what it meant, and he showed me. It was the first time I did heroin. My brother Kenny called 911 when I foamed at the mouth and had a seizure.

I was twelve.

I do remember the feeling I had at first. Warmth, bliss. It's indescribable, just a feeling. One that can't be put into words.

Wait. It can. *Scrumptious*.

It's a miracle I'm alive. I like to think I've straightened out, and I have as far as the drugs, but I'm only straight in the way you smooth out a piece of wrinkled paper. It's still a rectangle, you can still write stuff on it, but you know it's damaged and imperfect.

"Do you want anything else?" Damon asks, and doesn't leave.

I stare at the plate, then pick up a fork. "Are you going to watch me eat?"

"What's your name?"

"Tessa. Tessa Smyth."

"Damon Moretti," he says and holds out a hand. "See, I finally got to introduce myself correctly." He winks as I shake his hand.

He leaves me to finish my meal, an incredibly juicy chicken with impossibly crisp skin. I inhale both of my veggie sides and scrape the last of the creamy whipped potatoes on the edge of my fork with a knife. Nothing left but bones. Asshole never let me clean my plate. It wasn't "ladylike."

My sparkling dish is empty in front of me while I watch the baseball game. A busboy clears it away, as Damon mixes and pours and goes in and out of the kitchen for the dinner rush, which isn't that busy—I've been to places before where the people eating at the bar are shoved from behind with drunk idiots waving dollar bills or flashing cleavage to get some attention. The rush here makes it feel busy, but not like in a big city.

Everyone filters out as the restaurant will be closing soon. It's Friday night and the young'uns have to start their hookups. Barbie and Bitsy are the last to leave, besides me. They whisper to each other and sneak flirtatious glances at Damon all night. As the cleanup starts in the main dining area, Damon comes out and brings them their check, then brings me mine. Barbie (the blond) announces loudly that they're going to some bar two blocks away, one that stays open till three A.M., in case anyone else is thirsty?

Subtle.

Alone now, I plunk down what I owe plus twenty percent. I grab my denim jacket when Damon approaches.

"Hey. You don't have to leave. I want to talk to you a little more," he says. "I was just trying to get them out of here. I know them. The dark-haired one, anyway. She always comes here and gets drunk and try to get me to meet her somewhere after." He shrugs. "Nope."

I chuckle. "Girlfriend?"

"Nope."

Crap. "Boyfriend?"

"Nope."

Asshole? "So what's the deal with you then?"

"I don't have a deal." His eyes are intense, and I know he means it. I'm about to *your-place-or-mine* him out of habit when I remember my place is a disgusting shithole motel for the night, and that I'm trying to break the cycle. "Can I get your number? I'd like to take you out. Show you around. You know, since you're new." He smirks.

Me: No. I can't do it again. Not so quickly. *Brain*: Nah, he's not like the others.

"I suppose I can use a friend in town." I grab the pen that's nearby on the bar and write my number down on a coaster. I hand it to him, and he holds it over his heart as I leave to call Hobart to take me back to paradise.

Damon is nice, and he's hot, but I'm not getting involved with anyone, even if they promise to love me. Especially if they promise to love me. I'll know real love when I feel it.

Words don't mean shit to me anymore.

9

James

When James got home, he assumed Candy knew something was very wrong because she didn't bark and yelp the way she usually did when he walked in after work. Maybe she always did it to protect Tessa. Tessa usually stayed with her all day, and now she was gone, and whatever happened last night, Candy witnessed. She wasn't used to James being there during the day, especially in the morning, like he was now. Even dogs had a schedule. He let Candy outside in the yard and waited for her to come back to the door before he started his investigation. He didn't want to lose track of her and find out she was sniffing around Nick and Gwen's place, hunting for bacon.

James didn't know where to start, or what to look for. Tessa was pretty simple. She didn't have much when they got together. What still bothered him, however, was the detective saying she knew whoever did this to her. What did Solomon already know?

He gulped, wondering if anyone told Solomon about the violence. He hoped no one knew what happened.

James ran up the stairs into their bedroom. Tessa had replaced the plain doors on all three bedrooms with detailed, ornate, heavy wood that made a *whooshing* sound every time he opened them. He stared at the small, boxy room. Again, all Tessa. She liked things neutral with pops of color, so the walls were a light gray, and everything else was violet. A violet satin bedspread, a deep purple chair in the corner that was basically an extension of her closet, housing outfits that she'd decided against wearing yet was too lazy to hang up. It always irked him, but supposedly that's what women did. He'd only lived with one woman, Desiree, before Tessa.

Desiree took him by storm when he was thirty. They'd met at a party—one of his old college buddies had an elaborate Christmas party every year—and he was drawn to her thirst for life. She wanted to be a journalist and worked a room like she was being paid. She was good at asking questions, a trait that James obviously didn't possess or he wouldn't be in his current predicament. They'd dated for a few months before she suggested they get an apartment together in Hoboken so she could be closer to the city, which they couldn't afford. Not that they were able to afford Hoboken either. She assumed he'd just quit his job and get one at a different bank in the city, which he did. Entry level again; a newbie.

About a year later, she informed him that she'd gotten an offer at the *Chicago Sun-Times* and left him high and dry. She moved on without consideration for the life they'd planned together. Left him with the apartment too, and a lease that he'd signed. He couldn't make ends meet and had gotten himself into a bit of a pickle—the rent took up almost his entire take-home pay with little left for bills and zero left for a social life. He ended up giving up the apartment and moving back down to the suburban area where he had grown up—the same county as Valley Lake. He was able to land his job as assistant manager at the bank, due to his experience, and coming from a New

York City bank held weight. However, for the time being, he had to get a roommate off Craigslist. It was not where he'd envisioned himself in his early thirties.

James should've learned from that situation not to move in with anyone so quickly, with someone you barely knew, but Tessa was—different.

First, James checked the home office where Tessa worked. Opened all the drawers, went through all her folders. It was mostly printed-out pictures of rooms— offices, bedrooms, living rooms. She'd had some notes in the corners, with her loopy cursive, denoting changes she'd make on certain items. Her computer screen stared at him, mocking him. He shook the mouse until the screen came to life. There was no password since they shared the computer.

She had her own email set up in Outlook, and when he guided the arrow over the program and pressed, her entire email popped up. He looked in her inbox, her sent items—nothing was out of the ordinary. Emails to random builders, trying to get appointments to decorate and stage homes, a few to local offices selling her services. Then one stood out from their neighbor Gwen.

To: Tessa Smyth
From: Gwendolyn Holloway
Date: Wednesday, September 25, 2019, 4:25 P.M.
Subject: Are you okay?

Just checking on you. I don't blame you for not feeling safe. You should go to the police and do it the right way. Call me if you need anything

To: Gwendolyn Holloway
From: Tessa Smyth

That was this week. The day before she went missing. James was puzzled, because Gwen had told him that she didn't see Tessa.

She couldn't have told Gwen about—

That was their private life. Now what was he supposed to do?

James beelined for Tessa's closet and opened the door in a fury. Her clothes were arranged by color. He thumbed through the hangers, checked inside all her pockets. He felt like he was snooping, and even though he wasn't, it didn't feel right. Opened her jewelry box, which she had hidden in the bottom corner of the closet.

Her wedding ring was in the top drawer.

The room spun before him, like he was on a merry-go-round, and he held on to the wall to steady himself as his heart raced. *Deep breaths*.

Footsteps padded on the stairs, and Candy was soon behind him to investigate.

"Come here, girl," James said, and sat on the edge of the bed. Candy jumped onto the mattress and sat beside him. He pet her head, soft, and looked into her eyes. "Do you know anything?" he asked, like the dog was supposed to answer. Like she was going to turn around, sit like a human, put on her glasses, and say, *Ok, Dad, here's where it gets interesting*, like this was a Disney movie. Her eyes were so trusting.

Ding dong. Candy jumped up on all fours and barked toward the door.

"Calm down, girl," James said and leaped up. Candy was around three—she was a stray at the shelter when he and Tessa adopted her, but she was already rabidly protective. He exited the bedroom and closed the door behind him. He didn't want Candy rushing the door.

James stumbled down the stairs and looked out the window. A woman stood on the landing outside the front door. She had her light-brown hair cut into a chic bob and wore a knee-length pink dress with a light-beige overcoat, though it wasn't buttoned or belted. Tessa always complained about people knocking on the door selling stuff or asking for donations. He was about to back away, but she caught his eye through the window, and waved like she knew him. She looked familiar.

He opened the door a crack, even though there was still a screen door separating them. "Hi. Can I help you?"

"Are you James Montgomery?" she asked.

"Yes."

"Hi. I'm Carina Killhorn with Channel 10 News. Is it true your wife is missing? Tessa Smyth?"

Her voice was raspy, like she was a two-pack-a-day smoker, and it made her sound old, even though she was only about his age. Now he recognized her. The glasses she wore had thrown him off, probably wearing them just to look smart. He'd seen her on the news before, pushy and rude, always trying to break the big story. And a missing woman in a small town fit the bill. This was her chance.

She held a cell phone out toward him, indicating she wanted him to speak into it. He was being recorded.

This was his gotcha moment. He knew it was coming. Someone at the police department had a big fucking mouth.

66

"I can't talk about this. There's an investigation. I don't want to mess up anything they're doing. Go to Detective Solomon at the Valley Lake PD."

"Right. So, are you going on record with no comment?" She smirked at him.

"No comment."

He shut the door just as another news van pulled up to the cul-de-sac and parked. Carina didn't leave his stoop as two other men, one with a camera and one with a microphone, made their way toward the door.

Son of a bitch. James ran into the office and grabbed the cordless phone that was attached to the landline that Tessa insisted they needed for her business. With shaky fingers, he dialed the police department and asked for Detective Solomon.

The line went quiet without a *hold on please* as he waited. After the doorbell rang again, and Candy barked maniacally from upstairs, Solomon finally came on the line.

"What can I do for you, Mr. Montgomery?"

James pictured the detective, smug, with his lazy left eye and fat nose pointing into the phone. "Jesus Christ, Solomon. I have reporters at my door. I thought this investigation was ongoing. What the hell is going on over there?" He tried to contain his rage, but it was hard.

"Mmm, we were afraid of that." Solomon paused. "Small town and all."

This jerk-off leaked it. James was a suspect and Solomon sicced his dogs on him to try to get him to slip up.

"I'm not answering anyone. I'm consulting my attorney, and I want to set up a press conference for later."

"You sure that's a good idea, Montgomery?"

67

He'd been relegated to his last name. He wasn't a person anymore. He was no longer a grieving husband. He was a suspect and treated as such. "I'm sure."

James slammed the phone down and went back to the front doorway, which was now crowded with three people staring at the door, wondering what they should do next. He opened it to address them. Instantly, that cell phone and a microphone and two cameras were pointed toward him.

"Get off my property. Come back at five P.M. I'll be giving a press conference with my lawyer."

The door slammed shut with a thud.

James's best friend since middle school was Evan Soderberg, who was a lawyer now, but he didn't specialize in criminal law. He was a jack of all trades, a civil litigator, but he'd know what to do. James needed advice, and Evan knew Tessa. He knew the real circumstances of how they met. He'd be happy to help.

Then James went upstairs, hugged Candy, and cried over what was happening.

10

Tessa

"Thanks for the recommendation, Hobart," I say, smug and feeling attractive.

Asshole didn't make me feel attractive, and only complimented me when he apologized for hitting me. He wasn't always such a monster. I mean, he *was* sorry. Sometimes. Always got me a nice piece of jewelry when things got totally out of hand too. Thank God, because I was able to hock it all for a big chunk of the cash I currently carry around.

Tomorrow I'm going to have to go to a drugstore and get a couple of prepaid credit cards to use for things like Uber and Lyft and other online-related things that a regular person needs daily. I can't continue to have Hobart at my beck and call, texting him at all hours of the day and night and expecting him to come running. It's almost midnight for Christ's sake. He's old. He shouldn't be on high alert, driving me around. Though it is nice to feel safe and taken care of.

It happened fast, because for once, an older man has my best interests at heart.

"No problem, Tessa. Food was good?" he asks.

"The food, the company, everything."

From the back of the car, in the dark, I open my purse and take out my compact and check myself in the mirror. The makeup held up well, and my bruise isn't visible. If Damon sees it, I'll have to make something up. Grabbing something out of the closet. Walked into a door. The usual shit that nobody believes. Yet we all say it, and everyone we tell nods sympathetically and recalls a story where nearly the same thing happened to them. Their stories are made up, but they help us hide our shame.

"You sure you don't want me to take you to a different place?" Hobart asks. "I don't like you going up there alone. People here—they ain't the regular people. The cops don't come but once every couple-a weeks. Someone calls, they don't come. A gunshot'll get 'em here a little quicker, but by then, they might as well bring the chalk and outline the body."

Crap. I don't want to get in the middle of a damn shoot-out. And what if that crazy girl is waiting for me with a brick? She saw me come out of my room, so she knows I'll be back at some point. What if she's *inside* my room with a brick? It's not like this place has a security guard patrolling the lot. An alarm won't go off if someone breaks a window or kicks in a door. It's not even midnight. The party in the lot is probably in full swing.

Hobart is right. I have to get out of that place. It served its purpose earlier in the day, and I had somewhere to keep my stuff while I walked all over town securing my shiny new ID. If Asshole actually had detail on me all day and someone saw me leave my cushy suburban home, they've already reported back to him that I'm in a different state in a scummy place. He's probably laughing.

You'll never leave. You're nothing without me. You're nothing anyway.

"You know what? I think you're right. I didn't really unpack. I can gather up my stuff in a minute or two. Would you mind waiting? And do you know another place that's a little safer?"

"We can go back to the area where you just had dinner," he says. "Much safer."

I think about my cash situation. I don't exactly need a place that puts a mint on my pillow, but I can't start blowing a hundred and fifty dollars a night, before all those stupid hidden fees and taxes. But I decide I can't sleep in the Empire overnight. It's got to be ridden with bedbugs and STDs and I bet there's a bloodstain under the bed. These things didn't occur to me earlier when I unpacked my Walmart stuff for my nap because I was on the high of getting away.

"I don't need a Ritz Carlton," I say with a laugh. "Obviously."

"There's one-a those chain thingamajigs. Nothin' fancy. A Ramada or somethin' of the like."

"Sounds like a plan."

The ride back to the dump is five more minutes, and I hear the parking lot before I see it. Hobart slows and pulls in. Crowds of people are leaning against every car in the lot, some sitting on the hoods and some directly on the top of the cars. Some are even dancing, pounding their feet to the beat of the music from the stereos and making dents.

It's not like anyone has a Mercedes.

Despite knowing how to throw a punch, my stomach flip-flops. I don't want to go through them to get my stuff, but they aren't exactly clearing the way for Hobart to drive closer to where my room is located.

"I'm gonna walk you up," Hobart says.

71

Usually a terrible line to try to fuck me, I see no ill intent in Hobart, and I would welcome bringing him to my room. He parks the car exactly where it is, and I'm afraid by the time we get back it'll be turned over. He puts the cab in park, gets out, and opens my door to the delight of the onlookers shouting *ooooh* and *ahhhhh* and *Grandpa's gonna get some pussy!* He takes my arm sternly near my elbow, a way I've been shoved around before, but he's doing it protectively, not in the *do as I say or else* way.

We shimmy through the crowd and go up the stairs and I quickly fumble with the door lock. The knob feels looser than it did earlier, and I wonder again about someone being inside. Or maybe it's just my nerves. When it opens, I invite Hobart in, but he declines and stands outside my door.

"Just hurry," he says.

My bag is still opened on the rickety dresser, and I take my hair products and makeup off the bathroom counter and throw them in. I never hung anything up or used the drawers, so everything should still be in here. I don't double check. My money is in my purse, so I zip the bag and drag it out. Sixty seconds. Max. Everything is going to be fine.

But of course...

"That's the ho that's tryna steal Marcus!"

The crazy girl is back. And she has two friends with her this time, who fall in line behind her as she approaches the bottom of the steps, and the melee begins. They start shouting over each other at me.

"Oh, girl, you in trouble, girl!"

"Think you hot shit, bitch?"

Hobart charges down anyway, and I follow closely. "Just gettin' her stuff and gettin' her outta here anyway. You don't gotta worry about this no more," he says.

Crazy girl doesn't negotiate as she tries to make eye contact with me beyond Hobart. "He yo' damn keeper? Cat got ya tongue?" She produces a switchblade, hits the button and extends the sharp end. "Maybe I should cut it out."

Fuck!

Before I even have a chance to panic, Hobart pulls a gun from his waistband and brandishes it in the air.

"GUN!" someone in the crowd screams, and everyone scatters.

"That's right. Ain't y'all so tough now. Get out of the way!" Hobart shouts.

All day I've been riding around with someone who was strapped. I hate guns. Unfortunately, I've had them pointed in my direction more than once. One mentally ill foster brother. One of the Assholes. Wait, two of the Assholes.

Of course, I'm grateful for its presence now.

I quickly follow Hobart to the cab and jump into the back seat with my suitcase, and he starts the engine and peels off.

"Sorry 'bout that." He looks at me in the rearview mirror. "You doin' okay?"

What's okay? My heart is racing so fast that Hobart can probably see my veins throbbing through my skin, and my fingers are tingling. The gun is comfortably lying on the passenger seat, in full view. Small, shiny, metallic. One that you see in the movies when they play Russian roulette, with the thing that spins. Not one of those guns with a clip that you smack into the bottom.

73

I've seen *John Wick*.

All I've been trying to do is get away from the violence in my life and start over. I never should've put myself in this position to begin with. I consider myself lucky that I've left the situation unscathed. I should go buy a lottery ticket.

"Yeah. Thanks." I pause, and I don't want to talk about it, but I have to ask him. "Why do you have a gun?"

His right hand drifts on top of it in the next seat, like he's making sure it's still there. "You can never be too safe. I drive a cab. Been robbed before. Had a gun held to my head before. I ain't takin' no chances no more. I got a wife. Three kids. Grown, but they ain't needin' to go to their old man's funeral."

Hobart has more in common with me than he realizes.

"I've had a gun held to my head before too," I say quietly.

"You been robbed?"

"No. Just asshole exes."

"Ah, kid. I don't understand that shit. Threatening a woman. How low can you go?"

I decide that even if I sign up for Uber and Lyft, Hobart is going to be my friend.

We arrive at the new hotel. Nothing but cars in the parking lot—no people, no parties, no music or drug addicts or prostitutes. I take my bag out and it thuds onto the ground.

"Thanks again. I don't know what I would've done without you today." I really mean that.

"No problem. If you need anything else, let me know."

I pay him his fare plus an extra twenty, which he tries to refuse but to be honest my life is worth more than the Andrew Jackson I throw at him. I may not see him much going forward since I'll be starting an Uber account, but I don't tell him that. I'll use him occasionally just so he knows I'm okay. I'll text him every once in a while, to make sure he's okay too.

It's after midnight when I check in to the new hotel, which seems to be only a few blocks from where I had dinner. The room is ninety-nine dollars tonight and tomorrow, and seventy-nine Sunday through Thursday. They charge me the full ninety-nine for tonight even though I just got here. But at least the place looks clean and safe, so I don't negotiate. I pay cash for tonight and promise to give them a credit card to keep on file the next day, which Ellen, the lady behind the counter, accepts because it's so late. And to be honest, I think my makeup is fading and she sees the black eye.

Sisterhood. She's probably seen people check in late because they were running from something. I'm grateful for the second time that night and vow to get the prepaid credit cards first thing in the morning.

Thankfully, this place gives me a keycard instead of a metal key, and it has an elevator that takes me to the fifth floor. The top. The penthouse, I guess, even though I'm positive all the rooms are the same. Inside, the room is contemporary. Ugly carpet, but there are artsy pictures on the wall, not water stains like the last place. The bed looks big and comfortable with a white down duvet, and I can't wait to sink into it.

It's been a long day. I've only been away from Asshole for twenty-four hours.

I wonder if he's caught on yet.

He doesn't know the betrayal that's about to fall upon him. The wave of accusation headed his way. I even gave my little evidence-planting buddy a burner phone to use for when I *do* call and text, so there is no proof that we've been in touch. I picture the Asshole, smug, assuming everyone is on his side.

They're not.

He deserves every bit of the shitstorm that is about to come his way.

11

James

James's best friend and civil litigator lawyer, Evan Soderberg, showed up at three p.m. and James walked him through the events of the day so far, starting with last night. Evan's face crumpled when James told him the details of Tessa's disappearance. He'd only met her a handful of times, but James knew he liked her.

Everyone liked Tessa. Even Evan's parents. There was nothing not to like.

James grabbed two beers out of the refrigerator and set them down on the counter. At the kitchen table, Evan readjusted his glasses and let out a sigh. "I think you're going to need a criminal defense attorney."

"What?" James said. "I haven't been charged with anything. I had nothing to do with this!"

If she ran, James knew why. But she wouldn't run over something as silly as him "pointing" a gun at her.

Evan raised an eyebrow. "You know the husband is always the first suspect."

"Suspect? They haven't found a body, Evan. I don't even want to think about that. Right now, she's just— missing."

"But there's foul play involved. I'd bet my last paintbrush that they're looking into you and everything about you." Evan did watercolor paintings as a side hobby and took his brushes very seriously. "Interviewing everyone you know. Trying to build a case. You better be squeaky clean, bro."

James knew what he meant, but was anyone squeaky clean? The doorbell rang again, Candy barked again, and James had already resigned to not answering the door. It was reporters. One after the other. All damn day. His exhilaration hearing the bell, thinking it was Solomon with information on Tessa, was replaced with him wanting to rip the damn thing out of the wall.

"You've got to help me prepare what to say."

Evan took his glasses off and let them hit the glass table with a clank. He pinched the top of his nose, then rubbed his thick beard. "Just be honest."

Easier said than done.

When five P.M. rolled around, James was showered and dressed and ready for the throngs of reporters outside his door. He wore tan slacks and a navy-blue V-neck sweater with a white collared shirt underneath. Respectable. An everyman. A loving husband with a missing wife.

He'd memorized his statement that Evan prepared, but still had it on a folded piece of paper in his hand. He didn't want to reference it—it showed nervousness—but he needed it just in case he fumbled his words.

"You ready?" Evan asked.

With a deep breath, James opened his front door and immediately camera flashes went off in his face like an Alabama thunderstorm. People all talked at once, pointing microphones and cell phones and cameras toward him.

Evan stepped in front of him and put up his right hand, indicating he was about to speak.

"I'm Evan Soderberg, a close friend and attorney. I've advised my client to give a statement. There will be no questions answered." He looked at James and nodded. "Go ahead."

James had the speech in his left hand but didn't open it. Instead, he cleared his throat and waited for silence. When he got it, he started.

"My name is James Montgomery. Yesterday, sometime before nine P.M., my wife, Tessa Smyth, went missing. I had an event with clients after work, and when I got home, there was broken glass in my kitchen and blood on the floor. Tessa's personal belongings were still in the house. I immediately called the Valley Lake PD, who came to investigate with a forensics unit. So far, we have no idea of her whereabouts."

He paused and people started shouting questions at him, which Evan told him to ignore, and then he continued.

"My wife Tessa is a beautiful person inside and out." He produced his favorite wedding picture, the one of them staring into each other's eyes and held it toward the cameras. "If anyone has seen her, please, contact the police department immediately. If anyone has her"—his voice cracked in his throat—"I'm begging you for her safe return. The Valley Lake PD has been nothing short of amazing, and I have full confidence in them to find out what happened to her, and I expect her safe return."

They knew when his speech was over because Evan clapped a hand on James's right shoulder, and James's posture relaxed. Over and out. His right hand was on the doorknob when, of course, everyone started talking over each other.

"Did you have problems in your marriage?"

"Can anyone corroborate where you were last night?"

"Did you notify Tessa's family?"

"Do the police think she was kidnapped?"

"Have you been contacted for ransom?"

He ignored them all—Evan said not to answer any questions. But of course that grating voice that Carina Killhorn had spoke volumes above everyone else.

"I heard you had blood on your shirt last night. Did you kill your wife, Mr. Montgomery?"

The other questions were docile in nature, for the most part, but this was out of line. Where did she hear that about the blood? Who opened their mouth? Despite being told not to talk, James whipped around, furious. "No, *Ms.* Killhorn, I didn't kill my wife. Why would you say such a thing?" He was mad, a vein protruding in his forehead, as Evan tried to guide him back inside. Everyone's eyes were now trained on James, a murderer as far as they were all concerned. He couldn't have that. James shoved Evan off him and looked directly at Carina. "You want to be good at your job? Go find my wife."

The crowd didn't like that—boos and hisses and general disgruntled moans escaped from their mouths— and the questions kept coming. More like the accusations. He'd screwed up. He should've just kept to the prepared speech. Emotions were good; losing control was not.

Emotions—he just remembered that Evan had told him to cry if he was able. He forgot.

But then it hit him like a freight train. He was being accused of murder. *Murder.*

Tears fell on his face as he was being guided inside, but it was too little too late. His little outburst was going to be everywhere.

Evan slammed the door shut behind them. "Well, that didn't exactly go as planned. What were you thinking?"

James's heart was beating fast, *thump thump thump*. Dizzy, he placed his hands on his knees and blew out a long breath.

"Sorry, man. I don't like being accused of being a murderer. You understand?"

Evan gave him a half smile, dejected, and pat him on the back again. "You want to grab dinner somewhere?"

Evan was James's age and still single, though he did well with the ladies. They liked his intellect, his soft side, and the hipster-meets-Wall-Street vibe he gave off. He looked like a liberal college professor with the beard and the glasses, but wore a tie most days, even if not the full suit. His schedule was always his own.

"Nah, man. Thanks. I can't go out right now. I'm afraid to even order in. I don't want to answer the door." James shrugged. "I don't even know if we have food here. Tessa did all the cooking."

Tessa did everything. Based on what little he *did* know about his wife, she was always left to fend for herself growing up in the system, which always gave her a mom complex. She didn't seem to want children, but she knew how to take care of a man. Cooking. Cleaning. Laundry. Errands. Food shopping. Dry cleaner's. Bail.

She'd mentioned overcompensating when she was beaten in the past. She couldn't get herself away from abusive men, no matter how hard she'd tried. She always said she was a magnet for men with nefarious motives, and she couldn't break the cycle. It was like everyone sniffed it out on her and took advantage from the jump.

Evan looked out the window, and people still hovered. "Once this dies down, I'll run out. Grab a pizza or something from Gianni's and bring it back here. You've still got beer, right?" He smiled.

James said yes, then washed out the mugs and put them in the freezer.

12

James

James woke Saturday morning sprawled on the couch, Candy on the floor next to him. He turned over to stretch, his bones and muscles creaking and cracking, especially his neck. The throw pillows that Tessa had picked out were more for style than for comfort. He tossed the fluffy blanket to the side, another thing more for style as he'd shivered half the night. Candy woke and stuffed her wet nose onto his face for morning kisses.

Last night was as good as it could be, considering the situation he was in. After Evan got back with the Italian food, he widened his eyes and nodded toward the front door. There were still people there. Watching. Waiting. James hit the scotch after that. He remembered pizza and some sort of pasta dish with a creamy white sauce, but not much else. Evan must've let himself out.

James rose and fed Candy first, then let her out in the yard while he tried to find his phone. Where did he put that damn thing? In the kitchen, he searched the counter where Tessa's phone was plugged into the charger before he gave it to the cops to scan, and his wasn't there. He patted himself down, as if it was on his person, but he was wearing sweatpants and a long-sleeve T-shirt, neither of which had pockets. Heading to the dining room, he saw it on the bar cart, right next to the scotch. Of course.

When he pressed the home button, there were too many text messages to count, a lot from numbers he didn't recognize, asking for comments. Fucking social media. Anyone could find out anything about anyone these days. There were also a ton of missed phone calls, but he didn't bother scrolling through the list—he rarely used the phone to talk anyway. He scrolled through the texts until he found Evan's, one saying he covered a drunken James with the blanket and locked the door behind him. What a good friend.

Then there was a text from his mother.

> Honey, Dad and I just got a call from someone named Carina Killhorn. We've been calling and calling! Is something going on? She said you murdered Tessa! Where are you?

Fucking Carina, that damn climber.

James's parents had retired to Florida about a year earlier, which fit, since they were in their sixties but acted like they were in their eighties. Five-cent coupons. Dinner at four P.M. They'd lived in the same area, less than a half hour from where James was now, their whole lives. His mother worked as a real estate assistant and retired at fifty because of her first cancer scare, which went on for ten years of cancer scares and two rounds of chemo, but there hadn't been a thing on her scans for the last five years, thankfully. His father worked right up until sixty-seven and a half. Worked on parts for a local military base for their machinery. Not the bombs and the tanks, but the machines that made them.

They'd never met Tessa. James planned to bring her down to Florida for Thanksgiving.

Now what was he supposed to say?

James's gut was wrecked as he thought about his parents having to deal with this shit. Especially after their first son, Tommy, his beloved older brother, died right before James was about to graduate from high school.

The eggs he burned didn't settle the butterflies in his stomach, and the sponge he used to clean didn't get the rot off the bottom of the pan. How did Tessa know what to do every time? He began to realize he was almost helpless without her, after only a few months. Maybe she was even better than he gave her credit for. He finally decided to pick up the phone to call his parents.

In the office, he picked up the cordless phone from the charger and pressed the green button and waited for the hum. His parents' number and Tessa's number were the only ones he knew by heart and was able to dial without looking them up in his cell phone. He dialed and while the phone line normally trilled for at least four rings, this time his mother picked up immediately.

"Honey? What's going on? Why didn't you call us?"

James pictured her sitting on her recliner, wrapped up in the blue, brown, and white patchwork afghan that she'd knitted when she was on her first round of chemo fifteen years ago. Yes, she probably still had it around her shoulders, even though it was likely a billion degrees down there. His father was probably crouched down, leaning into her so he could listen as James spoke. They'd never learned how to properly use a speakerphone.

"I don't know, Mom. I didn't want to bother you until I had all the details."

"What details?" She coughed, which worried him. "So Tessa is okay? Oh, that Carina person. She scared the bejeezus out of us."

How was he supposed to start this conversation? "Is Dad there?"

"Right here, son," his father said, just as James predicted.

"Look, don't listen to anything that witch says. Don't listen to anything you see online."

His parents didn't know how to search for news articles online. His father still got up every morning and got a newspaper and still thought that was the most current way to get news and information. James remembered excitedly telling his father years ago that Henrik Lundqvist, the goalie for the New York Rangers, got a seven-year contract extension and his father didn't believe him. *It wasn't in today's newspaper*, he'd said, not realizing the story broke midday and it wouldn't be in the paper until the next day.

This mess with Tessa wouldn't be in a newspaper in Florida. It was local news. And it wasn't even real news yet. They hadn't found a body, and people go missing every day.

"Listen, guys. When I got home Thursday night, Tessa wasn't here. I noticed some suspicious stuff, so I called the cops. They're investigating, but it doesn't look good. Then someone leaked her name and then they got my name and now it's all just a big mess. They're accusing me of something I didn't do."

His mother waited for another coughing fit to subside before she spoke again. "But the lady said Tessa is dead and that you murdered her."

He gripped the phone, turning his knuckles white. "Don't listen to that. She's missing. Not dead." James gulped loudly when he said that.

"Okay. So, you're still coming for Thanksgiving?"

James shook his head. He loved his parents, but they just weren't getting it. They were old-school. Married thirty-six years. Still believed in kids riding bikes and playing outside after school, with mothers who stayed home and served warm cookies while the kids did their homework. They knew nothing of today's world.

When he married Tessa, as quick as it was after they'd met, he'd told them they'd been dating for a while and decided to be spontaneous—the reason for the parents not getting a proper invitation to the courthouse. The truth was he had a girlfriend when he met Tessa. Joanna. They'd been together for about six months and his parents didn't know many details about his relationships, so he let them assume she was the same girl.

And they still thought he was coming for Thanksgiving and bringing Tessa. His conversation wasn't landing.

"I hope so, Mom. This will all be figured out soon."

The coughing started again, violently, and there was a rustle on the other end of the line. "When do you think she'll be back?" That time, it was his father.

"Dad, is Mom okay?"

"Hang on, son." A muffled conversation took place for a few seconds, and then his father came back. "Mom's been a little run down lately. We're taking her for some tests."

James's heart stopped. "What's wrong? Why didn't you tell me?"

James pictured his father, once strong and stocky, now frail and a couple inches shorter than he was when he built the big bad machines. After retiring to care for his wife, he immediately moved them down to Florida, where the warm winters didn't take such a toll on either of them. No more snow shoveling or fireplace maintenance. Now they were in a nice community of people their own age, where they did neighborhood events like shuffleboard contests and potluck dinners.

"I didn't want to worry you for no reason. Same reason I assume you didn't call us yesterday," he said.

When James's mother was first diagnosed with cervical cancer, the easy fix was a hysterectomy—it wasn't like she was having any more kids. The doctor suggested a short round of chemo, which she did. It was the easy kind, as if any of it is easy, but at least she didn't lose her hair and eyebrows. Just some thinning and shedding, and she didn't look sick. A few years later when it came back, it was bladder cancer, stage two. A quick laparoscopic surgery removed the mass and then she went on a much higher dose of chemo. That one wreaked havoc on her looks and her entire immune system. But it worked, and her hair grew back thick and silver, and she was religious with her anticancer meds.

He hoped it wasn't back; he suddenly wanted to see his parents. James never got the speech from Solomon, the one that said *Make sure you don't leave the state.*

Still, the timing was horrendous. What was he supposed to do?

"Jesus, Dad." James refused to choke up with his father on the line. The man was going through enough. "I have to talk to the cops here and figure out what's going on with Tessa too."

"So she just disappeared? I don't know why that woman would say you murdered her."

"Me neither." Blood. Hair. Broken glass. His father didn't need those details. "Look, just do me a favor. If anyone calls, just hang up on them. They're trying to paint a bad picture of me. We'll find Tessa. She's probably just cooling off somewhere. We had a bad fight last week."

Shit. He'd said that without thinking. If someone called his father and he didn't immediately hang up, he'd repeat that information, thinking it was exonerating James.

His father didn't know that was a death sentence if any of the reporters found out.

After they hung up, James turned on the TV and just as he'd suspected, his outburst was on the local Channel 10 station where Carina worked. It was only the snippet of him acting out, not the entire press conference, because a man begging for the return of his wife doesn't get ratings or clicks. The violent husband with no control who probably killed his wife is what people want to see. The one who broke protocol and yelled at a woman.

On his phone, he searched the articles online, and true to the way the world worked nowadays, everyone had an opinion. People he'd never met, who didn't know him, had something to say about every intimate detail of his life. His peers. His neighbors. The people who came into the bank for a home improvement loan or to cash Granny's ten-dollar birthday checks. Now, everyone knew him as Scott Peterson.

MK1984: I bet he killed her. It's always the husband.
He's not even sad. Douchebag

AllisonCleaver5: You're sooooooo 100% right! I hope they fry him!

shellyDGTS214: Someone should teach that fucker a lesson. See how he likes it

KevinKane3: Maybe we should wait and see before accusing him. The guy's wife is gone!

shellyDGTS214: Just like a fucking man to defend him!

LisaAbbalate: Seriously! Fuck you Kevin!

MomOfThree3: This is gonna be just like that story from forever ago. The guy that killed his pregnant wife and dumped her in the SF Bay.

shellyDGTS214: Yes! Laci something. I bet this douchebag has a girlfriend too

JessOnFire: Totally!! How convenient he wasn't home when his wife was "taken." I bet him and his girlfriend hatched the whole thing to give him an alibi

shellyDGTS214: Where's your wife, James Montgomery?!!!!!

JessOnFire: They should check the yard for fresh dirt. We demand answers!

The pitchforks were out.

James thought back to their wedding day. Only months had passed since the day he and Tessa went to the courthouse. Her saying she wanted a long dress to cover the bruises on her legs. Her extra time in the bathroom with the makeup, covering the rings around her neck. Carrying a single daffodil because her wrist hurt too much to hold a full bouquet.

Maybe they never should've married. It was quick. It was almost deceitful, and a scumbag move on his part, since Joanna found out they were broken up when she discovered he was married to someone else. She lived an hour away and hadn't heard from him in months—he'd ghosted her. Just disappeared, out of the blue. Another cowardly shit move. She drove to town unannounced, and his old roommate said he'd left and moved in with a girl. Joanna found him at a restaurant with Tessa, having a romantic dinner, and confronted them.

Tessa hadn't known about Joanna. Actually, the night he met Tessa, he said he'd just broken up with her. He lied. But he managed to convince her to stay, even after she found out the truth. It was her leftover insecurity from all the other Assholes she dated.

James called the precinct and got the same runaround from Solomon.

"I'm feeling like more could be done here, Detective," James said into the phone. "Again, I'm willing to cooperate with anything you need to do."

Solomon cleared his throat. "That's a funny thing, Montgomery. We're gathering some information from your friends and coworkers. We'd actually like you to come down to answer more questions."

"That's fine by me." James broke out into a sweat. "What time?"

"No time like the present, right?"

James swallowed heavily, pushing the bad feeling down to the pit of his stomach where it belonged. If he asked to bring Evan, or asked for a public defender, he'd look guilty, and he was trying to avoid that. "I'll be there shortly."

He hung up and finished the last of the coffee that had grown cold because he'd spent too much time reading online about what a bastard he was, then went upstairs to shower and dress before seeing the detective.

From the master bathroom window, he saw two reporters at the edge of the cul-de-sac.

"God dammit," he muttered to himself as he buttoned his shirt, a crisp white one fresh from the dry cleaner's. Before he left, he checked all the locks and windows—they'd see him leave and he didn't want them lurking around his property, trying to find a way in, barking about an exclusive from inside the Montgomery home.

"Hey, girl," James said to Candy, as he headed to the door in the laundry room that led to the garage. "Protect the house, okay?" She looked up at him, her eyes so big and innocent, and mushed her head further under his hand, indicating that she wanted him to stay and pet behind her ears. It was something Tessa always did. "I can't, girl. I have to go."

He was backing out of the garage when the reporters came barreling toward the edge of the driveway as he made his way down. They didn't block his way but shouted questions at him as he drove out. He refused to make eye contact and kept his windows up. *Don't give them a reason.*

Again.

In his car, he left the satellite radio on, tuned into a Howard Stern on repeat. He didn't want to put any of the local stations on; God forbid they were in the middle of a talk session and mentioned the "*So did you see how that husband with the missing wife went crazy?*" He was better off steeling himself after the comments he'd read online.

When he walked into the police station, Solomon was waiting in the lobby. He looked drunk, with that bulbous red nose and lazy left eye, which was on full display, with his glasses tucked into his left shirt pocket next to a pen. The cigarette stench clung to him like week-old milk.

"Mr. Montgomery," Solomon said, including the Mr. this time as if James was finally worthy of respect. "Good to see you. You want to come with me?" His left arm extended in a grand gesture toward a door, one James hadn't been through yet. Solomon walked ahead of him and swiped a keycard and the red light outside turned green, and he opened the door.

This was a different hallway than the one he'd walked through yesterday. It went past office cubicles and a small kitchen with a refrigerator and a microwave, no doubt where some pencil-pusher heated up fish, and then they turned left to a narrow hallway where Solomon opened a door. There was a woman in a smart pantsuit sitting at the long metal table.

A tape recorder was in the center, and a camera was in the corner of the room.

"Have a seat, Montgomery," Solomon barked.

James looked at the woman. Forty, give or take, blond bob with gray roots, and she wore a navy blazer. She stood to shake his hand and she was much bigger on the bottom than on the top.

"James Montgomery, I'm Detective Leondra Garvey. I'm assisting Detective Solomon on this case." She was curt and professional and nodded toward an empty seat, which James took.

"Since you're being so helpful, I'm assuming you don't mind if we record this?" Solomon hit the button before James could answer.

James's mouth was dry. The camera was already on, a light streaming from under the lens. "Sure thing. I have nothing to hide." How many lies would he have to tell before they all caught up with him, the proverbial snowball that turned into a boulder that fell down the mountain and crushed him?

"Good." Solomon ruffled through some papers in front of him, then looked at Garvey. "You have that statement? The one from—" He stopped there and raised his eyebrows.

"Yep. Right here," Garvey said and slid a paper across the table, where Solomon caught it and inspected it.

What could they have been talking about? He hadn't done anything—

"How well do you know Rosita Morales?" Solomon asked.

Here we go, thought James. "We're coworkers."

"Mmm. For how long, then?"

"Don't know. A year or so, I guess," James said with a shrug.

"Mmm."

Solomon said nothing. Just stared. Waiting for James to say something, but Evan's advice replayed in the back of his head. *Don't volunteer anything. Just answer the questions.* James wouldn't lose this round of chicken, and Solomon submitted.

"You didn't really answer my first question, Montgomery. How *well* do you know her?" Certain words were accompanied by an index finger slamming on the table.

"What do you want me to say here? That we have a history?" James asked. "It's barely a history. It was one time. And I stopped it before it got too far."

There was much, much more he could say about Rosita, but chose not to.

"Mmm. And when was that?"

"Before Tessa, if that's what you're implying."

"How long before?"

James squirmed, even though he tried not to. He was being filmed. "Right before. Maybe a month."

The detective nodded.

"Look, I had a girlfriend when it happened. Rosita had been coming on to me for months, but I always said no. And nothing really happened, anyway. High schoolers get more physical than we did. It was a lapse in judgment. That's all. And again, before Tessa. What does any of this have to do with finding my wife?"

"Ah, I see how this was her fault," Garvey chimed in. "She 'wore you down.'" Detective Garvey used air quotes in the description.

"I never said it was her fault. It was no one's fault. It happened once and it was nothing. Some kissing and roaming hands and then I stopped it, against her will to be quite honest. Now, what does it have to do with finding Tessa?" James repeated his question.

"We'll be asking the questions, Montgomery," Solomon said. "So, there was nothing going on between the two of you? No reason you'd want to get rid of—" Solomon paused with a smirk, then rephrased. "No reason for Tessa to leave?"

"No." James looked directly at him, fire in his eyes. How dare he?

"Do you own a firearm, Montgomery?"

Fuck. James paused as Tessa's voice played on repeat. *Don't point that thing at me!*

"No," James said.

Were they able to see the sweat forming at his temples, or was it starting to show through his shirt in his armpits? He didn't blink, like a psychopath, and his mouth was like sandpaper as he was dying for a sip of water. He didn't dare ask, even though the water cooler in the corner with the little paper cups mocked him. Like slow motion in a movie, everything went silent. He could almost hear a single drop of water fall from the spout.

Drip.

Drip.

Delicious, wet water. So close, yet so far.

"We have reason to believe you do, Montgomery. You wouldn't mind if we searched your house?"

"Not at all. With a warrant, of course."

James had watched too much *Law & Order*, and mentioning a warrant immediately made him look guilty. Let them ransack his house, drawer by drawer, book by book, floorboard by floorboard.

They'd never find it, anyway. He'd kept his promise.

"Why would you think I had a gun?" James asked, even though he was sure that's what the email between Tessa and Gwen was about.

"Mmm," Solomon said, his go-to answer for anything and everything under the sun. Then he looked at Detective Garvey, raised his eyebrows again, and she thumbed through her papers. They stuck together, and she licked her forefinger, over and over, page after page, until her eyes lit up. She slid a piece of paper over to Solomon and he retrieved his glasses from his left shirt pocket and put them on. They slid to the tip of his nose and then his eyes shifted north to look at James.

"You know a Gwendolyn Holloway, I presume?"

He was right. Tessa had told her what had transpired between them that past week. Why couldn't she keep her fucking mouth shut?

"Gwen is my neighbor. Next door neighbor, but they're a bit of a ways down the street." *Answer only the questions that are asked of you.*

"They?"

"Yes. Gwen and Nick. Her husband. We're friends. All of us." He didn't dare look Garvey's way. She'd been eyeballing him ever since he'd lied about the gun.

"Mmm. Gwen has reason to believe you have an illegal firearm." Solomon took his glasses off. "I guess I don't have to tell you that an illegal firearm, is, well, illegal, do I, Montgomery?"

"I don't know why she'd say that, to be honest."

Garvey flipped through her papers again, studied one sheet that caught her interest, and pulled out a highlighter, which she used on a few of the lines, then slid it toward Solomon. He caught it with a whoosh before it skidded off the table and he zoned in.

"Says here, Tessa went to Gwen earlier this week. Complained about a gun in the house. Apparently, you two had quite the fight about it."

James scoffed. "Please. I called Gwen first thing Friday morning. Check the phone records. I wanted to know if either of them had seen a strange person or car on the street, or if they'd seen Tessa. They both said no. Maybe you should look into reasons they'd be lying?" He had to get Solomon off the illegal gun questioning, even if it proved futile. "I mean, if Gwen told me she hadn't seen her, then why would she tell you something different? Who's lying here, Detective?"

Solomon looked up from his pages of statements and peered directly at James. "Well, that's what I'm here for, Montgomery. I'll decide who's telling the truth. So," he continued with flourish, pointed at the camera, and then at James. "I'm asking you again. Do you own a firearm?"

James flashed back to three weeks ago. Talking with a client, Carl Rittenberg, after he'd secured a loan for his jewelry business. The guy was a straight shooter and James liked him. Talk of the loan turned into talk of the business turned into talk of how to protect the business. New Jersey had archaic gun rules, and Carl had recently applied for a carry permit. Illegal in the state for the most part, but he had extenuating circumstances: He dealt in diamonds. At any time, he could be coming from or going to a wholesale place. At any time, he could be carrying a half a million dollars in cash or a half a million dollars in diamonds. Anyone who scoped him out knew that. Anyone with less than good intentions knew where'd he'd be, and where he was vulnerable.

Carl didn't want to wait three months for a legal permit. He'd mentioned to James where he was able to secure a pistol in the meantime. The early bird gets the worm, but the second rat gets the cheese. Carl refused to have a broken back in a metal contraption.

"I don't own a firearm," James repeated.

Whoever made up the term *silence is deafening* must've had a time machine and must've come to a front-row seat in this room. James didn't want to be cliché and say that you could hear a pin drop, but it would've sounded like a crack of thunder at that point.

"Did you have blood on your shirt Thursday night?"

Fuck. "Who told you that?"

Solomon slammed his hand on the table again. "I said I'll be the one asking questions."

"I had a nosebleed."

He looked at Garvey and laughed. "A nosebleed. Do you believe this guy?" His attention turned back to James. "We're going to need that shirt."

"Is Judge Nguyen back from vacation?" Garvey cut in and asked Solomon. "We could probably have that warrant signed imminently."

"It's at the dry cleaner's," James said. A flash-forward of the jurors' disapproving faces danced in his head.

"Well, wasn't that lightning speed? Your wife is missing but you remembered to run your laundry off to the dry cleaner's?" Solomon asked.

"You're barking up the wrong tree. You should be looking for my wife. Are we done here?" James asked. "I really need to spend time with Candy. She's confused." Garvey gave him a look, one that said *Oh, the stripper girlfriend you're hiding?* "Our dog," he clarified.

Yes, Candy needed him. But he had to get rid of that gun. Completely and totally rid of it. Not just out of the house.

Solomon and Garvey exchanged a glance, and Solomon slapped both hands on the table. "I suppose you haven't heard the last from us, Montgomery. Don't go too far."

James stood and waited for both detectives to do the same before he exited the room. They followed closely behind, right on his heels as the saying goes. He could almost feel Garvey's hot breath on his neck, and their accusatory eyeballs scorched the back of his head.

James had to get home. The gun was out of the house, for sure, but he had to make sure the detectives wouldn't look *there* for it. Because of course that would be the next place to search.

13

Tessa

My day was productive. I did everything I had to do, which included rising at six-thirty A.M. even though I barely got any sleep. I wanted to walk over to the pharmacy a couple of blocks away and get my prepaid cards. I got two five-hundred-dollar ones—one for online stuff, and the other for the rest, including Ellen at the front desk. I knew she was on the eleven P.M. to seven A.M. shift, and I didn't want her to get in trouble for not having me checked in properly. She did me a solid last night. I'll have to pay cash once I check out, since the card won't cover the large hotel expense. And on Monday, I'll have to start looking for a job.

Damon texts me to "hang out" tonight, and I tell him yes, since the bruise is getting easier to cover. The yellow has faded to a point that I can tell him it's a no-sleep bag of under-eye water that refuses to budge, and he'll believe it. The swelling on the lump is still there, unfortunately, and I spend most of the day lazing around in the hotel room, running back and forth to the ice machine to try to keep it from getting any larger, even though that ship has sailed. When housekeeping knocks, I tell them I don't need a made-up bed or turndown service but request more clean towels and turn in my used ones.

Today, there is a bit more of a chill in the air than the last few days, which is finally normal for this time of year. I even open a window in my hotel room before I shower to get some of the stuffiness out. The hotel is set back off the main highway, so there are some trees, which are nicely lit up for incoming guests. The view is bland, but if I crane my neck to the left, I can see lights that line the main part of town, where people gather for romantic dinners and to clink martini glasses filled with rainbow-colored liquids.

Better than the red flashing "vacancy" signs I'm used to. I think every foster sibling, and even my half siblings, were probably used to the same things.

I often think about Sara and Tara, and what became of them after they took off. We lost touch in my teens, and they weren't always in the same foster homes as me. They've got to be in their midthirties by now. I wonder if they're still together. If they ran off and met brothers or friends, if they ended up getting GEDs or went to college and got stable jobs and have summer homes on the beach on the same block. They could be doctors or lawyers, mothers or trophy wives.

Doubtful.

I think Sara was knocked up. Tara is probably dead of an overdose—Lord knows she ran out of the last Hell House with a needle practically sticking out of her arm.

The things we had to do to cope.

Kenny is probably hiding from all his baby mommas. Working construction or dealing drugs or taking bets. Something off the books. It's not like the government will be able to garnish his wages if he gets paid in fistfuls of cash. He was never one for stability. I was closest to him at the time; we're only a year apart. Less, even. Irish twins, they used to call us. Aside from the actual twins, obviously, we were the only ones with the same mother and father. The twins had a different dad than us. So did Christopher, who was half Black. He had a hard time growing up as a mixed kid, who looked more African American than white, while living in a white trash world.

Christopher may or may not be out of prison. Maybe he did his time, learned his life lessons, and now works for youth groups, telling his story about growing up in the system and tsk-tsking them about their crimes and regaling them with tales of his own mistakes. Maybe he met a nice counselor who understood him and wanted to save him. Maybe he or she did.

Or maybe he was shanked while innocently taking a shower.

It's nice to dream about reuniting. Gatherings under the Christmas tree. Exchanging Hallmark cards on birthdays.

And I'd bet every last seven thousand four hundred seventy-seven dollars I have left in my bag that none of them have given one last thought about what the fuck happened to me.

Okay. Maybe Kenny. *Maybe.*

For now, I put the finishing touches on my makeup. I press two fingers onto the lump on my head. The swelling has gone down, but it's still a lump.

All of the Assholes brandished my bruises like a badge of honor. *Yeah, I hit my old lady when she's runnin' her mouth. She'll learn for next time.* Then they'd clink their beer mugs and take their whisky shots with their buddies. One Asshole, who lived in an apartment over a bar with two other guys, used to shove me around in front of them. Laugh about it. Let them order me around too. *Get me another beer, Tessa* or *I want chicken wings, bitch* or *Hide this coke and keep yer fuckin' mouth shut.* They all lived paycheck to paycheck, only splurging on high-end rims for their piece of shit pickup trucks or games for their Xbox.

I thought if I did what they said, the assholes would have no reason to hit me.

Unless the beer wasn't cold. I certainly paid the price for that when their refrigerator broke. Ever since the cast came off, I've been freezing mugs.

I move my hair to the right to make sure the lump is covered and swipe on a coat of sparkly pink lip gloss, the shiny kind that makes my hair stick to my lips if there's a gust of wind. My cheeks are flushed pink without any help from a bronzer. I'll have a real friend in town already, and hopefully Damon can put in a good word to be a waitress or something.

My phone beeps with a text message that my Uber driver is two minutes away, so I close my hotel room door behind me and head to the elevator. Inside, I check my face again in a compact mirror to see how it fares against harsh fluorescent lights. The lights in the bathroom in my hotel room are soft and perfect for putting on makeup, but that doesn't always translate to the real world. But I'm good. No caking.

I see Jerry and note the plate on his silver Honda Accord, and it all checks out. He has Damon's apartment address plugged into the app, and off we go.

It's only a ten-minute ride, thankfully in the opposite direction of yesterday's shithole motel situation. We're only on a highway for five minutes and I watch my new home pass me by. The supermarkets, The Walmart. The Home Goods, my favorite. Then we pass a stretch of land that has the banks, the professional buildings, and the doctors' offices. Jerry turns off the highway and we roll down a dark, tree-lined street. When it opens up, there is a hospital, a few strip malls, and then an apartment center, which the Uber app tells him to turn into.

There are four buildings in the complex, and I know this because we pass three of them and Damon's is the last one. They don't look super fancy, all standing five stories. From the dark, they look like white stucco on the outside. There's a keypad by the front of the main door to each building, so I'll have to be buzzed in.

I thank Jerry and jump out of the Uber, being careful not to slam his door. Once, about three months ago, Asshole and I were getting out of an Uber that took us home after what I thought was a fun night of dinner and drinks with our neighbors. The driver thought I slammed the door too hard, and it dinged Asshole's perfect five-star rating.

I learned the hard way never to do that again.

At the keypad, I search for Damon Moretti and hit the button. There is a buzzing sound that indicates it's okay for me to open the front door. He didn't even confirm it was me through the call box. Once inside, I wait at the elevator and when it opens, an attractive couple walks out. They aren't holding hands, and both wear their frustration with each other on their faces like a pressure cooker about to blow. I give them a quick smile, which they don't return, and get in the elevator.

When I get to the fourth floor, there is a *ding* from the speaker above me and I follow the sign to the left to go to apartment 4D. The carpets in the hallway are brown and old, like something from the living room of Foster Family Number Whatever, because they hadn't updated the house since it was built in 1960. Fluorescent lights hang overhead, which I was afraid of, and outside each door there is a little brass light. The one in front of 4B is broken and casts a dark shadow, making it look like the entryway to Hell House. I knock on the door to 4D.

Footsteps approach, and Damon opens the door, shirtless and in jeans. "Hey. I need another minute to finish getting ready," he says, then walks away without properly inviting me in.

O-kay then. Opening the door shirtless? Is this supposed to be some twisted date? Because I thought we were just going to be buddies.

The door is still open, so I invite myself in and close it behind me. I place my purse on the granite counter. The counters look new, but the appliances look old. White. Rusted in the corners. Electric stovetop, not gas. The tile on the floor is fake linoleum. The place is nicer than a lot of the places I've lived in. A quick scan shows a living room with a small eating area next to a single door with a knob, which I assume goes out to a small balcony, but the four small windows on the door are covered with a solid blue curtain so I can't be sure. To my left, there's a hallway that I believe leads to the bathroom and two bedrooms. The carpets run throughout the whole place, except for the kitchen, and look like they're in need of a decent shampoo. There are two candles burning, one on the counter and another on the cocktail table in front of the couch. It smells like Christmas. At least the Christmas I got to see in school, when I went.

Most of my Christmases smelled of rail gin, stale beer, and baked beans.

When Damon reappears, he's fully dressed, his dark hair perfectly full and loose, not slicked back as he had it in the bar. He's wearing a white T-shirt and blue jeans, and a belt with silver studs to match his boots. His tattoo on his arm shows, and it's a picture of a heart with a dagger through it, blood dripping down the tip.

"Nice place," I say. "How long have you lived here?"

He shrugs. "Couple of years. You want a beer?"

"Sure," I say. "Is your roommate here?"

"Nope. He usually just stays at his old lady's place."

I sting at the term *old lady*. It's so white trashy. Maybe I was wrong about Damon. Wouldn't be the first time the radar broke.

Damon takes two beers out of the refrigerator and opens them and hands me one. I immediately get anxious remembering Asshole's anger over his frosted mugs, but Damon just sips it from the bottle, so I do the same.

"What's our plan for tonight?" I ask.

After swallowing his sip, he licks his lips. "What do you like? Dinner and a movie? Is that a proper date?"

So, it's a date? Do I want that? Is he like the others? "I can eat," I say.

"Cool," he says, and places his full beer on the counter. "Let's go."

He's nothing like the Damon I met in the bar, and I'm trying to figure out if that's good or bad. Broken radar and all.

We head out and walk to his car, a blue Mustang. He hits his keychain and there's a beep and two flashing yellow taillights, so I know it's open. He doesn't open the door for me, just heads to the driver's side and gets in. Which is fine—I'm not used to being treated with chivalry anyway.

Yet, it always crosses my mind when it *doesn't* happen. For some reason I still think I live in a rom-com, with no past to dictate why I would. Goals.

There is a tapas place right across the way from the theater, so we get a quick bite there. Out in the wild, he's more relaxed than he was in his apartment. Damon talks mostly about himself. Thirty-five. Divorced, which is good to know. Ex-spouses can be such a pain in the ass, as I've come to discover. He says his regular day job is cable and Wi-Fi installation, and usually works from seven A.M. to three P.M. Monday through Friday, and only bartends on Friday nights. For quick cash, according to him.

He doesn't ask me much about myself, which is honestly welcoming. The only thing he asks me is where I'm from, and I lie to him. It's not like he's going to check.

After the movie, he asks me back for a nightcap. Experience says this will end badly for me. However, he never got handsy on me once all night—didn't even try, so I assume we're still doing the getting-to-know-you thing. I'm sure he won't flip into some animal.

It's a quick ride back to his place, and when he opens the front door, there's a girl in the kitchen. Tall, medium build, mousy brown straight hair. She startles me, as I didn't expect to see a woman in his place, but she enrages Damon.

"What are you doing here?" he says immediately. "He's not here, I thought he was at your house. Go home. God, I fucking hate that he gave you a key." He looks at me. "This is my roommate's girlfriend."

Jesus. Calm down, buddy. He certainly acts differently in front of strangers. Pretends to be a good guy? Should I get out of here?

He looks back at her. "Can you leave? I have company."

"Relax, Damon. I know he's not here. I was just leaving him a note," she says, points to a pad on the counter, and heads to the door. She stops and looks at me. "Girl to girl, I have to warn you against this one. He's an asshole."

Asshole. Man, I love me an Asshole with a capital A, huh?

"Get out!" Damon shouts and slams the door behind her. "We never got along. Don't listen to her."

He drops his keys on the table and then heads to the TV and turns on the cable box until it gets to a slow music station. Then he presses the remote-control button until the volume can surely be heard by the neighbors. His earlier rage turns me on a little, because I'm wired that way. He spins me around and kisses me. Hard. Rough. Without remorse, and without asking, which is also how I'm used to it.

He removes his shirt from the back of the neck and his gaze pierces mine and we fall onto the couch, him on top of me. He goes for my belt. At this point the couch pillows are under my back and making me arch, which I don't want to do—it's practically an invitation.

"Hey," I say and push back a little. "Let's take this slow."

Ignoring me, he goes for my belt again, and my stomach turns inside itself. Goosebumps develop on my skin, not the good kind, when he aggressively kisses my neck.

"Hey, wait." I try to push him off, but that just makes his grip tighter. "Damon, stop."

Now he's biting my neck, not listening. Not stopping. Fussing with my tucked in shirt, trying to lift it over my head. I push it back down with my free hand. He's got the other pinned above my head.

"That hurts," I say. "Damon, *stop*."

I think quickly about what Kenny taught me. Palm of my hand up. Break his nose.

Before I can act, my tiny wrists are gripped into one of his strong hands above my head. I sink further into the couch, making it hard to try to get control of the situation. I scream *stop* again.

He works his zipper. "You wanted to come here tonight. You started it."

I'm struggling beneath him, tears falling. My muffled sounds beg for help, but there is no help. There's nothing. There's just him, pushing his pants down and trying to get mine off. I'm kicking every step of the way. I try to knee him in the groin, but the way I'm pinned makes it impossible. His face is on my breasts, my shirt and bra now up around my neck, and he's vulnerable for one second and I make my move. My right knee goes up as best as I can lift it, and he wails.

He stops.

Then he hits me. Closed fist. Opposite side of the lump I already have, so it's a matching set. I shut my eyes and I try to scream bloody murder, but I can't. My vocal cords are constricted under his fingers, his thumbs pressing into the soft spot. How does a man know exactly where to shut you up, every time? I'm about to black out when suddenly, he's off me. Thrown across the room and into a wall.

"What the fuck are you doing to her, Damon?" a man screams.

My face is wet from my tears, I'm coughing, I'm sure my throbbing eye is turning purple, I think my wrist is fractured, and I'm trying to figure out what the hell is going on in the chaos. The front door is wide open, and a man is in the apartment, landing blow after blow on Damon.

"You sick fuck!" mystery man screams. Another punch lands. "Leave her alone!"

When Damon is finally subdued, he wipes the blood from his mouth and looks at the guy. "What the fuck business is this of yours?"

The guy looks my way, then back at Damon. "Yeah, I can tell she's totally into it. Girls don't cry and scream during sex. You don't hit women who say no—you stop." He looks at me again but doesn't come close. He stays near Damon, his arm out toward him in case he tries to get up and attack. "Are you okay?" he asks me.

I'm holding my eye and wiping my tears, trying to pull my bra and shirt back down. "No, I'm not okay. Who are you?"

The man looks at Damon. "His roommate. Call the cops."

"No." I can't call the cops. I can't explain who I am. Where I'm coming from. "No, it's fine. Just get him away from me."

Damon is still on the floor against the wall, knowing better than to jump up and continue the fight. "Fuck you, man," he says to the guy. Then he stands and pulls his pants up, grabs his shirt and yanks it over his head. "Don't be here when I get back. I want you out of here." Without a care in the world, Damon walks out the open door and slams it behind him.

The guy looks at me and puts both of his hands up defensively as he slowly walks toward me. "I'm not going to hurt you."

"I know," I say, then click my jaw. The pain sears into the back of my neck. "Thank you. I don't know what I would've done if you didn't walk in just now."

His expression is solemn, caring. "Can I look at your eye?" he asks.

I nod, and he comes closer, slowly, cautiously, still with his hands up. Then, a gentle hand touches my shoulder and another points my head toward the light in the kitchen. "This is going to leave a mark. And you're bleeding. Do you want me to take you to the hospital?"

"No." No insurance, fake Social on my ID, don't want to be found. No.

There's something in his eyes. Something special. Something gentle and loving. I've never seen it before. Also, they're the same exact color as mine. Gray. Unique.

"Hang on, I'm going to get some ice."

He stands and goes to the freezer, takes out a few ice cubes, and puts them on a clean rag he takes out of a kitchen drawer. They clink against each other as they roll into the rag and he approaches me again, slowly, gesturing toward my face.

"Is this okay?" he asks. I nod, and he swipes my hair away and winces when he sees the damage. "Jesus Christ. I'm so sorry."

I hold the ice rag against my head. "Why? You didn't do it."

"Hang on. I'm going to get the first aid kit."

He runs to the bathroom and I hear drawers and cabinets being opened and closed, and he comes out with a kit overflowing with bandages and ointments. I sniffle, but I don't want to wipe my nose on my arm because that's gross, and I'm trying not to be completely pathetic in front of my knight in shining armor. He stops and grabs a box of tissues off the kitchen counter and sets them down beside me, then sits cross-legged in front of me.

"Is it okay if I touch you again?" he asks, nodding toward my cut head and my purple eye and neck.

"Mmm hmm," is all I can muster as I grab a tissue to delicately wipe the snot away.

I think he must be a doctor, or at least in the medical field, the way he gingerly takes care of me. In silence, he disinfects the cut and uses two butterfly bandages to close it and then applies a waxy ointment on top.

"I can put a gauze pad over it if you want," he says, then holds the ice over my eye again.

"No. I'm okay. Thank you."

"Fucking Damon. I'm so sorry he did this to you. What's your name?"

"Tessa. Tessa Smyth. I met him yesterday at the bar."

He shakes his head back and forth. "That's where he finds them all." Then he takes a deep breath and introduces himself. "Nice to meet you Tessa. I'm James Montgomery."

14

James

Driving back from the police station, all James thought about was Tessa. He'd tried to fill in the holes in her past, who her ex that she was running from was, but part of him didn't want to—the poor girl had been through some real shit. Hell, when he met her, she was being beaten and almost raped by his former roommate.

It was fate. From day one. How could he know her for barely four months, and her sudden absence left such a huge hole in his heart?

Unfortunately, he'd heard about Damon, after he'd moved in with him—it was why he mostly stayed at Joanna's place, even though she lived so far away from work. He didn't want to be associated with the guy that didn't take *no* for an answer. It was the worst-kept secret around town. Supposedly, he'd abused his ex-wife, and that's why Damon was divorced. A good-looking, mysterious, troublemaking bartender, he was an entitled prick and assumed he deserved women to be at his beck and call. He didn't like it when they weren't. James had never witnessed it until he saw Tessa on the ground, being choked, bleeding, and Damon trying to forcibly get her pants off.

The image still made the bile rise from his stomach to his throat. That was his wife.

James remembered the way Tessa looked at him when he took care of her that night. She was a wounded bird, and so grateful that he wasn't there to take advantage of her, like every man in her life before him had supposedly done. He knew nothing of her checkered past at that point, and he may have fallen in love with her right then and there. Her doe eyes, even though one was swollen and the other looked to be healing. Her beautiful lips, even though one was bleeding. Her long neck, even though there were purple and blue rings forming around it.

Now, all he thought about was getting her back.

There could be a million reasons why she'd disappeared, since she'd had so many abusive exes, including one that she was running from the night they met. But James only thought of one real problem: Damon Moretti. But he couldn't tell the cops that *yet*.

With James's current bad luck, now that the news about Tessa was out, now that his *name* was out, he wouldn't be surprised if Damon himself went to the cops. To scream about James pulling a gun on him last Thursday night, the night Tessa went missing.

Tessa hated guns—she'd had her share of guns pointed in her direction. When she opened up about her nameless last husband—Asshole—she'd said that he pulled guns on her all the time. And someone she knew from back home mentioned to her that the ex was still looking for her. So James got a gun for protection. When he let Tessa know and showed it to her, wanting to teach her how to use it in case she had to in a pinch, she shrieked her disapproval and told him to stop pointing it at her—like he'd ever do such a thing. He assured her he was doing it for her own protection. Then he promised her he'd get rid of it.

He sort of did. At least, he got it out of the house, like she'd asked. He kept it in the locked glove compartment of his car, until he could figure out a better place to hide it—he wouldn't be without it—not if Damon or the other nameless Asshole came looking for her. And the night she'd disappeared, he had left a note on the table before he left for work that morning, one which he immediately burned when he discovered she was missing.

> *Tessa—I got rid of the gun. I never want you to feel unsafe. I'll be home as soon as I can tonight. I love you. James*

He couldn't let the cops scouring his place know he'd had a gun in his possession, because it was illegal. He didn't want to bolster their belief that he was a suspect. He hadn't done anything to Tessa. He'd give his right arm to know she was safe.

Still, rage took over when he saw Damon at Jupiter's while he was out with Rosita and the two guys from VistaBuild, Andy and Kyle, last Thursday. As usual, Damon was hassling a girl. He didn't see James—in fact James had only seen Damon once since the night that he beat Tessa, and that was a few days later, when James was moving out. Tessa was staying at a hotel nearby, and James stayed with her until they got married, two weeks later.

Quick.

Fate.

Love.

Damon had followed the girl out of Jupiter's that night. She was alone, a would-be victim. James wouldn't let

Damon fall into his old antics, so he excused himself from his current company. Grabbed the pistol from his glove compartment and when he found Damon pinning the crying girl to the back of a building, he put the fear of God into him.

The gun wasn't loaded—James wasn't stupid, and he wasn't about to kill a man. Even an attempted rapist piece of shit like Damon. But seeing his face in the bar brought back the memories of his hands around the throat of the woman he loved, and he lost it.

In the back of the building, over the woman's cries, even Damon was able to hear the click of the trigger being pulled back—a warning. Felt the pressure of the cold steel barrel against his head. Heard the threats that poured out of James's mouth.

Damon literally pissed himself while the woman ran away. For an added threat, James cracked Damon over the head with the gun. Left a mark, made him bleed, as Damon had done to many other girls. A huge mistake, considering it was Damon's blood that Andy noticed on his shirt when he went back into the bar. But worth it as Damon looked up at him with wide, glassy, frightened eyes, and James added, "Don't let me see you again, motherfucker," and backed away, still pointing the pistol at his head.

He hoped it would be a while before Damon tried to harass another woman.

When Rosita called him out on disappearing from the bar for a little while, James made up the story about having to move his car. If Rosita told that to the cops, surely, they'd be able to check street cameras and see where his car was all night. He hoped she kept her mouth shut.

He didn't mean to lie. He wasn't some county vigilante, but fuck Damon Moretti.

Tessa disappeared around that time. According to the
forensics team, it had to do with the freshness of her blood
in the kitchen.

Did Damon seek revenge? He knew James and Tessa
were married. Did he look up their address, knowing that
James was out in town without Tessa, and that she'd be
home, alone, vulnerable? Did he sneak to the back, bust
open a kitchen window, and drag poor, unwilling Tessa
across the floor, punching her, causing her to bleed all
over their floor?

Was Tessa's disappearance James's fault?

15

Tessa

This man, this James Montgomery, is complete and utter perfection.

I'm all cleaned up and safe. James offers to drive me home, but I want to call Hobart—he's the only person I trust. But the way James looks at me, with his dark hair, his five o'clock shadow, his loosened tie on his button-down shirt—I fall under a spell. I can't put my finger on it. It's not the same. I don't fall because he's dangerous and mysterious and *bad*.

It's because I think he's good.

This is something that's never happened to me before.

Sure, I've tried to see the good in people that I knew were going to fuck with me—truck drivers and construction workers and "professional video game players"—but there's something inherently perfect about this man. He's hot, but he's also gentle and doesn't come at me with lines and smarmy bullshit. Genuine.

"Come on, Tessa. Let me drive you home. I promise you can trust me. I'm not like him," James says. "I'm not."

His pleading eyes are sincere. And he hasn't tried to touch me since he wrapped me in a blanket as I sat on the couch to recover. He even made me tea. He didn't talk to me while I drank the tea, not because it was awkward, but because it wasn't.

I finish the last of the Earl Grey, not my favorite but the only kind that was in the cupboard, and place the mug on the glass table in front of me with a soft clank. Then I look up at his caring face, while mine is stricken with panic. What will he do if I leave a ring on the table?

"I'm sorry. Do you have a coaster?" I ask, my first words to him since he fixed me.

Rings on the tabletop have never been a plus in my past situations. I'd be reminded of the coaster by having it smacked into my face.

"Don't worry about it. This place obviously isn't fancy." He smiles at me, and it's real. "Hey, I don't feel right putting you in an Uber after—after everything tonight. I promise you can trust me," he says again, which in my situation has always been famous last words.

But I do trust him.

"What are you going to do about him?" I ask.

He lets out a long sigh. "I'd like to go to the police, but I'll respect your wishes if you don't want me to. I guess I'll pack up some stuff tonight and stay in a hotel. I have to get out of here. I swear if I see his fu"—he stops, looking at me and wanting to be a gentleman—"his damn face, I don't know what I'll do."

I press my lips together, still tasting blood from the split one, and nod.

"Do you live around here?" he asks.

I shrug. "I'm new in town. Just got here a few days ago. I'm staying at that big hotel off Main."

"Where were you before?"

I shake my head softly. I can't tell him. I don't even know him. "Around. Needed a change of scenery."

"I see." He nods. "Well, I'm going to pack a few things, and then I'm taking you back to the hotel. Looks like I'll be staying there a while too." His hands go up again, quickly. "I'm not stalking you. I just have to figure out where to sleep for the next few days."

My thoughts go back to the girl who was here earlier tonight. "Don't you have a girlfriend you can stay with?"

"Nope. We broke up tonight. That's why I came home early. Thank God," he says, nodding toward the floor where I was attacked.

"Oh. She was here when Damon and I first got here. She was in the kitchen; said she was leaving you a note. I think it's still on the counter."

"She was?" his eyebrows knit together, and he rises from the old wingback chair and goes to the breakfast bar. He finds the note, reads it, and balls it up and throws it in the garbage. Runs his hand through his thick, wavy hair and scratches the back of his neck. "Well, that's that."

"Do you have any family you can stay with?" I ask.

A shadow casts over his face. "No. My parents retired to Florida. And Tommy—my brother—he's been dead for fifteen years."

I open my mouth simply to remove my foot. "I'm sorry." Change the subject. "Why did you and your girl-friend break up?" Sure, good move, T. Make him talk about one depressing thing after another. Rude of me to use him to get my mind off my current situation.

He laughs and looks at me. "Aren't relationships always complicated?" He shrugs, smirks. "Things happen for a reason, I guess."

I nod, thinking that if they didn't break up, I'd be raped and possibly dead right now.

"Well," he continues, "like I said. I'm going to pack some stuff. I really hope you let me take you back there."

I could almost hear him saying once again I could trust him… or maybe that's what I wanted to hear in that moment. That would be the third time, and you know what they say: Third time's the charm.

"Okay. Thank you," I say softly.

I sit quietly as I hear him shuffle around in his bedroom and the bathroom. Hangers scratching against poles, drawers opening and closing, things shaking around in the bathroom. A zipper closes with a squeak—a long one, must be a suitcase—and then another shorter one, perhaps a duffel bag. The wheels to the case thud against the floor as they roll into the living room. James pulls the handle to the navy-blue bag, and he has a matching navy-blue duffel over his shoulder, worn crossbody, and is also holding a garment bag. Called both right.

"This should get me through the week." He grabs his keys. "You ready?"

I stand and follow as he opens the door and moves through.

He turns back to me. "Let me stay in front of you. Just in case. I don't want that jerk-off hiding behind any corners and trying to surprise us."

It has never occurred to me that a gentleman always lets the woman walk in front of him. Because I've never been with a gentleman. Asshole may have been an alpha male with a stable job, but he was also a narcissist who got off on humiliating me and making me feel small. Opening doors for himself and leaving me to enter after him was par for the course. He didn't give a shit if the door slammed in my face.

James moves cautiously through the hall and to the elevator, then takes every precaution through the lobby and through the lot to his car.

He opens the door and I slide in and buckle up. He pops the trunk and loads his luggage before rounding to the driver's side. When he turns the car on, the satellite radio is already on the Howard Stern Show and he quickly flips it to a Top-20 type station.

"Sorry about that," he says.

I happen to like Howard Stern. "You can put it back. He's funny."

"Oh yeah? Most women find him offensive. And I feel like you've been through enough shit tonight."

I chuckle. "Nah. It's just a persona for radio, I think. I saw his movie. The one he acted in, about his life. I think he's loyal. Went back and got everyone from his past as soon as he started to make it. And they're all still with him. For decades." I train my gaze out the window as he pulls out of the lot that I hope to never see again. "Loyalty is important."

He's quiet for a quarter minute, then flips the station back on. "You're something else, Tessa. I never looked at it that way."

The short ride to the hotel is filled with conversation about the show, and it's easy to talk to him. He pulls into the lit-up drive and stops at the top of the semicircle near the front door.

"Does Damon know you're here?" he asks.

I shake my head. "He wasn't much for talking."

"Okay, good. Go inside. I'll wait until the doors close behind you."

"Oh. I thought you were staying here too?"

"I am. I don't want you to have to walk from the other end of the lot after I park. I bet you just want to get inside and curl up in bed."

"Yeah, you nailed it." I smile at him and reach for the handle.

"Hey. Wait one second," he says, then puts the car in park and gets out and rummages through the trunk. It slams shut and he comes to my side and opens the door for me, and hands me a Yankees hat. "Just in case you don't want anyone to—you know—see."

I nod. "God, I must be hideous." I punch the inside of the hat and then place it on my head. That was something Kenny always did before he put one on, and I was the adoring, copycat little sister. Old habits die hard. I lift my head extra high to see James's eyes under the lip of the cap. "Thanks, James. I mean it. For everything."

"Take care of yourself, Tessa. And," he pauses and reaches for his wallet, a small black leather one that folds in half. Inside the inner pocket he retrieves a business card. "My cell is on there. Let me know if you change your mind about going to the police. I was a witness." He shakes his head softly again, in disbelief, then he smiles. "Or, you know, if you just want to talk or hang out or something. That's okay too."

"Thanks. Maybe I will." I turn to go inside, and as soon as my hand is on the door, he calls my name again, so I whip my head around. "Yes?"

His smile is crooked and shy when he says, "I just wanted you to know you're not hideous."

I'm laughing as I open the door, and when I'm in the lobby I'm aware of the bright lights, and thankful for the hat. I pull it down farther over my forehead and keep my head down as I head to the elevator.

Once inside my room, I beeline for the bathroom and look at my face. Jesus, I can't go out at all tomorrow.

Disaster.

I take pictures in the mirror with the cell phone, just in case. It's always good to have evidence.

I took pictures of bruises when Asshole got really rough. The hospital reports would never be used as evidence, since I was always adamant about the fact that I "fell" or "walked into something."

The nurses knew; they had to. They probably saw that shit on the regular. They didn't even seem shocked by the third-degree burn on my arm from the boiling water, as the first ex-husband's arm was around me, telling the nurses I'm clumsy. He was the tattoo artist. We were only married for three weeks total. I did it to get out of Foster Home Number Whatever, but decided that being burned was worse, so I went back. The marriage was annulled but it was never legal anyway since I was underage without parental consent. Whatever that was.

Plus, I'll never forgive him for what he did to me. It was worse than the boiling water.

I grab one of the burners to see that a text came in from Asshole's coworker Maribel Lopez—the one he's been having an affair with. The one who, now, wants to see him go down almost as much as I do. I look at the screen.

It's done. Now we wait.

16

James

When James got home, there were no reporters waiting in the driveway. He felt the tension ease from his shoulders as he pulled the car into the garage and brought the gun inside with him. He wanted to take Candy on a run, but he couldn't risk her barking and giving him away while he completed his mission. While she explored the yard, he changed into a T-shirt and sweatpants, and grabbed his armband to strap his phone into. His headphones were on the kitchen counter, and when he plugged them into the phone, he blasted Linkin Park in his ears to drown out the swirls of accusation in his head. With one last peek out the front door, his head swiveled left to right. No one was there. No one was waiting for him.

He let Candy in and refilled her water, and before he left for his run in the park, he duct-taped the gun to his lower back. Not the most perfect—or comfortable—way to handle it, but he certainly couldn't brandish it while waving to neighbors.

It was a perfect afternoon, the onset of fall, and the fresh cut grass smell was still thick in the air. The smell reminded him of simpler times, when all he needed to do to earn a few bucks was clip the neighbor's grass. He started a slow jog on his way out of the neighborhood. While he normally stopped to talk to neighbors weeding their lawns or to pet dogs being walked, this time he kept his head down as he exited the cul-de-sac onto the main street.

James ran cross country all through high school and college, and even ran the New York Marathon once in his late twenties, when he was in peak shape. Running was the one thing that put his mind at ease, pushed everything else bad out of his brain. When he was so focused on his pace and his heart rate and pushing himself to the brink, it was impossible to think about anything else except how to survive long enough to get home without passing out.

This time, James had a mission.

He ran three and a half miles to the park. It was one of those parks that had set up paved trails, a hockey rink, basketball and tennis courts, and, in the summer, a water spray park for the kids. He and Tessa often walked the grounds with Candy over the summer.

He knew exactly where to go.

Candy, being a herding dog, liked to go off leash and explore. She was a good girl and always stayed next to either James or Tessa on their walks. One time, a squirrel ran out in front of her and she zigzagged into the adjacent woods, making chase. The squirrel was faster, of course, and quickly climbed up a huge tree. When James and Tessa found Candy at the foot, barking like a dog possessed, they laughed, then marveled at the tree. It didn't look like it belonged in New Jersey, with a trunk ten feet wide, sturdy branches billowing out from every angle and taking root in the ground. It looked like one of the trees near downtown St. Petersburg, where his parents lived in Florida.

The gigantic hole in the middle of the multiple trunks and branches looked like a nature-made fort. Like the Keebler elves lived inside. An actual tree *house*.

So James ran the trail he and Tessa and Candy were on that day. Passed other joggers enjoying the end-of-September weather. People walking dogs, kids riding bikes. When he got near the turnoff into the woods that Candy had taken, he paused, his hands on his knees, huffing and puffing in an exaggerated manner as he looked for other people. He turned off the anger music that pounded in his ears. The silence of the park, save for a few bees that buzzed by, shocked him on such a nice day.

When the coast was clear, he turned right, crunching deep into the foliage, and found the tree. The majestic beauty was perfection, and the ideal hiding spot. He winced as he ripped the duct tape off his chest, then removed the tape from the small revolver. It was a .38 caliber, and he had the six bullets it came with in his pants pocket. He wiped the fingerprints from the gun with his sweat-covered T-shirt and placed it in the center hole of the tree—the Keebler elves would just have to deal with it. He scattered the bullets in the same place and covered everything with fallen leaves.

Again, he looked left to right. Nothing. No one. No random dogs chasing animals through the woods. Even the bees weren't buzzing in there.

Back at the edge of the woods, near the concrete trail, he looked both ways again, like a child crossing the street, and no one was there. Just in case there was someone in the distance that he didn't see, James stopped and did some calisthenics and stretches, so any passersby would think he just stopped to give his aching muscles a rest.

Not that he was hiding an illegal gun.

His feet hit the pavement for a fast walk, and he turned the anger music back on before he picked up speed again. Another half mile or so on the trail, then another three and a half miles back from the park to his house.

Mission accomplished.

17

Tessa

I spent the entire Sunday lying in my hotel room, and only went out once to walk to the McDonald's down the block, because I needed to eat something. Now it's Monday morning, and I can't even look for a job. Not with my face looking the way it does, thanks to Damon. As per usual, the lumps on my head have settled into the shape they'll take for the next few days, and the purple and blue marks I'm used to are taking hold. My split lip can't be covered with lipstick. In fact, it makes it look reptilian.

I stare at Maribel's text. *It's done. Now we wait.* For how long? I decide to call her. My anxiety bubbles in my subconscious as the line trills. She says she wants to help, but can I trust her?

"Are you alone?" I ask in a semi-disguised voice when she picks up.

"Hey. Hang on," she says.

The phone plunks into an abyss, and I know she's at work with Asshole, trying to hide the burner before being discovered. "Let me call you back in a few minutes. I'll go for coffee," she whispers, then hangs up.

Waiting never bothered me. Biding time.

However, these five minutes are excruciating as I picture her, tall and blond, in her clicky-clacky expensive heels that Asshole probably bought her. He liked women to look a certain way, and even I fit the mold for a little while. Maribel Lopez was half Puerto Rican on her father's side but somehow got her white mother's less-dominant genes. She had her father's height but her mother's features, including the dirty blond hair and light skin. The first time I met her, I thought she was a model, so I sort of understood Asshole's fascination with her. Right now, she's probably ducking the little cheap phone into her Zac Posen bag, then popping her head into his office to tell him she's running out, and does he want anything? Supposedly that's how it started.

Maribel told me everything when I approached her a couple of weeks ago. She had no choice, really. She was his "work wife" at the hedge fund. She knew me, his *actual* wife. I followed her home one day, when Asshole was out with clients, and she stopped in her driveway when I pulled up. She didn't act paranoid when she saw me get out of my car—she was good at her deception. Maybe she thought I was just coming over to say hello, so she did what every mistress trying not to get found out does. Be accommodating. Smile. Lie.

She stopped at her door and gave a little wave. Likely shitting her pants, but still. As I got closer, she saw my black eye. Her face registered shock when I came into full view.

When I told her that I knew about the affair, and that Asshole did this to me repeatedly, she believed me.

She didn't go off on a tangent about how I'm crazy and that they're in love. How I didn't deserve him. She wasn't jealous or confrontational, as mistresses usually are. She was immediately sympathetic, invited me in for coffee, and I even cried in front of her. She apologized profusely, saying she got caught up in his charm and it had been going on for a few months.

Of course, I already knew that.

One thing about the men I've dated in my past is that I know a cheating man. The signs. The late nights. The shower when they come home. The complete disregard for my feelings.

He may as well have worn a red *A* on his chest. It would've been less obvious.

One night when he passed out on some twenty-five-year-old scotch, I went through his phone, as most suspicious wives do. All the evidence was there, as most cheating husbands needed to validate themselves over and over by rereading the sexy text messages from someone other than their wife.

What Maribel didn't know was how he treated me. Of course, in the beginning of their affair, she said he gave her the same sad sob story that every horrible man with a handcuff on their fourth left finger said: *She doesn't pay attention to me, she doesn't work, I buy her everything, the sex is dwindling, I'm a rich virile man with so much to give.* And Asshole *is* charming—it's how I fell for him too, but that's a whole other story.

So, one night at work, she stayed late. So did he. And what's the term the guilty use? One thing led to another.

Uh huh. His dick led itself right into her wide-open legs.

But I digress.

She said she asked him if he needed anything when she was leaving, and he pounced like a cat onto a tabletop. After months of them flirting, she said she made an error in judgment.

Sixteen times. Sixteen times in two months. That's a hell of a lot of error.

But she did believe me, and I'm thankful for that. Her rage grew as she held my hand and let me talk about all the times that he put me in my place.

When I told Maribel that I was afraid of leaving, she wore her guilt over the affair like blinking neon, and said she'd help me if I needed it. She'd even go a step further—she'd help me stick it to him. She even agreed to keep up pretenses for a couple of weeks while we figured out my next move. Fuck him a few more times. And after I disappeared, and he looked guilty, she'd go on record about their affair. Ruin his life. Really put the pressure on him.

And keep me safe.

I've never had a real friend, but I imagine this is what it's like. Someone who has your back. Girl power and all that.

When the phone rings, I answer with flourish. Giddy. Smiling even though she can't see me, but she'll hear it in my voice.

"Hey," I say when I pick up.

"Hey. I've only got a few minutes. But I did exactly like you wanted," Maribel says, and I hear the relief in her voice as well. "Drew didn't tell me that you were missing Friday night, but he knows something is up. Just like you wanted, I texted him over and over, promising vile sex things. He didn't answer me until late at night, probably when he realized you were just gone with no explanation. But we know what a pig he is, so he came over. Didn't tell me you were missing though. He actually said that you were bitching at him about something and he left and came to me instead. Because he loves me." She scoffed.

"God, I feel like such an idiot for believing him all those months."

"That's what Drew is good at. Making you feel like an idiot," I say, thinking of all the times I fell prey to his misogyny and narcissism. Then, a twinge of self-pity creeps in. "He just went over to your house for sex, after he saw the blood and the hair?" She can't see me shaking my head, but I'm doing it. "I could be dead, and he doesn't care. He's glad I'm gone."

When I met Drew, I was a waitress at a dumpy little breakfast place near his office. One that, according to him, had the best sausage, egg, and cheese on a toasted croissant in the county. He flirted, I flirted back. It went on for weeks, until he asked me out. Mr. Hedge-Fund Man wanted to rescue the stupid little sandwich slinger.

No, he didn't want to rescue me. He wanted to control me. He needed someone to take out his machinations on, and I fit the bill. Really, where was I going to go, once he started beating me? I'd been upgraded from a studio apartment—with a Craigslist roommate who dealt coke—to suburban utopia. He figured that, after a taste of champagne, I wouldn't go back to tap water.

He was right. For a little while, anyway.

"So, you planted the gun?" I asked.

"I did. I had to fuck the ever-living shit out of him Friday night. Made me sick. But he did pass out and I put his prints all over it. Yesterday, he told me you were visiting family for the weekend and he invited me over, so I went over there and planted it, in the back of his closet, behind those ratty shoes he never wears but refuses to throw out. The ones from college."

It pains me for a second that she knows intimate details about those shoes, and why he won't get rid of them.

She continues, "I left a bunch of my hair everywhere too. And my grandmother's ring behind the bed." She pauses. I know how much that ring means to her, but that tidbit was my idea, and a good one. She'll get it back when this is over. "He'll never know it's there, but once I tell the police about the affair, he'll deny it, of course. I'll tell them my ring is missing and to look for it. Plus, my hair is in your bed now. My underwear is wedged between the mattress and the box spring."

"Okay. Good." This must be so hard for her. The man she fell for is a monster, and that discovery hurts her as much as it hurt me. "Hey, are you okay? How are you doing?"

"I'm fine," she says quickly. "We all make mistakes. Mine was the worst, but I'll make sure he pays for what he did to you. And what he'd probably do to me if I continued to see him. I'm still so sorry."

"Stop. I don't blame you."

"Where did you end up?" she asks.

I pause. "It's better if you don't know. Plausible deniability."

Maribel doesn't need to know I'm over a hundred miles north, in New Jersey. Especially because I told her I was headed south somewhere. I want this as far away from her as possible.

"Okay," she says. "I'll do the other part this week. Probably Monday, if it all works out."

"Great. I won't bother looking online for news yet. Let me know when my disappearance is official."

"I will. Take care of yourself, Tessa. Start over. Meet someone who treats you the way you deserve to be treated." She sighs. "I'll try to do the same."

We say goodbye and I hang up.

Find someone who treats me the way I deserve to be treated. I don't even know what I deserve anymore.

On the dresser, his business card calls to me. James Montgomery. It says he's the assistant manager at the bank in town, and I want to thank him again for last night, but I don't. Not yet.

But I will. Even if I have to hide who I am.

18

James

James felt like a rat in a cage at home. He didn't want to leave again, so it was just him and Candy, flitting around from one room to the next. Flipping between watching television and reading the paper. And staring at the phone, waiting for it to ring, waiting for Detective Solomon to call and say that they found her.

Or worse, that they found her *body*. James pushed it away. He didn't like to spend time with negative thoughts like that—Tessa was a survivor, if anything. He wished he could do something. He would *not* be planning his wife's funeral. What also gave him anxiety was the constant threat that Solomon would show up with a warrant. Even though they wouldn't find anything, he didn't need to be *that* person in the neighborhood. The one with the missing wife, the suspected murderer with cops showing up to ransack his residence.

And yes, he also spent time looking at the now three hundred-plus comments on the article. He tried not to, but it was futile.

Some were downright vicious. And the girl who was going nuts on the page earlier in the day didn't relent.

shellyDGTS214: don't know why they haven't dragged that ape out of his house in cuffs yet!

People don't go missing like that, this isn't the city! He totally killed her.

HelenCarrera: I know right!

TheBoo800: I've seen him in the bank. Always had that creepy look to him

shellyDGTS214: @TheBoo800 A murderer had a creepy look? I'm shocked!

JohnKlein6969: You people need to get a grip. I thought in this country it was innocent until proven guilty?

shellyDGTS214: Then why was he at the police station again @JohnKlein6969? I heard they brought him in for questioning again! Yeah sounds totally innocent. Fucking murderer!

JohnKlein6969: YOU HEARD @shellyDGTS214? Stalk much? Jesus maybe you did it

shellyDGTS214: Fuck you and your patriarchy @JohnKlein6969. Wouldn't surprise me if the murderer is your friend!

SweetVictoriaXO: I don't know him but I'm not necessarily convicting him yet either

shellyDGTS214: I'm sure dead Tessa would love to know that even women turned on her. Fuck you too @SweetVictoriaXO!

Dead Tessa. His chest squeezed at those words.

That Shelly woman was the ringleader and attacked anyone else who didn't share her already made-up mind. The hits just kept coming, and James didn't know what to do.

Then it hit him. He needed to speak to Gwen.

Outside, the street was buzzing more than it had been earlier in the day, when he went for his run. Now there were couples weeding, kids riding bikes, people walking dogs. He put on his New York Rangers hat to hide, thinking that would suddenly turn him into a hockey player, maybe power left winger Artemi Panarin, and no one would know that he was James Montgomery. The friendly Lovett Road killer.

James went out the back door. He could cut diagonally through the woods and end up near Nick and Gwen's shed, then go around the side of it to the front door. He didn't want to walk in plain sight on his street under prying eyes right up their driveway like he was stopping in for coffee, even though going around this way made him look like a cat burglar. As he turned the corner and approached their stucco house with the yellow door, he had to calm his shaking hands. He took a deep breath and rang the bell. Footsteps approached and Nick's face appeared at the window. The locks clanked and he opened the door a sliver.

"Hey James," Nick said, hiding behind the door. His shifting eyes said *go away*. "What's up?"

"I was hoping to talk to Gwen."

Nick looked behind him, where James's superman powers let him see through the big door to Gwen's disapproving face. The urgent whispers began.

"Gwen, it's important," James said, louder, making sure she heard. "You know I wouldn't come here otherwise."

More whispers. Then the door swung open and Gwen appeared.

"Make it fast, James. Caleb is still sick."

She stood in the frame, Nick now behind her. She wore black yoga pants and what probably used to be a white V-neck T-shirt but it was now gray in the armpits. Her blond hair was pulled into a bun, but the stray hairs around her face had escaped her hair band and made her look wild-eyed and fierce. The mama bear, shielding her family from the murderer.

James's eyes pleaded. "Can I please come in, Gwen? I'm worried sick. I need to talk to you about Tessa."

Gwen's face scrunched, but she took two steps backward. "Fine."

James stepped into the front hallway, and Nick shut the door behind them. Gwen nodded her head toward the kitchen and walked in. James followed. Caleb sat in a highchair, and James thought again that he looked too big to be treated like a baby. There was a pile of colorful, crunchy cereal spread out on the tray in front of him and a bottle full of milk to his left.

"Hi Caleb. I hope you're feeling better," James said.

"He's fine," Gwen said curtly, then unhooked the tray and the belt from around his waist and picked him up. She stood there, holding him, staring daggers at James.

This was not to be a family discussion, and he didn't want to talk in front of their son. "Can we have some privacy?" His eyes drifted to Caleb.

Gwen huffed, then handed Caleb over to Nick. "Can you set him up with his blocks in the family room?"

James had seen Caleb walk before, so he knew that he could, but Gwen seemed to think that the kid was made of Swarovski crystal and barely let his feet touch the floor. Do four-year-olds still play with blocks? And drink from bottles? James really didn't know, but again, Gwen always seemed intent on smothering the poor kid and keeping him a baby forever.

Nick took Caleb from her arms. "Come on, buddy. Let's see if we can match the circle to the hole this time."

Caleb's round face smiled at James, and he waved as his father carried him to the next room.

"Like I said, make it quick." Gwen all but tapped her foot.

"Can we sit?" James asked.

Another huff, but she sat at the table and motioned for James to do the same.

"Look, Gwen. I know what Tessa told you. I know that you told the cops about the gun."

"Good." Her eyebrows rose, showing the lines of over-bearing motherhood on her forehead.

"It's not what you think." James paused. "Do you know anything about her past?"

"I know that she's had enough violence in her life, and I don't know why you seem intent on continuing the pattern."

"Jesus, Gwen. I'd never hurt Tessa. I got that gun to protect her."

"From some bum in a side alley? She doesn't need her husband going gangster on her."

"Well, it's gone. I got rid of it. Just like she asked me to. I didn't want her to feel uncomfortable. Unsafe." He knew his admission was a direct conflict to what he had told the cops earlier. "I wish you hadn't said anything to the cops. This is a private matter."

She shrugged. "She came to me, James. Upset. And to be honest, I don't know how to feel right now. I'm not convinced you didn't hurt her."

"I'm trying to find her. Please, Gwen. Just tell me if you know something about her past."

Gwen's face gave it all away. She knew what Tessa wanted her to know, no more, no less. "She had a pattern with men. Bad men."

"I know."

One eyebrow rose. Accusatory. "How do I know you weren't part of the problem? Of the cycle?"

"Because I wasn't." His voice deepened, but he quickly reverted. "Did she ever tell you about the night we met?"

Gwen shook her head. "Just that she met you through your old roommate."

"Let me fill you in on a few details."

James took a deep breath and began the story from the beginning. Gwen gasped when James told her about finding Tessa being beaten and almost raped by Damon. He even told her about seeing Damon the night Tessa went missing. He left out the part about threatening him with the gun, but said he'd gotten his point across with his fist. Gwen sunk her face into her hands, and when she looked up, her eyes were misty.

"She never told me any of that."

James could barely hear her voice.

"She didn't tell me a lot of things either," James said. "That's why I can't piece together what's going on. Did she ever tell you her ex-husband's name?"

"No. She didn't tell you?"

"Nope." He shook his head. "I think I'm in some real trouble because of what you said about the gun. You made it sound like I threatened Tessa. I'd never do that. I just wanted to protect her." James felt like if he said it enough, he'd drill it into her head. She needed to know the truth. "It's gone. I told the cops I never had a gun," he said, speaking to her now like a neighbor. A friend. "Is there any way you can tell them you misunderstood what Tessa said to you?"

Her eyes went wide. "You want me to lie?"

"No. Yes. I don't know." James's eyes closed tightly and he pinched the top of his nose. "I just wish I knew something. Anything. I want to find her, Gwen."

She put her hand on top of his, a gesture that went further than she knew. It comforted him and showed that she was back on his side.

"There's one thing she complained about."

James opened his eyes and looked at her. "What?"

"That girl in your office. Rosalita?"

"Rosita. What about her?"

"Yeah. Rosita. She thought there was something going on. At least that Rosita was after you."

This wasn't the time or the place to go into what had happened between him and Rosita and he wouldn't offer any information. This was now a fact-finding mission on his part. "Why would she think that?"

"Because Rosita threatened her."

"Threatened her?" His face flushed, and he balled his hands into fists. How dare she?

"Yeah. It was in the beginning. Right after you got married."

"What did she say? Tessa never told me this."

"Something about you and her and your job."

"Gwen, please. I need to know exactly what was said. It's important. Think."

Gwen's eyes went up and she bit her bottom lip in thought.

"Right. It was after you got promoted to manager. At the celebration party. She told Tessa that the job should've been hers, and that she better watch her back."

James was incredulous. "Are you kidding? Right before that is when Rosita—"

Stop.

Nope. He couldn't tell Gwen what he knew about Rosita and how hard she tried to get that job.

But he was certainly going to confront Rosita.

19

Tessa

I called James at work a few days after the incident, once my face healed enough where I could cover up the really bad parts. He seemed delighted, and there was additional pep in his voice when I told him it was me, as if I could even see him sitting up straighter. Extra caring, he asked me how I was doing and again told me he'd go to the cops with me to file a complaint. Said he moved all his furniture into storage the night before and was officially staying at the hotel until he could find another place, as quickly as possible.

I'm meeting him for a drink after work today, and he said he'll help me around town trying to get a job. When I told him I was an "interior designer" he said he'll let people coming in for business loans know to contact me if they need a push in the right direction. So I should go online and get some business cards. I hear they're pretty cheap nowadays.

First, I google Drew, and for the first time, his name pops up with a headline:

LOCAL HEDGE FUND PROFESSIONAL UNDER SUSPICION FOR MISSING WIFE

A-ha!

I click the link and read the blurb.

> Local citizen Drew Grant, of Homer & Foster Financial, has recently come under suspicion in the disappearance of his wife, Tessa Smith. Married for four years, she went missing almost a week ago, yet Drew never reported it to the police.
>
> "She'd run off for spa weekends without telling me. I thought it was the same thing," Drew said when asked by reporters camped out in front of Homer & Foster in Wilmington, Del.
>
> He said when she didn't return home by Monday night, Drew tried her cell phone and found it disconnected. He then called the local station and asked to open up a missing persons case. When questioned about the delay, Drew waved us off with "no comment."
>
> Initial reports say blood was found at the scene. All inquiries should be directed to his lawyer, Kristina McMahon of McMahon, Stern, and Torelli.
>
> Detective Mason Grenning is leading the case. Please call with any tips or email the police department.

I'm sorry? Running off for spa weekends? This Asshole has got to be kidding me. I call Maribel's fake cell from the burner phone. I wonder why she didn't let me know about this breakthrough. When I get the automated voicemail, I hang up. She's probably with him, like we planned. Either they're in his office playing footsie, or he's got her at some extravagant lunch at that place he likes by the river.

Waiting for Maribel to call back, I go online and order business cards, impressed with the selection on the website. They have my name, one of my burner cell numbers, and a website I called TS5Designs.com, which I'll have to do next. The title *Interior Designer* is in fancy script and I like the way it looks. I opted for the thicker stock with a swanky border, in yellow and gray— a combination I now love. When I approve the layout, it makes me feel accomplished. Grounded. Whole.

I already sense things taking a turn for the better. Even a slight taste of the good life with Drew makes me want to do better. He made sure I was invested and felt taken care of before he put his fists on me. One year of seeing what life *could* be like has set me up for my future.

I guess I should thank him for that.

Next, I buy the website name, having checked the availability before getting the cards printed. It's from one of those free website hosting places, but for seven bucks a month I can name it whatever I want without having a dot-blogspot that makes it look unprofessional.

For now, I keep the page clean, with my contact info and a few obscure close-up pictures of photos from my old house. A chic but heavy crystal vase filled with orange tulips. A gray wing chair on a fluffy red carpet with a three-foot-tall gold globe next to it. Brass lion head bookends on a white marble mantel stuffed with the classics. All things I put together when I decorated my old home. I also rip off a few images from Pinterest of lofted rooms and modern walk-in wine lockers, but really, who's going to ask if those are *actually* my designs? I just want a few images on a slideshow for anyone who looks.

By the time Maribel calls me back, I'm giddy with achievement.

"Hey Mar," I say when I answer. "I saw the news article."

"Oh good." Her voice is flush with relief. "I wanted to tell you yesterday, but I was too busy comforting him. It made my skin crawl."

"So, how did he tell you?" My curiosity has the best of me.

"Well," she starts, "I was with him every day since Thursday, the whole weekend including Monday night at your house. I asked why you weren't complaining that he was gone all weekend, you know, like he always said you did, and asked if you were still visiting family. Then he told me he didn't know where you were, but he was sure it wasn't serious. I made him call and report you missing."

"Good. The article mentioned blood. So, you took care of that too?" I ask, hopeful but relieved because I know she got it done.

"Yes, I emptied part of the vial you gave me on the floor by the back door, then quickly wiped it away with a dry paper towel when he was on a work call with China in the home office on Monday night. I was able to scatter the rest in the trunk yesterday when I borrowed his car to grab his lunch."

He was treating her like a damn slave too. Why should she be running out to get his lunch? My stomach lurches.

"Then yesterday I called the cops from a new burner, just like you asked. Disguised my voice, said I was a friend of yours and I knew for a fact that he beat you and they should get forensics in there because I thought he killed you. Once he's under more pressure, I'll go to the cops about the affair."

"Good. I read online that he told the police I was at a spa weekend."

"Yes. So it'll make him look even worse when I tell them that he told me you were visiting family. Like he can't keep his stories straight."

"He can't. Liars lie. That's what they do."

Drew was digging his own grave, and he didn't know it. Covering for an affair and for abusing me was going to immediately make him a suspect for murder.

"Keep me posted, Mar. If you need me to do anything else, to help you nail him, let me know. We're in this together."

"I know. I'm grateful that you came to me before this happened to me." She pauses. "And I'm still so sorry about the whole thing. You know him; he won't stop looking for you once he's officially under suspicion. I'll help you with whatever you need to stay hidden."

"Thanks. And I'm sorry for putting you in this position. You know. Having to pretend."

She laughs. "It's not easy, but good things rarely are."

We hang up, and I get ready to meet James.

Earlier, I told him I'd meet him at a restaurant in town, because I didn't want him to get the wrong idea about me if I let him pick me up. It's going to be weird enough coming back to the same place, albeit on different floors.

I dress casually, a white V-neck tee and jeans, and black ankle boots. My makeup covers the bruises that he knows are there. I head out early and walk fifteen minutes to the center of town. The weather is perfect, a week or so until Memorial Day weekend, and the sun is slightly setting westward, creating an orange- and daffodil-colored sky behind the taller buildings, which are now a black silhouette that looks like a painting.

I find the restaurant, Jupiter's, on the corner of Main and Second. It's huge, half the block, and very nice inside. One section in the back has tables with white linen tablecloths and plastic flower centerpieces, surrounded by three walls of windows that are opened to let the warm spring air inside, which gives it an even bigger, open feel. Immediately, I think of my Pinterest board and different ways I would decorate. Instead of the huge crystal chandelier in the center of the room, I'd urbanize it a bit with track lighting in various colors, setting a sexy ambiance for diners in the center of town.

The room in the front, just past the hostess stand, is large as well and busier. The bar in the center has three sides, made of sturdy oak, and there are high-top tables scattered around that seem to be first come, first served. I get a good look at the locals and smile. There are girls clinking cosmo glasses, men ordering pints of tap beer, and older gentlemen in suits swirling scotch in heavy cups. I find a solo empty seat at the bar and I'm right about to order a red wine when there's a tap on my shoulder.

"Glad you could make it."

James Montgomery. He looks better than I remember, especially since I'm looking at him through non-swollen eyes. He's wearing slacks, a button-down shirt, and a tie. He smiles crookedly, which I decide I love about him, and extends a hand to me. I shake it, thankful he didn't have the gall to come right at me, a virtual stranger, and kiss me on the cheek.

"Hi, James," I say. "Come here often?"

He laughs. "My office is a couple of blocks away, so yeah, I've been here once or twice." He winks at me and doesn't mention my makeup sliding off my face, so I secretly hope it isn't.

I want to look pretty.

"Can I get you a drink? Or do you just want to sit and eat?" He looks at his watch, which he wears on his right arm, so I assume he's left-handed. "I made reservations, but we're a bit early. If you're hungry I can see if they'll seat us now."

He fumbles over his words and it's adorable. "Let's grab a drink first," I say.

"What's your poison?"

Assholes. But usually red wine. "I'll have a Chardonnay." I decide to make the change everywhere.

"Coming right up."

He squeezes into the empty space beside me. Gets the bartender's attention, Donald, who shakes James's hand before taking the order.

James certainly knows a lot of bartenders. Thoughts of Damon creep and crawl on me like a spider and I feel like that eight-legged fucker is about to bite and the room starts to spin and I'm about to scream and then—

"Donald, this is my friend Tessa. She's new in town. An interior designer. Does Michael need any help with the renovations? I've seen her stuff. She's amazing. I'm helping her get started with a business loan, and you should have Michael snatch her up before her prices double." James winks at me again. "She'd like your best chilled Chardonnay. I'll take the pilsner on tap."

"Sure thing, James," Donald says, then looks at me. "Do you have a card I can pass along?"

I'm completely taken off guard, but I act confident. I've done a lot of acting my feelings in my day. "They're on order. I've only been here a week." I go for broke. "I have a website if you'd like me to write it down?"

"Absolutely. I'll let Michael know."

Donald hands me a pen from behind his ear and a small pad he takes orders on. I write down my brand-new website, so thankful I at least had to chutzpah to start that today, and hand it back to him. He pockets the piece of paper and runs for our drinks.

"Thanks, James. You really didn't have to do that," I say, even though I'm so, so grateful. Because I've pretended to be in this position before, I know only three states require a title act to practice if you want to call yourself an interior designer, and New Jersey isn't one of them. Fake it till you make it.

He waves his hand in the air around him in nonchalance. "No big deal. I'm glad to help. Even if I had to tell a little white lie. I'm just trying to help a new friend."

"That was quite a risk. How do you know I don't paint walls orange and install brown and beige carpets and hang framed Confederate flags on the walls?"

"Oh. Well, do you?"

"Not the orange walls." I stare at him seriously, but his expression is so horrified that I give up too easily and laugh. "Wow, I can get you to believe anything, huh?"

"Feisty!" he yells, then puts his hand on my shoulder, but quickly removes it. "Sorry. I didn't mean to get in your space." He tries to take a step back in the crowded bar, bumps into someone and apologizes, then turns back to me. "You look better. But how do you feel?"

"I'm okay." I'm about to say *par for the course* but I don't. This man's parents did a fantastic job raising him, and suddenly I'm curious. "Where did you come from, James Montgomery?"

He shrugs. "Jersey boy my whole life. Grew up not too far from here. Moved to Hoboken for a while with an ex—" He pauses. "But now I'm back here. And clearly looking for a new place to live," he says with a chuckle. "You'll have to help me decorate when the time comes."

"Gladly."

I smile up at him, completely taken with his face. He's good-looking for sure, but that's not it. He's not Hollywood-hot, and most people probably wouldn't give him a second glance if they passed him on the street. But I'm lost—when I look at him, I see the man who saved me. I need to know everything about him.

And I'm about to ask. But of course...

"James, is that you?"

A woman walks up behind him, and she legitimately puts her hands on his waist and *turns him around* to face her.

"Oh. Hey," he says awkwardly. That's it.

"I didn't know you were coming here today!"

This woman is overly excited. Women know when they're being ignored on purpose, and that's exactly what she was doing to me. And then, knight in shining armor to the rescue, yet again.

He shifts his body back to my direction. "Rosita, this is my friend Tessa. She's new to town." James looks at me with that smile again. "Rosita and I work together at the bank."

"Nice to meet you Rosita," I say. Kill them with kindness.

I get a close-lipped, tense smile in return. "Yeah. Hi." Her lips don't do all the talking, as most is done with her eyes. The up-and-down scan of my outfit, and I know she's stifling the laughter about my being in a T-shirt and jeans while she's in some va-va-voom designer wrap dress with huge emerald earrings that don't match, but look classy against her medium-toned skin. Her long, brown-to-blond ombré Real Housewife curls overshadow my razor-chopped bob with the box dye, the *bangs*. She turns to James, reverting from Queen Bee back to damsel in distress. "Can I talk to you for a second? Privately?" Her shiny lips are pursed between a pout and a *gimme-a-kiss* stance.

Okay. Terrific. My knight is having a workplace affair. I should've known he was too good to be true. I should've known that all men—

"Actually, Rosita, can it wait? I just got here and left Tessa waiting long enough. We're about to sit down for dinner and I don't want to be rude to my date."

She's not used to being blown off—I can tell by the way her face twists—and she's especially pissed by being blown off by James.

"Your date? What about Joanna?" She looks at me, smug. "He already has a girlfriend."

Wow, what an evil bitch this one is! I thought girls were supposed to stick together. She doesn't say it as a warning to me for chicks-before-dicks camaraderie; she says it to make me feel bad about myself.

"Joanna and I broke up, Rosita. Tessa knows about her. Now, if you don't mind?" James says, his hand on my shoulder.

She's not happy. In fact, she looks like he just slapped her across the face. I have tons of practice with that expression. "Mmm hmm. Well then. I'll leave you to it." She turns on her leather high heels and walks off, without saying goodbye.

Turns her down nicely? Check. Lets her know we're having dinner together? Check. Lets her know I'm his date? Double check. I wasn't sure in the beginning, but now I am, and I like it. Another tally added to my virtual jail cell wall.

"Sorry about that," James says. "She can be... difficult. We're both assistant managers now but one of us will be promoted to manager in the next few weeks."

"Ah," I say, because I don't want to seem nosy getting involved with him and a coworker in the first ten minutes. "I don't think she liked me."

"She only likes people who can get her ahead in life. Don't worry about her."

When the drinks arrive, we clink glasses and, like a gentleman, he asks me about myself again. The usual. Where I'm from, why I moved, how I got started in interior design, what's the biggest project I've ever had, where do I get my inspiration, was I artistic as a child. The list goes on and on. I'm as cut and dry as can be. *South of here. Change of scenery. Designing my ex's firm. Life around me. Yes.*

Yes, I tell him I was artistic as a child, because I can tell he's into me and I don't want to spoil it for him right now with the truth. The truth being I barely even got to play with crayons as a young child because my mother spent her money on beer and pot in the beginning, then gin and crack as I got older. I didn't play with many of the neighborhood kids because I'd be in the same outfit for days and they shunned me, even in the trashy neighborhood I was from. I had Kenny and my half siblings, and we were all in the same boat, albeit together, until my mother really fucked up and we all got separated. Then I got to spend my teenage years being passed around like a sex doll and a social experiment to see how little food I could be given from the monthly check without actually starving to *death*.

Not exactly marriage material, you know?

"Yes, I used to draw all the time. Then I started writing stories to go with my drawings. Then, I started painting and I liked the way I could complement different hues with one another. I first fell in love with color in a new way after I saw *The Wizard of Oz*. Seeing the film transform from black and white to color was magical. It's still my favorite movie."

That explanation on color was repeated verbatim. Drew had allowed me to go to a one-day conference that was in town, about design careers. Obviously, I wasn't doing enough to make myself worthy of him, so he tried to make me better. I see now that he was trying to control me. Anyway, the keynote speaker said something along those lines about the color, and I committed it to memory years ago. It's the same thing I tell everyone.

As we sit for dinner, I defer to asking him about himself, afraid my real persona will shine through. He sounds like he was written from a nineties sitcom. An athlete. A scholarship. A fraternity guy. A traveler.

"Played baseball and ran track in high school," he says. "Even ran the New York Marathon once."

"Wow. That must've taken dedication."

"I got a partial athletic scholarship to Rutgers for track. After I graduated with honors, I moved back in with my parents afterward for a little while. Traveled. Ran around with my buddies. Got a job at a different bank, then moved to Hoboken with a girl and got a job at bank in New York. That's the year I ran the marathon."

Don't ask, don't ask, don't ask. "What happened with the girl?"

"She got a job in Chicago and took off." He shrugs. "What's your ex story? We've all got one."

"I—" I take a sip of Chardonnay. I'm not a fan, but I take another sip anyway. "He was an asshole. I don't really want to talk about it, if that's okay."

He places his hand on top of mine and caresses it, comforting me.

I offer to pay for half when the check comes, but he waves me off like it's the most ridiculous thing he's ever heard, and I'm grateful. There's enough money left for dinner, and then some, but I have to watch my spending until I get a job.

When I look at my watch, it's almost eleven. Where did the time go?

"Have you been to the shore yet?" he asks.

"The beach?"

He laughs. "Here, they call it the shore. Only place in the country."

How quaint. "No. I know it's not too far from here, but I've been... indoors," I say, motioning toward my face, which I hope is still hidden under my makeup.

He winces, sympathetic, and holds my hand across the table. "I'm sorry, Tessa."

I fall for him right then and there. Maybe I did earlier, but something about him makes me want to love him, and I want him to love me. I want it so bad I can taste it.

But who would want this to love? Maybe he's another Asshole, another hound dog sniffing out my insecurities, wanting to take advantage and use me like everyone else. He knows I wouldn't go to the cops about Damon; he knows he can get away with beating me.

His pinky lightly strokes the top of my hand. "It's not too late to go to the police. About Damon. I'll drive you right now."

He's not a hound dog. He's a fluffy puppy. A loyal Golden. An emotional support animal. He should be wearing a sash.

"Thanks. I'm okay."

We stand up and he gestures his hands as if he wants me to walk in front of him, placing his hand on the small of my back the way I see the lead in the romantic comedies I've watched do. He says goodbye to Donald. The bartender looks at me and raises a thumb and forefinger to his ear, likely indicating I'll be hearing from Michael regarding design possibilities. I'm so grateful to James and I want to kiss him. But I can't.

"Do you want to go for a ride?" he asks. "The beach is only fifteen minutes away. Have you ever seen an East Coast sunrise on the ocean?"

"No, I haven't. Sunrise is quite a ways away," I say.

"We can take a nap in the car and wait. I'll set an alarm."

I don't know why, but I agree.

We get in the car and he says he's taking the long way there. He points out places of interest. *If you go that way, that's where Bruce Springsteen grew up.* Five minutes later, *I spent a lot of my twenties in the beach bars over in that town.* Five minutes after that, *Over there is where I played hockey when I was ten, but I was too clumsy on skates to be the next Gretzky.* I'm instantly jealous of his upbringing. I can't even fathom what it would've been like having two loving parents supporting anything I wanted to do.

It's still dark, the sky black as tar, and James eases the car into a parking spot facing the ocean. The thump of the waves onto the shore pound so hard in my ears that

I feel myself moving. The moon is hung high in the sky, almost behind us, shining a bright white glittering line on the water in front of us.

It's quiet otherwise.

When his arm jostles, I think he's going to make a move, but he just turns the radio station to Howard Stern.

"We can listen to this until we fall asleep," he says.

And I do. I must be asleep, because I'm having happy dreams. I can't even describe them; I just know that I feel safe. What could be minutes or hours or days later, as I'm gently shaken awake, I'm smiling. I don't even forget where I am as my eyes open and the sun peeks over the horizon. I know I'm with James Montgomery, and I'm comforted.

"Hey. I didn't want you to miss it. It happens fast," James says.

He lowers the volume on the radio as the burning ball of fire turns from a dot to a semicircle to a full circle, the ocean melting around it. The waves no longer roar, but tickle onto the sand, *bloop bloop*. And in mere minutes, fast like he said, the sun goes up, up, up.

My first live sunrise.

I turn toward James, and my eyes let him know I'll accept a kiss. One that I so desperately want, even more than I want to see Drew suffer.

"Did you like that?" James asks.

The sides of my lips curl upward. "Yes," I say breathily. *Kiss me!*

"Good." He smiles at me, then turns on the engine. "Let's get you back home so you can get some real sleep. I have to be at work in a couple hours."

Right. It's Friday.

We leave the Stern repeats on as he drives back to the hotel, where we both reside. He parks, opens the door for me. He again guides me inside, and after we exit the elevator, he walks me to my door.

"I had a really nice time," he says.

"Me too." My breath must stink from sleeping. I don't care if his does.

When he gets closer, he hugs me and kisses me—on the cheek.

"I'd like to do this again sometime, if you would," he says.

I pounce. "I do. Are you free tonight?"

He nods. "I'll text you."

We lightly wave, and I slide the keycard into the door handle, and it lights up green. I collapse on the bed behind the closed door.

In. Fucking. Love.

When I wash my makeup off, I peer at my face in the mirror. Even the bruises can't hide the happiness. The entire night was better than any damn movie I've ever been jealous of seeing.

Now, if only I could find out the deal with this Rosita girl.

20

James

Rosita.

James fast-walked from Gwen's back to his house with fiery determination. He slammed the door behind him, and Candy barked.

"Sorry, girl," he said as she met him in the foyer. He leaned down and pet her head, cupping her neck in his left hand, and then kissed her. "Daddy didn't mean to slam the door."

She cocked her head like she knew what he meant. Then she looked past him at the door again, likely wondering why Tessa didn't follow him in. Tessa had never spent a night away from Candy, much less days at a time. She had to be confused.

James sighed. Candy wasn't the only one.

He went right to his phone charging on the counter and looked in his contacts for Rosita. He was about to press her name and dial her up, but on second thought, put the phone down. He couldn't go into this hotheaded. His heart was racing, and he needed to prepare what to say.

What the hell was he supposed to say?

Why did Rosita threaten his wife over a promotion? Was it because Rosita had a thing for him? She had made a move on him when he was with Joanna, knowing full well he was taken. And yes, James succumbed to her advances once. For a couple of minutes, anyway. One hundred percent his fault. When he stopped it from going too far, that pissed her off even more. She said something about how they could be a power couple, since one of them was due to be promoted anyway.

One, James didn't want to get involved with a coworker, and two, he had a girlfriend. Yes, their relationship had been on the rocks for a while and yes, she lived far away, but potentially banging Rosita in her townhouse when he stopped over after work to give her some papers she conveniently "forgot" when she ran out early didn't solve anything.

So he made an excuse about how it wasn't right, he was still with Joanna, and he left. Rosita called him two minutes after he walked out the door and left a raging voice mail, which he should have saved. He hadn't thought he'd need "proof," showing Rosita's obsession and clearing him of murder, and he also hadn't wanted Joanna accidentally stumbling upon it. He wanted to break up with her officially, but he hadn't done it yet. He didn't want to be "that guy."

As fate would have it, if you could call that heinous act "fate," he came home to Damon trying to rape Tessa a few days later.

That night, he had been out with a couple of college buddies. Joanna knew he was out but texted him saying she was waiting at his apartment, which he'd never invited her to. He texted her to go home. She left a note on the counter before leaving, saying she missed him, and she knew something was wrong and she wanted to talk. When he immediately fell for Tessa, that massive love-at-first-sight stuff you only hear about, he stopped dealing with Joanna altogether. He saved Tessa, and the spark was immediate. He couldn't help it. She was his person. His life had changed on a dime.

Yes, he lied to Tessa and said he came home early because he and Joanna had just broken up.

It was the best lie he'd ever told.

And Rosita was *not* happy to find out James was married two weeks later. Not even to Joanna—to someone he barely knew.

He didn't realize how badly Rosita had taken the news.

Fuck it, he thought, and dialed her.

"James," she said when she answered. "What's up? Tessa come back?"

So casual.

"No, Rosita, she's not back yet. And the cops don't know anything about where she could be. Just that you and I had a moment a few weeks before I got married. What did you tell them?"

"The truth," she said with a hint of anger in her voice.

"The truth? Really? The whole truth and nothing but the truth?"

Rosita gasped lightly, but James heard it, and he knew she knew what he was referring to. That *other* thing.

"That has nothing to do with anything." Her words came faster, laced with annoyance. "What I do with my life is private. They specifically asked me about *you*. So, I told them what happened. I mean, it was right before you met Tessa, anyway. You had a girlfriend. I couldn't exactly paint you up as some great guy. Why should I offer up any more information about anything else? It has nothing to do with anything." She repeated herself, which she often did when she was scrambling.

"What did you say to Tessa?"

"Excuse me?"

"After I got promoted. You threatened her."

"Says who?"

"Tessa told my neighbor. I just found out."

"Oh, please. We're supposed to be listening to a neighbor about what a missing person supposedly said? That's hearsay."

Rosita also clearly watched too much *Law & Order*. Why was she so indignant?

"Do you know what happened to Tessa? I'm warning you, Rosita. If you're hiding something, I'll find out."

"Oh *God*, James. Come on. I was with you Thursday night."

"You arrived late. We left the bank at the same time. Where were you before?"

The line was quiet. It spoke volumes.

"Jesus, Rosita." James knew exactly where she was. "I knew it."

"It's none of your business."

James blew out a deep breath. "The cops are trying to blame my missing wife on me. You know I wouldn't do anything to hurt Tessa. Why are you trying to make me look like a shit? Because I said no to you?"

"Get over yourself, really."

"What did you say to Tessa?" His voice strained.

"Nothing! Honestly, she started it. She said something about you being manager and how proud she was, and I know she was making a dig at me for being passed on. I said something about women having to stick together and she laughed. So, I told her she should know better than to laugh at me."

164

"Uh huh," James said, then used her own words against her. "And I'm supposed to just listen to you? How convenient that Tessa isn't here to defend herself."

"Well, when she comes back, ask her."

She said it, but James heard in her voice that she didn't mean it.

"I got an email from Andy and Kyle from VistaBuild. They picked us. They're coming back next week." She changed the subject. A tactic.

"What?" James pressed the home button on his phone and saw that he had emails. He scrolled through them quickly. Nothing from VistaBuild, at least nothing confirming *his* win. "I don't see that email."

"You weren't on it. I guess they saw you on the news."

"Not likely." He gripped his cell tighter. She told them. Her, or Trey. Traitors.

Rosita had quickly diverted the conversation about her personal indiscretions into one about how she was going to take over this project. At least she stabbed him in the front.

"When are they coming back?" James asked.

"Tuesday. They have to secure the paperwork with their in-house legal on Monday. But James." She paused and took a breath. "I really don't think you should be there."

His entire life was collapsing around him. "This is *my* project!"

"Is it more important than your missing wife?"

Bitch. Nothing was more important than his missing wife. Rosita had him by the balls and she knew it. Optics were everything. Perception became reality. No, it wasn't more important than Tessa, but he couldn't lose his job and his wife at the same time. What purpose would he have to get out of bed?

"I'm going to make sure they find out what really happened to Tessa." He said it as a mild threat to her, and he hoped it landed. When she didn't say anything, James disconnected the line without saying goodbye.

Rosita had to be involved, somehow. A woman scorned by him, for a relationship and a job. He just had to prove it.

21

Tessa

Early Friday evening, I smooth down the front of my black dress. It's sleeveless and has a turtleneck, and I bought it today at one of the local stores down the block. For whatever reason, the rings on my neck are getting darker, probably in that worse-before-it-gets-better phase that unfortunately I know so well. It looks worse than it feels. James had asked me to be ready early. I tug my denim jacket on over my dress and exit my room.

When I step off the elevator, James is waiting in the lobby holding a dozen roses. There are four each of red, pink, and white. They're wrapped beautifully, stuffed with baby's breath and long greens, laid out in gold lace with a huge red bow bundling it all together. They clearly didn't come from a checkout line in a grocery store.

I smile a goofy grin. "Hi."

He holds them out for me. "For you. Although their beauty no longer compares in present company."

Heat rushes to my face. What is it about this guy? He knows everything right to say, and how to make me feel like the only woman in the room. In the world. He's dressed more casually than the night before, in slacks and a button down but no tie. He must've gone up and changed after work.

"Thank you," I say. "These really are gorgeous."

He leans forward and kisses my temple. "You're worth it."

Such a departure from the other things I'd been worth. A six pack. McDonald's. Jewelry that left green stains on my skin and was probably stolen to boot.

"How did you sleep?" he asks.

I raise my eyebrows. "Really well! I was actually woken up by a phone call. Your bartender friend already relayed my information to Michael at Jupiter's. They're closed on Mondays, so I'm going over there Monday afternoon to meet with him to go over some ideas."

It took me by surprise, how it happened so fast. Michael said he knew James and trusted his referral, and wanted to speak to me as soon as possible, because he was ready to proceed with a renovation. He said the restaurant slowed down between Memorial Day and Labor Day, since most of the people who usually frequented ended up going to the beach. He planned to close for most of June and then have limited open days until mid-July. He'd already chosen an architect and a construction company for structural renovation, but agreed that he needed more of a theme and flow when it came to design and wanted to see what I had to offer.

"Where are we off to?" I ask, cradling my beautiful flowers in the crook of my left arm.

"Have you ever been to the city?"

"Which city?"

He laughs. "*The* city. New York."

"Only on television."

"Well, then you'll love the night I have planned. Shall we go?"

His left arm bends out and I hook my right arm into his.

My face likely resembles Jack Dawson's the first time he took in the sight of the Titanic as we approach the city from the main highway. The traffic is brutal—I've never seen anything like this before. Where are all the cars coming from, and can the city really accommodate all this? I grew up in western Virginia, which not many people know. Traffic only happened when too many cows blocked the road. No, it wasn't quite that bad. The trailer parks were in the middle of nowhere, yes, but even we had gas stations and convenience stores, not just errant farm animals.

When we finally get into the actual city, the traffic is worse. James says thankfully we're on the "west side" because that's where our plans are. He finds a garage (holy shit, it's so expensive!) and I leave my beautiful roses on his back seat as we walk out onto the block.

"Good, we're close," he says, then takes my hand. I don't even flinch.

Here I am. I made it to New York City. It's loud, it stinks, and the colors and the lights are overwhelming. People are everywhere. Everywhere! Some are rushing, still in work attire, bopping and weaving between the drones of people who stop to stare up at the tall buildings. Some are obviously tourists, posing for pictures with giant M&Ms or other mascots. A group of hippie-looking men with long locks are smoking pot, right there on the street, right in front of a patrol cop. Or maybe it's a parking cop. Still, clearly not afraid of the men in blue.

We have a quick dinner in a small, crowded Italian restaurant. James tells me it was where he'd go with his parents and his brother when they were younger. Dinner and a Rangers game for the family, every fall, until they left for college.

Sounds lovely. James never opened up to me about his brother, and I don't want to press, just in case it's a horror story. His eyes mist over as he mentions Tommy, and I just want to change the subject, so I offer it up. "I'm the youngest of five. 'Tessa' means 'fifth child.'"

"Oh. Wow. Big family."

Shit. Why did I do this again? "Yeah, sorta. We all kind of went our separate ways."

"You don't talk to them much?"

This time I stiffen, and he notices. He stops quizzing me and places a hand over mine. "It's okay. You don't have to talk about it."

I take him up on that and we finish dinner with small talk.

"I have a surprise," he says after we share a chocolate soufflé, one that he knew to order in advance. "Do you trust me?"

"I do," I say, and I mean it.

"You sure? I don't want you to be scared." He takes a sash out of his back pocket and raises his eyebrows. "May I?"

I hesitate. "You want to blindfold me?"

"Just for a minute."

A blindfold is a trigger for me, and the room whizzes before me in my dizziness and I feel like I'm breathing in a coffin. It's been like that ever since Drew decided on a "fun" sex game, where he tied me up and blindfolded me, then got a phone call from a client and left to take it in his office. I heard the conversation getting heated, then the front door slammed. He didn't come back for seven hours.

James's crooked smile melts me. He isn't going to hurt me. Not in front of half a million people, anyway.

"Okay."

He ties the sash around my eyes. In seconds, the rest of my senses become heightened. The music is louder, the street-meat smell is more pungent, and I even taste the cologne of passing men. James grabs my elbow.

"Don't worry, it's still just me. Let's go."

I'm walking unsteadily, like a baby deer, as we slowly walk through the crowds. He laughs the whole time, shouting "excuse me, she's getting a surprise!" to the people who are probably staring in horror or delight. It's less than two minutes when we stop, and I feel him untying it.

"Tah dah!" he says. My eyes readjust and I see we're in front of a theater. *Wicked* is playing. "You said *The Wizard of Oz* was your favorite movie. I thought you'd enjoy this."

What? My favorite movie is *Legally Blonde*.

Oh. Right. I told him that design story about the color. The one I swiped off someone else.

That's not James's fault. As far as he knows, he did good. And he did, because he did it for me, did something he thought I would love. The theater in front of me goes misty, because tears spring to my eyes. No one has ever done something like this for me before. Ever.

"I—" Jesus Christ, I almost say I love you. "I don't know what to say."

I have to stop there, or I'm going to make a mess out of whatever this is we've started. Falling too fast never ends well for me. But my God, this man.

The play is my first, and I feel like Cinderella. The whole time, I lean forward on my seat and I swear I look like a five-year-old watching a cartoon. When it's over, he asks what I want to do next, saying the city never sleeps and he'll take me anywhere I want to go.

"I want to go back to the hotel," I say. It's the only place I want to be. There. With him. Alone. Together.

He takes the hint, and we leave. Back at the hotel, I take my roses from the back seat and we go inside. It's late, almost midnight, and the employees in the lobby stare at the young couple. The young couple in love.

At least I am.

He takes me to my door and starts with the same *I had a really nice time.* That's what I think he's about to say, anyway. I stop him midsentence and pull him toward me for a kiss. One that he returns, in the most feverish, romantic way. Our lips are still connected as I reach a hand into the front pocket of my purse for my keycard and wave it at the door until I hear the beep, and I slide the handle down and open it, pulling him inside my room.

My jacket comes off, and I reach for his belt.

"Wait," he says, breathless. "We don't have to do this. That's not why I did this tonight."

"Then why did you?" I ask.

"Because I wanted to make you happy."

I finish his belt and undo his pants, then unbutton his shirt and throw it on the ground. My dress comes off.

Oh no! Wait! Not—

He turns me around and wipes the hair off my neck and kisses it and then—

"What's this?" he asks.

He's horrified. He's seen it. What a way to ruin a moment. It's been ruining moments for fourteen years. Wait, that's not true. It's ruined moments for me. Most men just laughed at it, assuming it was true.

"Oh," I say.

Then I start to cry. I sit on the bed in only my bra and panties, my face in my hands.

"Tessa, shhh." He sits next to me, in boxers and an undershirt, and puts his arm around me.

I whimper for a few minutes, and he stands and goes to the bathroom. He comes back with a glass of water and tissues, and I take both. I have to explain it.

"I was married for a few weeks when I was a teenager. To someone older. I had to get out of that Hell House. I was in a foster home and I—" I stop talking for a minute to gather my thoughts. I don't want to tell him too much. Not yet. "He was a tattoo artist. I asked him for a lower back tattoo the night we got married. He drew the design, and I approved it. One of those things they call a tramp stamp. Which, honestly, would've been infinitely better. I was so happy when it was done a week later. I made him take a picture so I could see it. When he showed me, he laughed."

There was no tribal design. Instead, tattooed on my lower back for the whole world to see, was *White Trash Whore*. In huge letters.

"Oh God." James was speechless.

"I've never been able to afford to remove it," I say through sniffles. "The marriage was annulled after a few weeks. It was never legal because I lied about my age. I had a fake ID."

I always have a fake ID.

Assuming I was branded for life, branded with the truth, branded with what I deserved out of life, I stayed for a few more weeks, until he threw the boiling water on me.

"I understand if you want to leave." I say it with a heavy heart. I'll never have a normal life, with a normal, wonderful man like James. *I'm a white trash whore.* That's why I end up with men who beat me and treat me like shit. It's all I deserve. I'm branded like fucking cattle.

James tips my chin up to look at him. "We helped Dr. Matthews get her loan for her dermatology practice. I'll make a call on Monday. We'll get you a discount on laser removal."

"I can't afford it, James." I need to think about every last cent. It's going fast.

"Don't worry about it. I'm here for you. We'll figure it out." He takes my hand. "Together."

We don't have sex that night. We fall asleep together, and I'm wrapped in his arms. It's the most freeing, comforting place I've ever been in. I feel more like a woman that night than in all my thirty-one years.

So, I jump him the next morning, and it's the best feeling I've ever had.

I'm going to marry this man.

22

James

Sunday the weather turned, and fall came in with a blast. The temperature dropped into the midfifties, and the wind howled outside James's windows all day. He didn't want to go outside, but he couldn't stay in his empty house anymore. It had become twice its normal size without them cooking breakfast together, or Tessa baking brownies for him, or them reading the paper together in bed on weekends. After walking Candy, he scanned a recent picture of Tessa on the computer and printed out a hundred copies, then went to the local hardware store for a heavy-duty stapler and duct tape. He handed a copy of the picture to every store owner he knew and peppered the light poles in town with her face. *M-I-S-S-I-N-G*, with Tessa's picture and his phone number, all over town. The cops weren't doing shit. Nothing but accusations and the runaround. If he had to take this into his own hands, he would.

After he got back, he didn't even eat. Well, not really. A little bit of the food Evan brought over Friday night was still in the refrigerator, so he picked at it. His stomach turned against him and he couldn't keep anything down.

Another lonely night in bed, just him and Candy. Party of two. Nights were the worst, without her there, safe in bed next to him. Where was she? Was she hurt? Alone? Cold? Did someone take her against her will? Was she wondering why James hadn't rescued her? His heart split into a million pieces every time his mind wandered in that direction.

He slept in on Monday. It wasn't like he had to get up and go to work. Even Candy rested beside him in Tessa's empty spot, likely enjoying the extra daddy/doggie morning. He didn't want to disturb her, but he slowly pulled Tessa's pillow out from under Candy's head and embraced it. It still had some of Tessa's scent—her shampoo, that coconut oil she liked to use as moisturizer—and he took a deep breath of memories before he got up. After checking his phone, for something, anything to let him know that his wife was safe, he was yet again dejected to find no calls, no texts. Not like he'd miss it—his volume was as loud as it could go. He didn't want to chance sleeping through something important.

He rose from the bed and went into the bathroom. His reflection was foreign. His gray eyes sunken, rings of worry surrounding them. He looked like he'd lost five pounds, all from his face. Hollow cheeks, dry lips, lackluster hair. He splashed water on his face and slapped his leg twice, to indicate to Candy it was time for breakfast and a walk.

Candy followed James downstairs, into the kitchen, and he prepped her meal—half wet food, half dry food. He looked at the clock—after ten. Half the morning was already wasted, yet he didn't know what to do with himself. It wasn't like James to be stagnant. He hadn't heard from Solomon since he was at the station two days ago. Did Solomon do anything besides harass James and smoke cigarettes?

Were they not telling James details because they thought he did something to her?

The phone rang. It sounded different, ominous, like he was in a horror movie and the monster was about to attack. The number flashing on the screen was from the bank and he answered immediately.

"James. It's Trey."

"Hey."

"Have you heard from Rosita?"

"No." He hadn't, but he didn't want to omit anything. "Well, I spoke with her on Saturday."

"About what?"

I sort of accused her of being involved in Tessa's disappearance. "She let me know about VistaBuild. That I won the project." Yes, he stuck in that dig.

"Really? She told you?"

"Yeah. What's this about?"

An obvious sigh. "She's not here. Not answering her phone. Andy and Kyle have questions from legal."

"What do you want from me? I'm 'sorting it out.'" *Jerk.*

"We're a little strapped here, James. Can you come in?"

"Oh, so now you need my help. Now that Rosita is gone?" He knew he sounded antagonistic, but really?

"I'm sure I don't have to remind you about the importance of this entire project to us. To the town."

"And *you* haven't been able to get a hold of her?"

"James, not now."

James assumed Rosita jumped through hoops every time Trey called. When they were competing for the manager job, everyone worked overtime. James didn't want to be the first to leave while Trey was in the office. He wanted to show his dedication.

James and Tessa had adopted Candy right before he was promoted. Tessa had called him, late one night when everyone was burning the midnight oil, and said Candy was vomiting and she wanted to take her to the after-hours clinic. James promised he'd be home in ten minutes. Left in a rush. Realized two minutes into his ride that he'd left Candy's new pet insurance papers on his desk, so he turned around and went back.

When he got inside, Trey was in his office, his head leaning back on his chair, looking like he was taking a nap. Until he heard a grunt. And then he saw Rosita on her knees between Trey and the desk.

"What the hell is going on?" James shouted.

Rosita got up so fast she bumped her head on the desk, and Trey scrambled for his pants.

"James. Shit!" Trey said. "Wait."

"Don't you dare say *it's not what it looks like*. Is this what I'm competing against for the job? I guess I'm the one that's screwed." James looked at Rosita on the floor, her expression half embarrassed, half smug.

"James. Wait." Trey stood, buckling his belt in record time. He smoothed down his damn sweater vest. "Listen. Wait. Fuck!"

No, of course his happily married boss didn't know what to say. Was this a consistent thing? An affair? Or was Rosita just trying to one-up James? He never asked. He walked out in disgust.

James was promoted two days later.

And Rosita never forgave him. All that "overtime," and she didn't get the job.

But now, what did it mean that she didn't show up for work? She was set to take over James's project. She should've been happy as a clam. That thing with Trey happened months ago. And it stopped. Right?

"I have to ask you a question, Trey, and I need an honest answer."

Another sigh, indicating he knew what James was about to ask. "What's that?"

"Were you with Rosita after work last Thursday? She showed up late to the thing with VistaBuild. And you showed up with Aleesha hours later."

"That's not relevant to—"

"Trey!" James cut him off. "Come on, man. Tessa is missing, and I just found out the other day that Rosita threatened her, and now Rosita is missing. Something is going on."

"Rosita isn't *missing*. She's just not here."

"You didn't answer me."

There were a few seconds of silence before Trey spoke. "Can you come in? We'll talk when you get here."

"Fine. Give me a half hour."

James hung up and quickly showered and dressed and headed to the bank. When he walked in, the coworkers he locked eyes with quickly looked away. *The Lovett Road Killer is here!* Small waves, a few close-lipped smiles and nods.

He walked right past his dark office and went right for Trey, who was just ending a phone call. The phone slammed into the cradle, Trey's face tense. He nodded to James to shut the door, which he did. He pulled up his slacks on both legs and got comfortable in the seat in front of him.

"No news on Tessa?" Trey started.

"Nope. Nothing," James said, but he was done beating around the bush. "What's going on between you and Rosita? I need to make sure she has nothing to do with Tessa being missing. Her whereabouts are unaccounted for during the time the cops think something happened to Tessa. I'll go to the board if you don't tell me the truth."

That was a threat he should've made months ago, but he admittedly dropped it once he got the promotion. He'd never know if he earned it or if it was hush money, and it bothered him.

"Nothing. I'm a happily married man, James." Trey nodded toward the picture of himself and Aleesha on one of the islands. "I love my wife and my kids."

"Where was she last Thursday?" He was more insistent. He wouldn't back down. Not now.

Trey's face stiffened, his eyes guilty. The kid caught with his hand in the candy jar. "Okay, okay. She was with me."

"Jesus Christ, Trey. So, it never stopped?"

"It did. I swear." He had his hands up defensively. "Then, I don't know. What do you want me to say?"

James shook his head back and forth. "How could you do this to Aleesha?"

James loved Aleesha. The first time they met was a few years ago when she brought in a batch of Bahamian rum ball cookies to the bank. She had that charming island accent and her hair was in long braids and she smelled of fresh roses when she grabbed him for a hug. James had been to barbecues and holiday parties at their house and she was a perfect, accommodating hostess, a fantastic cook, and did part-time administrative work for a doctor's office while the kids were in school. The complete package. Trey was a lucky man, and James couldn't believe he'd jeopardize his marriage and his children for Rosita.

"I wish I had something clever to say, but I don't." He shook his head softly, looking at the picture again. "Aleesha is a better person than me, I guess."

You guess? "Not good enough. But whatever. So, you were with her on Thursday? When?"

James could tell Trey didn't want to give up the details, but at this point it was that or his job. Which paled in comparison to James and his freedom.

"She left when you did, yes. We had plans to meet at her townhouse. We knew we had to… rush… She had to be with you and Andy and Kyle, and I had to go home to…" He let the statement fade, not wanting to say he had to go home and be a doting husband and father before he came back to meet them at Jupiter's with his wife mere hours after he stuck himself in Rosita's mouth. "But yeah. She went right to the bar. We were together for about a half hour."

James was disgusted at the entire situation, but he didn't dwell. Fine. It wasn't Rosita who had anything to do with Tessa's disappearance. But then why was Rosita missing too?

"You have no idea where Rosita is today?" James asked.

"No, I don't. And while that's a huge concern for me, so are the questions from VistaBuild's legal team. Can you help us out?"

What James wanted to do was storm off and leave Trey to clean up the mess. After all, he'd probably told VistaBuild to leave James off the correspondence until further notice. But it *was* his project, no matter what Trey or Rosita thought. And to be honest, he needed a distraction while the cops sat around with their thumbs up their asses. There was nothing else he could do at the moment.

He was elbow deep in contracts when his phone rang, the number to the police department popping up. He answered in half a heartbeat.

"Hello, Mr. Montgomery. It's Detective Solomon. You have a second?"

Was he kidding? "Yes sir. I have all the time in the world. Is there news?"

A scoff answered him. "Yes, there's news."

A lump formed in James's throat. He swallowed it down. Oh God, please don't be bad news. "And?"

"And? Did Tessa have any identifying marks? You know, scars, *tattoos*?"

James didn't like the way Solomon spoke the words. "Yes, she had a tattoo on her lower back. But we were removing it. She only had two or three sessions left."

"And what did it say?"

"Why do you assume it said anything?"

"Well, Mr. Montgomery. We found a woman who fits Tessa's description. Will you meet me at the morgue to identify the body?"

23

Tessa

It's been nine straight days of ecstasy, in every meaning of the word.

After our first morning together, we barely left my hotel room for the rest of the weekend. *I love you*s were exchanged. By Sunday, I would've taken a bullet for him. And by Sunday night, James asked me to "move in" with him. Why pay for two hotel rooms when we were going to be together in one? We were wrapped up in each other, fanatical, obsessed. New love.

Out of nowhere, I cared only about James. I didn't even care about Drew anymore, or about him trying to find me. I didn't contact Maribel the whole week.

She hadn't contacted me either. A fleeting moment passed where I thought of her, and, God forbid, if he did something to her. But then it was gone, and I was focused on James again.

I got the job helping Michael redesign Jupiter's, and what a challenge it is! I must've spent more time online self-teaching design in the last week than I had all the three years I pretended to be a designer when I was with Drew. When I'm not online, I'm in the hardware store comparing paint samples to see how colors complement one another—it's how I discovered yellow and gray were so pretty together. Or, I'm in furniture and lighting stores getting ideas, and visiting other restaurants.

To be honest, I think I'm going to be good at this.

James is a godsend. We meet for lunch every day. If it's raining, he'll come to the hotel with takeout, so I don't have to leave and fight the elements. If it's a beautiful day, I'll meet him in town, and we'll grab a fast lunch at one of the bistros that offers outdoor seating. When I promised him a home-cooked meal one day, he said we had to get out of the hotel.

And he wants us to move in together, for real.

As if he hasn't done enough, he says he's taking a half day and has a surprise for me, and to dress up. This is how he is on a random Tuesday. I can't wait to see how much more perfect my life can be with this man in it. I want to be the new and improved Tessa.

New Tessa will wear gingham aprons and work in the backyard garden and have a stable job. She will cook dinner for her man, and we'll take romantic vacations together to sunny islands that smell of coconuts and have swinging palm trees, and we'll get an adorable puppy to love.

I can't wait to meet her one day.

When James gets "home" at one-thirty, I'm in the bathroom applying concealer to the stubborn bruise around my neck. I'm already dressed in heels and a flowy pink sundress that I got for twenty-two bucks in town, and the sight of his face still melts me as it has for just over two weeks, since the day I laid eyes on him, when he came to save me from Damon.

"Tessa," he says as he kisses my temple, so genuine and tender I get chills. He looks me up and down. "God, you look beautiful. You always look beautiful." His grin is sheepish, and he looks about twelve years old when he drops to one knee. "I can't even wait until dessert to do this."

Drops. To. One. Knee.

My right hand covers my wide-open mouth—*Catching flies?* my mother used to say—so I close it. He grabs my left hand.

"Tessa, I never, ever thought I'd want to do anything like this, especially so fast. But I know I love you, and I know I want you to marry me. Will you marry me?"

The diamond ring he brandishes is thin and looks more like a wedding band than an engagement ring. The diamonds go all the way around the circle and combined they're probably less than half the carat weight of what Drew put on my finger, because he wanted to weigh me down with his threats. It's plain too. Just a bunch of tiny diamonds on a white gold band.

It's the most beautiful thing I've ever seen.

Scratch that. The second most.

I look at the most beautiful thing I've ever seen—James's eyes—and without thinking, because I don't have to think, I say yes.

He stands up and hugs me, so loving.

I've never felt more loved than I do in this moment. I'm Elle Woods.

James kisses my neck, still sore. "Well, what are we waiting for?"

"Meaning?" I ask.

"Let's go to the courthouse at city hall. Now. I just want to be married to you. I don't want to wait. Or, do you want a big wedding? We never talked about stuff like this. Do you want to wait until we can get your whole family into town? I'd love to meet them. Plus, I think there's a three-day waiting period after we apply for the license. Let's do that right now."

Now? "James, that's so fast. I don't have anything in order." Like, the fact that I'm still legally married to Drew. Then again, that's on a different Social Security number. Would he ever even know? Would the government even know? Don't they just stamp the paper and file it away at city hall?

"No," I say quickly. "I told you, my family and I have kind of drifted apart." I have no clue where to even attempt to look for them.

"Even your mom and dad?"

Especially. "Yeah. I know I told you I was in foster care for a bit. I don't want to—"

"It's okay," he interrupts. "We don't have to talk about it." He hugs me, then pulls back to smile at me. "Well, my buddy Evan is on vacation for the long weekend. My parents are in Florida. I don't want to tell anyone at work. But we'll need a witness. Any ideas? Maybe Pablo from room service can run to the courthouse with us. We've gotten to know him pretty well the last week or so." He says it with a chuckle, but he probably means it.

I don't even have to rack my brain. "I know exactly who to call."

When Hobart pulls up to the front of the courthouse, he parks the cab and ambles toward James and me, happy and holding hands. He looks exactly as I remember him, and he grins as he walks toward us.

"Miss Tessa. I'm so glad you called." He extends his arms, inviting me in for a hug, which I give him. "Marriage, huh? You sure this isn't too fast?" His face is amused and concerned at the same time.

I grab James's hand again. "Hobart, I'd like you to meet James Montgomery. He's the most amazing man in the world. Next to you, of course," I say with a wink, then look up at James adoringly. "My knight in shining armor, if there ever was one."

James and Hobart smile as they shake hands. "You got yourself a good woman here, Mr. Montgomery."

James's arm is around me and he kisses my head. "I know. She won't tell me how you two know each other."

Hobart glances at me quickly and keeps my secret. "Tessa and I go way back," he says with a chuckle.

The application process is swift. My hands visibly shake as I hand over my fake ID, but people do this all the time. We all sign on the dotted line and we're told we can return on Friday. Hobart promises to come and give me away, as much as one can do that at a courthouse wedding.

The days pass quickly, and I don't get cold feet. A little apprehension about the ID, but I know I'm doing the right thing. It's just like a fairy tale.

On my wedding day, I wear a flowy off-white dress that I got in town, another cheap find but it's perfect for the day. The last of the rings around my neck don't need too much concealer, and when we get to the courthouse, I'm beaming. Hobart is already there, and he's wearing a sports jacket over a T-shirt. It's a bit battered and has suede on the elbows, but he looks proud and handsome. There is an older Black woman next to him, clutching his arm, her gray hair half pulled away from her face.

"Tessa, this is my wife, Pearl," Hobart says as we approach. "She knows all about you."

"Come here, darling," Pearl says and pulls me in for a hug, then whispers in my ear. "Thank you for asking him to do this."

187

I introduce them to James, and off we go.

Me, with my family.

I feel complete. The puzzle is finished. All four of us are each a corner piece that will hold my new world together.

After I'm married (MARRIED!) the four of us go to dinner near the shore, since the beach season is officially opened, being the Friday of Memorial Day Weekend. James tries to pay, but Hobart and Pearl insist that dinner is a wedding present for us. They also tell us their daughter Sasha does appraisal work for a realtor and she'll put us in touch with someone who can find us a home quickly. We certainly can't live in the hotel forever.

After dinner, Hobart and Pearl go home, and James and I go to a packed Jersey Shore bar and dance the night away. Just him and me. That's my honeymoon.

It beats the week in the Bahamas that Drew and I went on four years ago. By a longshot.

I feel it so deep in my bones, so sure of my life, for the first time. Nothing else in my life mattered until this point. In fact, it got me here. I'm so grateful I'd take another beating from Drew, just to end up here again.

I love James Montgomery, and I'm going to grow old with him.

24

James

A shiver ran down the length of James's body as he stared at the wall of drawers. The room was dank, the lights low and bluish, and the air smelled of rot and antiseptic, cigarette smoke wafting off the detective. The silence bothered him, as Detective Solomon stood quietly and judged. He hadn't said another word to James after his greeting and a quick *follow me*.

Minutes had passed when the autopsy technician walked into the room, introduced himself as George, and put on gloves. James listened to the way the rubber gloves smacked onto his wrists as he tugged them on, and afterward George looked at a clipboard and made a note.

"Ready?" he asked.

James nodded and caught a glimpse of himself in the mirror on the wall. He didn't know if it was the bluish lights in the room, but he looked absolutely yellow. Jaundiced.

Daffodil.

He didn't realize his eyes were closed until the creak of the drawer opening made his eyes go wide as the toe tag became visible. Then the plastic that was wrapped around the body. There was no way this could be Tessa! She's not dead, in a bag. She's at a design convention that he forgot about. *That's it!* That had to be it. *Please, let that be it.* He relaxed as the drawer came closer to his body. *It's not her.* Without warning, George yanked the cover open to reveal the person's face. He understood why they needed an identification. The woman was cut up beyond belief.

At first sight, James almost fainted. His fingers gripped the edge of the slab with white-knuckled rage.

He hadn't seen rings around a woman's neck that dark since the night he met Tessa. Were they dark because her face was so, so pale? Lifeless? Expressionless? Dead.

But—it wasn't Tessa.

James felt so guilty when he was *glad* that the tortured and bloody woman in front of him on the table wasn't her. He almost cried and hugged the strange dead body to apologize, and to thank her for not being Tessa. He couldn't stand the thought of this being her. At that moment, the rage came back. He was going to find her, no matter what he had to do. She'd never end up wrapped in plastic and stuffed in a drawer.

"No." It was all he could say.

Solomon looked at him, his forehead crinkled. "You're saying this isn't your wife, Mr. Montgomery?"

Was someone holding Tessa, doing this to her? Was there a serial slayer out there, kidnapping women and cutting them up? Did someone have Tessa, and were they inflicting pain? He'd give anything to trade places if that were the case. She'd been through enough and he couldn't deal with the images swirling in his head. James's mouth opened again, but this time the bile that had been storming in his stomach came rushing out in an instant, half on the plastic all over the floor. He didn't care when it splattered on his pullover and his shoes. He wished it landed on Solomon. That jerk-off wasn't doing a goddamn thing to help Tessa.

George grabbed a bottle of water from a nearby mini-fridge and handed it to James, whose face was drenched with sweat; it dripped into his eyes.

"No," he said again quietly. "It's not Tessa."

Solomon raised his eyebrows. "She was found at the edge of town, by that park near Huntsville. A woman was jogging the long trail with their dog, and the dog went crazy. Pulled his owner right into the woods. There she was. Shot," Solomon finished, matter-of-factly, almost disappointed it wasn't Tessa.

Solomon had to know it wasn't her before he called. The woman's hair, matted and bloodied as it was, wasn't even the same color or length. He brought James here to look at this body to fuck with him. *Tell us where you hid your wife's body, murderer!*

The bag was zipped back up and the drawer was closed. Back to the refrigerator, Jane Doe. Just like that. Someone else's problem. Solomon addressed him again. "Wait, Montgomery, didn't you say you don't own a firearm? But the neighbor still says you do?"

Solomon was trying to trip him up. Fucking Gwen. "I don't have a firearm. This isn't Tessa. Can you please tell me what you're doing to find my wife?"

This woman wasn't Tessa, but someone still had her. He tried to remember the last time he saw her. The morning he left for work, she was still in bed, not feeling well. She wore a ribbed tank top and yoga pants. Wait— was her robe on? Or was she just snuggled up under the comforter?

He couldn't remember. And that killed him. The fact that he had to identify a body made this become all too real.

He internally berated himself for never pressing Tessa for details of her life—how could he go about finding her now? He had no idea where she grew up, who her siblings were, who her foster parents were. He didn't know what her favorite subject was or why she didn't drive.

All he knew was that he loved her, and he was going to find her. No matter what it cost him.

He'd saved her once. He was her knight in shining armor, so she always said. He'd failed her in the worst way. He couldn't shake the feeling that she was screaming for him to save her as someone took her, and if he didn't find her soon, that was going to haunt him for the rest of his life.

At least, until he made someone pay for taking her away from him.

25

Tessa

Walking down the block with two days' worth of groceries, I treasure the end of the cul-de-sac where our new house is located. The house isn't huge; it's a three-bedroom, two-and-a-half-bath colonial, and it's rather old. Built in the eighties, Sasha had said. But the location is perfect, less than two miles to the main part of town, and the changes we need to make are cosmetic. With my new design business, I can do it all. I'm almost finished with my project at Jupiter's, so I can dedicate the entire next month to updating our space.

At the top of the driveway, I punch the code into the garage door opener—our anniversary, naturally—and load the groceries through the laundry room, whose opening is attached directly to the kitchen. I place the bags on the counter and put the vegetables and meats into our refrigerator. The kitchen is decent but will eventually need an update. The appliances are black and there's a beige-and-black granite countertop with a black porcelain sink. The floor and backsplash tiles are a matching peach hue. I bet this was a dream kitchen in the nineties, which is when the last family moved in. They raised their kids here, grew old here, and finally sold it once they empty-nested and realized they'd be happier in a senior adult community where they didn't have to worry about shoveling show or mowing lawns. They were motivated, accepted our initial offer, and we closed two weeks later.

I note the time, and I have at least an hour to start dinner. James wants me to learn how to drive and get a car, and eventually I'll have to tell him why I can't do that. I should've come clean in the beginning, when we got married. About my fake ID and how I procured it. But that would've opened up a whole other can of worms, one that I was happy was still closed and sealed.

That being said, I haven't heard from Maribel at all. I haven't even googled Drew. It's because I'm moving forward and I'm happy. But the sick part of me that's been abused not only for the last four years but for the last fifteen needs closure.

I google him. Nothing.

The burner phone I use to communicate with Maribel is hidden in a knee-high winter boot in the back of my closet. After dusting it off, I try to turn it on, but it doesn't go on—likely out of juice, since it's been sitting here for a month. I plug it into the charger, the lights blink, and I wait for voicemail or text notifications from her. She must be wondering what happened to me.

I wait.

Nothing.

After ten minutes, the phone is at almost fifty percent charge, so I know I don't have any notifications. She's not looking for me.

Or. Or Drew did something to her. I text her.

> Hey! I haven't heard from you. Is everything ok?

194

I wait anxiously for a reply, hugging my knees into my chest while I lean against the bed. Then, I rush downstairs to the office and google Maribel Lopez. The regular stuff pops up. Her LinkedIn, her private Facebook, her private Instagram handle. Nothing about a murder or a domestic disturbance.

Thank God.

I text her again.

> I'm afraid Drew did something to you. Are you ok?

I wait for a few minutes and then decide it's time to check out caterers online. We're having people from the bank over on Friday night after work, just a couple of days from now, to celebrate James's promotion to manager. It happened on Monday, and I beamed when he told me— like I need anything to be prouder of him. He wasn't as happy as I thought he'd be, told me with a smile and then shrugged, like it wasn't a big deal. I knew he was competing with that girl Rosita and it was a huge deal that he won.

We're only having twelve people over, so I don't go crazy ordering. Three different salads: One lettuce, one pasta, and one vegetable mix, two trays each of baked ziti and chicken francese, and a cookie platter for after. That will go along with the congratulatory sheet cake I ordered from the bakery, personalized for him.

The best part about all of it is that I paid for it with my own money. The job at Jupiter's got me a three-thousand-dollar consulting fee, which I'm not sure is good or bad, but I earned it myself. I had a thirty-thousand-dollar budget to make the space industrial and clean. I opted for black and gold linear pendant lights hanging from the ceiling, and picked a rich red for the walls, speckled with gold. I suggested new furniture, and no linen tablecloths, but made the room look richly elegant with sleek black tables and black metal chairs with red cushions, red dinnerware, and gold cloth napkins. It came out warm. Sexy.

And because I met my wonderful husband, I was able to get the job, because he believes in me. And I believe in him, and I want to show my gratitude in every way possible.

My thoughts are interrupted by a buzz. From the burner phone. Like an athlete, I hurdle to the other side of the kitchen where I'd placed it on the counter near the stove.

> Can I see you?

It's from Maribel. My first thought is *thank God she's alive*, and my second is immediately *no*. I write back.

> Maribel! I was worried about you. Why do you need to see me? I'm hundreds of miles away

I wait.

> Can you talk?

I call her, and she answers on the first ring.

"Hey, Tessa. I haven't heard from you in a while," she says.

"I know. I've been getting my life together."

"How's that going?"

"So far, so good!" I pause, still guarded, even though it's her. "Just doing my thing. What's going on over there? With Drew?"

She scoffs. "You know him. He has everyone in his back pocket. He's called in favors from local law enforcement around here. It's pretty much dropped, as far as the cops are concerned. No one cared about the affair when I told the police. Everyone thinks you left him."

"But what about the article? The blood?"

"They questioned him. He had an alibi. A hundred people saw him at that gala. Without a body, there's nothing to go on."

"Oh, Jesus." I say it, concerned, but I get over it quickly—Drew is my past. I can't let my need for revenge bleed into my current life. I no longer care, and I won't get dragged into it anymore. "All's well that ends well."

"You seem better," she says. "What have you been doing?"

I can't give away too much. I just need to let her know that I'm okay, and she will be too. "I got a job. I've been hanging out at the shore. Made some friends. Met some neighbors. It's all good. A new beginning. One I never thought possible." My voice lowers, out of the shame of my past. "For someone like me."

Someone like me. What a loaded statement. According to the mold, I'm supposed to be on welfare and pregnant with my fourth kid, from a third baby daddy. Addicted to drugs, working at the checkout at the grocery store, and constantly trying to make ends meet.

Still, I want something just for myself, so I don't tell her about James.

"Thanks for your help, Maribel. And as long as you're free of him, you've won too."

"I know. I guess this is goodbye?" Her voice cracks.

I feel like we're in a movie, and this is the dramatic ending. But this is a happy ending. "It is. I wish you well. Maybe someday, our lives will cross paths again."

"I'd like that," she says. "Take care, Tessa."

"You too."

I hang up.

In the garage, I ruffle through some boxes—we're not entirely unpacked yet. When I find James's tools, I take out the hammer. And I obliterate the phone.

26

James

James drove straight from the morgue to the shore to clear his head. And to replay every damn second of the past four months—the good, the bad, and the ugly.

Except there wasn't any bad, and definitely no ugly. Their life was good. He didn't think he'd ever get to have anything that good ever again.

He parked the car in an empty lot. While the weather at this point in the season could either be eighty or fifty, the "beach season" was over, and the place was a ghost town even though it was pleasant today, with temps in the upper sixties. Opening the door, the smell of salt and seaweed hit his nostrils and instantly calmed him. With the thunderous crash of waves in the background, James removed his shoes and socks and left them in the car, then rolled up his pant legs to his midcalves. He balanced on the edges of his feet as he walked across the rocky parking lot and finally, his toes were in the cool sand.

Then he fell to his knees and pounded his fists on the beach in front of him, the same place he took Tessa to watch her first sunrise. With the thought of someone torturing her like that poor woman he just saw, it became too much to bear and his eyes opened to the ocean in front of him. He stood and took a step. Then another. Before he knew it, his feet were wet, and then the coolness spread to his upper thighs.

He walked into the ocean. His eyes closed, the water now chest high, soaking into his clothes. He kept his hands glued to the insides of his pockets. A wave crashed over his head, and for a few seconds, he held his breath—survival instinct. The wave retreated, but he stood his ground like a statue. Another wave. Every time the waves retreated, they buried his feet farther into the earth. The sand barreled him in above his ankles, and he couldn't move.

Another wave was on the horizon, first a bubble of water, rising higher as it got closer, turning cylindrical. This was the one that would bury him.

And right when the wave was about to take him, he was dragged backward. Hands on each shoulder. His heels were now digging in the sand in the opposite direction. He was on his back, on the dry sand, where two burly men in plaid flannel shirts with the sleeves cut off stood above him. One slapped his face.

"You okay? Sir, say something!"

James coughed and turned to his left, blowing the water out of his nose.

"What were you doing out there?" the other man asked. "We were fishing over on the rocks and saw you going under. Didn't even move your arms when the waves hit you. You okay?"

Jae sat up and placed his forearms over his bent knees. "Yeah. Thanks. I got confused."

The two men exchanged a glance; the first man thrust a bottle of water into James's hand and threw a towel over his shoulders. "You're lucky we saw you. That could've gotten ugly real fast. This morning's riptide is no joke."

James unscrewed the top of the water bottle and finished it in two long swigs. He rubbed the top of his head with the towel and stood, handing it back to the man who gave it to him. "Thank you."

"No, keep it man. The wife makes me bring the cheap ones fishing. I think she got it at the dollar store. We won't miss it."

"Thanks," James said. "Thanks for everything."

"You okay to get out of here?" towel man asked.

James, dripping with ocean, rolled the towel over his shoulders. "Yeah, I'm good. Parked right over there." He motioned to his right with a quick head nod. "Really, thanks again."

Back at the car, James was sopping wet and covered with sand. Luckily he always kept a spare set of running clothes in his trunk in case he decided to go on a spur-of-the-moment jog. He dried himself as best he could with the wet towel, then hooked it around his midsection as he disrobed in the parking lot, behind his open door. He didn't have extra boxers, so he had to free-ball it in his comfy black pants with the white stripe down the side of the leg. He tugged a clean T-shirt over his head, one that he got in college with the name of his favorite bar on the front. He couldn't part with it. It was a running joke between him and Tessa that he still hung on to it.

She handled it with kid gloves, knowing how much it meant to him.

He grabbed his phone; Evan had texted him that he was at his place, waiting in the kitchen. He knew their garage code and had waited for him at the house before. He'd heard through the grapevine that there was a warrant about to be executed.

Fuck. It was almost five o'clock. How long was he crying at the beach before he went into the water?

There were two cars at the end of the cul-de-sac as he pulled up to his house. A proper police vehicle and a town car. As he approached, all doors opened. Solomon and Garvey got out of the town car and two officers got out of the cruiser.

"Nice day, Montgomery," Solomon said as James stopped in his driveway and got out to greet them. "Out for a run?" He said it sarcastically, like he hadn't just made him identify a body hours before. Solomon was practicing psychological warfare on him. He had to know that wasn't Tessa, but he made him go look anyway.

"Just clearing my head," he said. Let them think what they wanted.

"Mmm. Well," Solomon said. "We got an interesting phone call since you left. An anonymous tip, if you will."

James swallowed, hopeful. "Tessa? Does someone know where she is?"

He scoffed. Angry. His eyes were accusatory. "No, not about Tessa. About Rosita. And you. Someone saw you go into her townhouse late at night. Before she went missing."

James crinkled his eyes. What was happening? He hadn't seen Rosita since the morning after Tessa disappeared. "That's not true."

"Mmm. Interesting. Especially since we went there on the tip. Found her, too. Shot."

Someone *shot* Rosita? "What? Is she okay?"

"No, Mr. Montgomery, she's not okay." He reached into his inner coat pocket and pulled out a yellow piece of paper, then slapped it on James's chest. "We have a warrant to search your house for an illegal firearm."

"Oh my God. Rosita's dead?" The color drained from James's face. "I swear, I had nothing to do with this!"

"Mmm. You swear, huh?" Salty.

Between Jane Doe, Tessa missing, and now a dead coworker with a bullet wound, James was a serial killer in their eyes. He let them in. They wouldn't find anything, and then maybe they'd get on with looking for his wife's true whereabouts.

Evan embraced James as soon as he walked in. "You okay, pal?"

James shook his head. "No. They said Rosita is dead. Someone called and said they saw me there. What the fuck is going on, Evan?"

"Jesus." Evan's eyes shifted to the cops filing in, evidence bags in hand. "Don't say anything. No matter what happens, just don't say anything."

James's eyes thanked Evan without a word.

Solomon and Garvey stood watch as the other two officers were joined by a team of agents. James sat at the kitchen table with Evan as they read through the warrant—pretty standard, according to Evan. He reminded James that they could only search places where a gun would fit, which, in reality, could be almost anywhere. They didn't have a right to look in his computer, and also not in jewelry boxes and other tiny compartments. James could have ten tiny baggies filled with cocaine in a one-inch-by-two-inch box and they wouldn't be allowed to arrest him. Not that James had any cocaine. He'd never even tried the stuff.

"Can I make you some coffee?" James asked politely. He might as well stay on their good side and not act smug when they didn't find anything.

Solomon and Garvey looked at each other, and Garvey shrugged, then answered. "Sure. This might take a while."

James thought it best to stay in the kitchen with Evan anyway. They could tear the place apart. He had nothing to hide. As the percolator bubbled, he sat at the table and opened the paper, trying to act normal. If there was such a thing now that Tessa was missing.

Unlike on TV, no one ransacked his house. They didn't flip furniture, cut into cushions, or break things. Aside from the subject matter of their presence, they were respectful.

Until the worst happened. A man came down the steps, holding a clear plastic bag marked EVIDENCE. Inside was a revolver. A *gun*. One that didn't belong to James.

"What's that? Where did you get that?" James asked nervously. He'd never seen that gun in his life.

Solomon stepped next to him with a smirk on his face. "Mr. Montgomery, place your hands behind your back please."

James, wide-eyed, stared at Evan. "What's going on?"

Evan's face was blank, registering as much shock as James.

"James Montgomery, you're under arrest for the murder of Rosita Morales."

"What?" James screamed as the cuffs clicked tightly around his wrists. "That's not my gun! You planted that!" James looked at Evan. "Evan. Help. This has nothing to do with me! Where's my wife?" he shouted.

"I'll take care of everything," Evan said. "Don't say a word."

Solomon patted him down.

"You have the right to remain silent. Anything you say can and will be used against you in a court of law."

27

Tessa

I'm on my knees in the laundry room, my face smothered with saliva. "Mommy loves you. Mommy is going to miss you. You're Mommy's good girl, aren't you?"

We adopted a dog last week. She was in the shelter for six months, they said. They named her Candy, and we kept the name when we brought her home. She's a cattle dog mix, and she took to James and me immediately. She's already housebroken and knows basic commands, and except for jumping on the couch no matter how many times we say *no*, she's a great addition to our little family.

I swore I'd adopt a dog when I was settled and could care for it properly. The poor dogs I had growing up—well, they were usually my mother's boyfriends' dogs—God, they were treated horribly. I saw one of the boyfriends kick the dog once, and it yelped and ran to a corner, tail between its legs, ears pulled back, face full of fear. There was nothing I could do about it then, but there's something I can do now. James will be lucky if this is the only dog I save, because I would've taken every single one in the shelter if it was up to me.

James laughs at my overbearing Mommy act. "She's fine. We'll only be gone a few hours." He places his arm around my shoulders, and we get in the car and head out.

"Are you sure this is okay?" I ask James, again motioning to the chocolate babka in my lap that I got at the bakery in town that afternoon.

He places his hand on my knee in the car and strokes it gently. "Yes, Daffodil. Mr. and Mrs. Soderberg will love it."

I love when he calls me *Daffodil*. I mentioned that it was my favorite flower when I used them as centerpieces at Jupiter's, and he's been nicknaming me ever since.

Evan invited James and me to dinner with his parents, as they are all excited to meet me for the first time. James mentioned that Evan and a few law school buddies who were still single had gotten a house in the Hamptons for the entire month of June, and he's been back for a couple weeks, catching up on work, so James hasn't seen him in a while. Evan was shocked when James sent him our wedding photo with "I'm hitched!" attached to the bottom and set this up for a proper introduction.

"They're going to love you as much as I do," James says.

I know how much Evan and his parents mean to James. He's told me stories about them growing up together, and how they were like second parents to him. Since James's actual parents are in Florida, I won't get to meet them until we go down there for Thanksgiving. Afraid of my ID, I told him I had a fear of flying and he agreed to drive, stopping for a night in North Carolina on the way down, and South Carolina on the way home, to break up the weeklong trip.

One day, I'm going to have to tell him the truth, the whole truth, and nothing but the truth. It's a weird thing to say about my husband, and the love of my life, but... but I've only known him seven or eight weeks.

We make a left to a quaint tree-lined street. The lawns are manicured, dogs and small children run under sprinklers, and some properties even have little white picket fences. The Victorian-inspired houses practically rotate colors like a box of Crayolas. One red, the next blue, the next green, the next white. It looks like something straight out of a children's picture book. We pull into the long driveway of a powder-blue house with white trim. There's a detached one-car garage at the end and James parks the car.

What a departure from the concrete jungle I called my backyard. A sprinkler in the summer was a leaky pipe. We constantly moved from shitty rental to shittier rental, or occasionally in with whoever my mother was screwing at the time. Most times those were trailers. All of us, mashed in, fighting over a jar of pickles or a bag of dollar-store cheesy poofs or a carton of week-expired milk. Zero supervision, as mom spent her time doing dollar shots or giving dollar blow jobs at the local tavern. Super fun.

James's arm is around me when he rings the doorbell and a guy around James's age opens the door. Evan.

"What's up, man?" he says as the door swings open and they hug. Then he looks at me. "You must be Tessa. I'm Evan. It's so good to finally meet you. Come on in."

Evan is tall and lanky, with a hipster beard and thick, dark-rimmed glasses, which are nerdy but not on him. He looks like he teaches interpretive dance at a community college. I know he's a lawyer because James told me, and I wonder if I should tell Evan about my history, my fake ID, and have him help me fix it all—but I'm not sure that James wants him to know about any of that.

We walk in and Evan embraces me, and I know I'm going to be put on the spot when he says, "Let's find out everything about the girl who got James married."

My stomach clenches, and I try not to let my nerves show as I meet Mr. and Mrs. Soderberg, but my hand is shaking as they take mine in theirs and lead me to the kitchen. Mrs. Soderberg's hair is cut into a bob, silver streaked with black, and she wears an apron around her black T-shirt and bone-colored linen pants. She takes the babka from my hands with a flourish, commenting on how I must've known it's her favorite, and kisses me on the cheek, welcoming me to the family.

Looks-wise, Evan takes after Mr. Soderberg, who is also tall, although less lanky, but he's also sporting a beard. Less hipster, more old-school. He's wearing a golf polo with a country club's logo and golf shorts. Same as Evan. Apparently, they "hit the links" earlier in the day.

In the wallpapered kitchen, there's a meat and cheese feast on the kitchen counter. Mrs. Soderberg offers me a drink, red or white wine, but I opt to start with a club soda, so I don't look like a lush. Plus, I don't want loose lips tonight.

When I reach for a small paper plate, Mrs. Soderberg notices the burn scar on my arm.

"Oh, dear, that looks like it hurt!" she exclaims.

My eyes go wide and my mouth is open and I'm about to say—God, I have no idea what I'm about to say—when James jumps in.

"She spent most of her teens pushing dough in and out of a pizza oven," he says, winking at me. No, he won't tell them that my ex threw boiling water on me when I was sixteen. He looks at his best friend. "And guess what, Evan? The place she worked as a teenager was also called

Emilio's. Just like where we used to hang out! Oh, man, Tessa, let Evan tell you the story about when we got there right before it opened that one time, and what we saw through the window. He tells it best."

And just like that, all eyes are on Evan as he regales them with the story. James gives my other arm a little squeeze. *Partners.*

It's a nice feeling, having someone in my corner. Drew didn't tell his colleagues that someone threw boiling water on me, either. He told them I poured it on myself because I'm clumsy and I couldn't cook if my life depended on it. Ironically, half the time I did fear my life depended on presenting a hot meal.

Over dinner—chicken parm, one of my favorites—I hear a lot about James as a teenager and college kid, which fascinates me. He played cool instruments—drums and a little guitar, not band-geek instruments like a tuba. He was in honors classes.

They even talk about his brother, Tommy. Tommy was two years older than James, and dated Evan's twin sister Pamela—Evan's a twin?—for a few months in high school. When James goes silent, Mr. Soderberg mentions that "it's a shame they never caught that drunk bastard" so I assume it was a hit-and-run. James looks at me, because he knows I don't know.

"It was a few months before we graduated," he says, nodding toward Evan. "Tommy was finishing his sopho-more year at Ohio State. He and some friends were heading out to blow off steam after cramming for finals. There was an accident. His friend that was driving lost an arm, but Tommy didn't make it after surgery. The two guys in the back seat were okay. Said it was a black truck, the kind with those huge wheels. Rammed into the passenger side at double the speed limit after blowing a stop sign. Then sat there for thirty seconds after the crash and took off."

Very detailed explanation, yes. I take it as James not wanting me to ask questions about it later because it makes him too upset to talk about. His eyes mist over. I'm not sure if changing the subject is insensitive but I don't want him to feel pain.

Luckily, Mrs. Soderberg mentions that she talked to James's mother in Florida and she's so happy that the cancer is gone—something else I don't know about. But at least everyone is in better spirits, talking about the medical miracle.

James seems to have had enough pain and loss to last a lifetime. I promise myself, right then and there, I'll make sure he never feels pain again.

For the most part, I get out of the evening unscathed—every time something came up that James knew I wouldn't talk about, even with him, he covered for me. Everything from answering about my exes: *Come on, a girl's gotta have her secrets* to answering about the town where I grew up: *Her high school had the same mascot as us. Remember when our lion backflipped at that pep rally...?* Not only did he trick everyone into thinking they were learning about me, but he also showed at the same time how much we had in common.

Even if it was all a lie. They didn't know that. But I *did* have so much in common with James. Just not *those* things. I didn't come from a happy home and eat fresh-baked cookies while I did my homework. I didn't attend pep rallies. I didn't graduate from high school.

The only thing they know, or Evan knows, anyway, is how James and I *really* met. The night with Damon, his old roommate. What could've happened to me. God, it seems like a lifetime ago.

I wonder what ever happened to Damon Moretti?

28

James

Of all the shitty things that could've happened since the moment he arrived home to an empty house the night Tessa disappeared, being arrested for a different murder was the last thing that James expected to happen. And now, there he was, wrists pinned behind his back and perp-walking into the police station. Thankfully, he supposed, they found the gun (whose fucking gun was that?) and arrested him immediately—there was no time for the media to get involved. Although, he had a feeling when, *if*, he got out of there, the vultures would be waiting to snack on whatever was left of him.

James was led down a hall and into a room, where he had to hand over everything personal to be sealed in a bag and locked away, possibly forever. He was observed as he took off his clothes and fitted with an orange jumpsuit. The administrators took his watch, his wallet, and Jesus, did his heart clench when he slid off his wedding ring. The portly woman behind the counter snatched it up in her fat little hand and threw it into a plastic bag with zero regard for what it was, what it meant to him. Then it was sealed and tossed into a bin, like garbage.

James didn't need his phone call, because thankfully Evan was at his house when the arrest was made, and as

James was being pushed into the back of the police cruiser, Evan told him that he'd get a criminal attorney that he knew to the courthouse for the arraignment, and to wait. To not talk, and to wait.

So, he didn't talk. Not when Solomon pulled him in a room and asked him questions about Rosita, or when he tossed postmortem pictures of her in front of him on the table. He didn't say a word. Solomon wasn't amused and threw his ass in a cell.

He waited.

He sat in a cell—a fucking jail cell—overnight, while the cops played goddamn TV detectives with a chip on their shoulder, trying to pin anything on the husband. All of this was a distraction, and it was taking away from the real issue: Tessa was missing, and what the fuck were they doing to try to find her?

He'd failed. He couldn't protect her. Instead, he was rotting in a jail cell for a murder he didn't commit, while someone was probably hurting his wife. *Where are you, Tessa?*

"Montgomery!" A cop shouted his name and he rose onto wobbly legs. "Time for your arraignment."

When James was led to the courtroom, he had mere minutes to consult with Robert Brown, the attorney that Evan had procured for him. James's mood lifted, because this man looked like a champion, from his custom navy suit to his shiny red pocket square. He was about Evan's age, and James assumed they were law school buddies or colleagues. They shook hands—another win. Robert's paw engulfed James's hand and pumped firmly twice, never breaking eye contact. He exuded confidence, something James was sorely lacking at this stage of the game.

"Hello, Mr. Montgomery. I'm Robert Brown. Evan filled me in, and I've talked to the DA. Obviously, say nothing except 'not guilty' when the judge addresses you. I'll take care of the rest."

"Thanks, Mr. Brown."

"Robert, please call me Robert," he corrected.

"Robert. I didn't do this. I didn't kill her. I never went near Rosita."

Saying her name out loud reminded James that he'd barely thought about the fact that Rosita was actually dead—all he'd thought about was that he was being blamed, and his mind had been engrossed with Tessa's disappearance. Rosita had issues, sure, but Good Lord, they were friends and he didn't want her dead.

They were called quickly, and the judge read the charges, which still sent a shiver up and down James's spine. *Murder in the first degree.* James abided by Robert's rules and only said *not guilty* even though a speech burned at the tip of his tongue as the rage of such a certain mistake ate apart his insides.

Robert went on to plead for bail, mentioning that James was an upstanding citizen who'd spent most of his life in the county, being born and raised here, and that he was a pillar of the community, the manager of the town's local bank, and didn't have as much as a speeding ticket.

The judge was not amused but took it all into account.

"Bail is set at two-hundred-fifty-thousand dollars. If met your client will be fitted with an ankle monitor and placed on house arrest until a trial date can be set."

The gavel pounded on the desk, and that was that. A quarter of a million and quarantined at home for however long. While Tessa was out there somewhere, and the cops weren't doing shit to find her, and now he was completely helpless.

"Hang tight," Evan said from a row behind him. "I'll have you out of here in no time. And just so you know, I went over this morning to walk and feed Candy, so she's good." He looked at James's new attorney. "Thanks, Robert."

Robert winked and made a little gun shape with his hand toward Evan's direction and double clacked his mouth, a gesture that told James they were old college or law school buddies. Colleagues without history didn't act like that in open court.

It took two hours for James to be released. He was handed his clothes and his plastic bag of personal effects and immediately slid his wedding ring back on. He put on his street clothes—something he never thought he'd have to call them—and braced for the shitstorm he knew would be outside.

Evan waited for him in the front.

"Robert had to go," Evan said. "He's working another case that needed attention, but he'll serve you well. I've known him a long time."

"Great. Thanks. I really can't thank you enough."

Evan placed an arm around James's shoulder. "Come on, man. We've been friends since sixth grade. I wouldn't leave you hanging." He cleared his throat. "Neither would my parents. I secured bond because they put up their house as collateral."

Of course Mr. and Mrs. Soderberg did that for him.

"Oh, Jesus, Evan. Can we call them so I can thank them?"

Evan nodded toward the door, where reporters were gathered. "Let's get you out of here safely first. It's a mess out there."

James blew a puff of air from his mouth. "Terrific."

"Just walk with me to my car. Don't say a word. James, they're going to try to antagonize you, like they did at your house a few days ago. Don't engage. Please," Evan begged.

James knew he had to heed Evan's advice this time.

His head low, James walked through the open door that Evan held with his right arm and quickly made his way down the steps. The questions and accusations flew, like he knew they would. *"Did you also kill your wife?" "Were you having an affair with Rosita Morales?" "Where did you get the gun?" "Did you kill Jane Doe?" "Where's Tessa's body?"* Over and over. Carina Killhorn's raspy voice was a decibel louder than everyone else's, or maybe James just heard it clearer because he hated her so much. How dare she call his parents and upset his ailing mother? He lifted his head and was about to go back at her but pushed the feeling down. *Listen to Evan.*

"Did she put up a fight or did you shoot her in cold blood?" Carina shouted.

James's blood fizzed so much in his body he was sure it was carbonated by then.

"Keep walking," Evan said reading his mind. "Excuse me. Excuse me!" he shouted as they went past the throngs of reporters, who kept hurling accusations even as James sat in the passenger seat and buckled his seatbelt.

Evan pulled out slowly, careful not to hit anyone, even though secretly James hoped his friend would roll his tires over one of Carina's pointy-toed heels.

"Well. That was a first," Evan said with a chuckle, trying to lighten the seriousness of the mood.

He sniffled and wiped his nose on his left arm. "Rosita is dead." The floodgates in his eyes opened up like a dam. Too many innocent women dead, and James was terrified that Tessa would turn up next. "Why aren't they looking for Tessa? Why are they wasting time with this bullshit?" He pounded a fist on the dashboard.

Evan squeezed his shoulder from the driver's seat. "I know, man. I'm sorry." He lowered the radio. "We'll stop at my parents for a few minutes, then I have to get you home. They're coming to fit you for the ankle monitor."

Evan's mother waited at the door. She opened the screen as they walked up the driveway and immediately took James in her arms.

"Oh, darling, get inside," she said, and ushered them both in.

"We don't have long, Mom," Evan said, pointing to James's ankle. "They're coming today."

Mrs. Soderberg made coffee and the three of them sat sullen at the round kitchen table. Mr. Soderberg was out practicing his golf swing.

"Thank you, Mrs. Soderberg," James said, savoring his last social gathering until God only knew when. He hoped he'd never have to talk to anyone through glass. "I don't even know what to say."

She placed her hand on top of his. "Now, now. Don't you worry about a thing. It's a misunderstanding. We know you didn't murder anyone. And they'll find Tessa. She was so lovely," she said, biting the corner of her lower lip. "She *is* so lovely. I can't believe they think you would hurt your wife or murder that girl."

"They found a gun in my house. It wasn't mine. I'm being set up. Something strange is going on, and I want to find out what it is."

"A gun? Oh, dear. Guns everywhere. We tried to talk Evan out of getting a gun, but you know this one, once he sets his mind to something..." She waved toward Evan.

James's face went blank when he looked at his best friend after finding out this brand-new information. "When did you get a gun?"

Evan rubbed his beard, then the back of his neck. "Years ago."

"Why?"

Evan shrugged. "I was in my midtwenties. Lived right by campus with a roommate who seemed a little shifty to me. I think he was dealing. He had people coming in and out all hours of the night. I saw one of them strapped once. Better safe than sorry. There's nothing wrong with protecting yourself. It's not like I ever pulled it on anyone. It's under lock and key in a safe in my condo now. Hopefully I'll never need to use it."

Mrs. Soderberg shook her head. "Those damn things. You're going to shoot your eye out, kid," she said, mocking *A Christmas Story*, as she rose to wash out the coffee pot in the sink.

With the water running, James was able to disguise his tone. "Evan, man, I think I'm in some real trouble. Look, I never told you, but I had a gun. It wasn't legal. It's gone now, though. I got rid of it last week. But someone knew about it." He paused. It wasn't just that Tessa had told Gwen—he'd pulled it on Damon. He still didn't regret scaring the ever-living shit out of that prick. "Two people knew. It's a mess."

"Crap. Why didn't you tell me?" Evan's face scrunched up, and he pulled out his cell phone and began texting. "Let me see what time Robert can get to your house."

Robert told Evan he'd be over after the workday, around eight at night. Evan drove James home in the afternoon, all the way to the top of the driveway where James quickly punched the code into the keypad and ran inside. The reporters didn't move past the sidewalk in front of his house, but they shouted the whole time. A missing wife and a murdered coworker were huge news in suburbia.

When he opened the door that connected the garage to the laundry room, Candy was waiting on her bed, and jumped up with excitement, wiggling her little butt until James bent down and scratched her behind the ears.

"Hey, girl. I know Uncle Evan came and saw you this morning." He petted her soft head, and her eyes questioned him as she looked at the door and then back to him. "I'm sorry, girl. Mommy isn't coming home yet. I swear I'll find her." Her ears stirred at the mention of "Mommy" and James cried again. Right there in a ball, on his laundry room floor, where Candy licked his tears, then settled in beside him. His companion.

James only rose from the floor when the ankle monitor company came and slapped it on. They wired his property and read him the rules. It was tight and the skin around it already itched. He needed to get his mind off the fact that he couldn't leave to look for Tessa, and against his better judgment, turned on the computer to see the headlines.

LOCAL MAN WITH MISSING WIFE, JAMES MONTGOMERY, ALLEGEDLY COMMITS MURDER

WHERE IS TESSA AND WHAT DID
SHE KNOW?

ALLEGED WORKPLACE AFFAIR
ENDS IN HOMICIDE

Right as he was about to wipe the entire desk clear with his forearm, sending everything to the floor, his cell phone rang. When he retrieved it from his pocket, he didn't recognize the number, and sent it to voice mail. Likely another vulture.

A minute later, there was a beep, indicating a message. Like a sadist, he hit *play*.

"Hello, this message is for James Montgomery. My name is Bella Johnson, and I'm a new reporter at the Valley Lake Blaze. I don't agree with your portrayal in the media. I don't think you are responsible for your missing wife, or for murdering your coworker. I'd like an interview to get your side of the story, without the venom attached. If you're interested, please call me back."

She left a number, which James jotted down. He'd have to speak to Robert about this tonight. Was it possible that someone was on his side?

When Robert got there at eight on the dot, James offered him a beer but he declined, so James opened one for himself. He grabbed a frozen mug from the freezer and winced. *Tessa*. At the kitchen table, Robert had James's charges and release forms spread out on the table, and a yellow legal pad in front of him, which he tapped with his expensive-looking pen.

"Okay. Go," Robert said.

"Well, here's the quick background. Tessa—"

"I don't want quick, James. I need to know everything."

"So do I." James pinched the top of his nose. "I wish I knew more about Tessa. We only knew each other two weeks before we got married." He paused, and noticed Robert's eyebrows go up, but he didn't say anything, just kept writing on his pad. "She was out with my roommate the night I met her, and thank God I got home and was able to—"

"What does this have to do with an illegal gun?"

Direct. "Well, I'm getting there. I got home early and Damon—my old roommate—had her pinned to the ground. He hit her. He was going to rape her, and I got there in time to stop him. He was a bad dude. She wouldn't press charges, which I know a little bit now is because of her past. She was running from an abusive ex-husband and didn't want to be found. I'm not even sure Tessa Smyth was her real name. She had a state ID card with her Social on it, so she got that somehow, and I didn't really question it. I know—I should've. But I was in love."

"And the gun?"

"Right. She always feared that the ex was after her, so I got a gun. I knew a guy who knew a guy and I'll never say any more than that. When I told her, she told me she hated guns and to get rid of it. So, I did. Mostly. I got it out of the house. I had it in my glove compartment, and then I saw Damon the night she went missing. Me, and my boss Trey, and Rosita—God, Rosita—we were out cultivating a client at Jupiter's, and I saw Damon there, hassling a girl. My blood ran cold, man. I wasn't thinking. He followed her out and I thought he was going to try the same shit, so I grabbed the gun, and I was right. Saw him pinning her in an alley. I put the fear of God in him."

"How, exactly?"

"I—I held the gun to his head."

Robert's eyes lifted from the pad, but not his head. "Well, this isn't good, James."

"I know. But I obviously didn't kill him. The girl got away, thank God, and I hit Damon over the head with the gun. But now that this is all out—he knows I had a gun. And I threatened him." James slammed a fist onto the table, making his glass of beer rattle. "And while the fucking press will say that's reason to believe I killed Rosita, I think it's a reason to say Damon wanted revenge and did something to Tessa. Why can't they find her?"

"Damon. What's his last name?"

"Damon Moretti. I lived with him for almost a year. Mostly stayed at my ex Joanna's house an hour up north. Damon gave me the creeps, the way he always brought girls around. Never saw anyone more than once or twice. Probably because he date-raped everyone."

"Let's not speculate here, James," Robert said as he dropped the pen. "This was all the night Tessa disappeared. This isn't going to look good. Now that you were arrested and your name is out there, this Damon may have already contacted the police with the information about the gun. If he hasn't—yet—me putting his name out there as a potential suspect for Tessa is going to open a can of worms. They'll say you were violent, in a rage, had an illegal gun on your person that night, and then your wife disappeared, and your coworker who everyone thinks you're having an affair with was found dead days later by a gunshot. They found the gun in your house during the search, James."

His shoulders sagged. "That wasn't my gun."

"Unfortunately, we can't prove that."

"Yes, we can. I know where my gun is. I hid it. It was nowhere near my house. No one knows where I put it."

"That proves nothing." It was a statement, not a question, and James was afraid that Robert was starting to doubt him. "How would anyone know you didn't have two? Or five? When did you hide it, exactly?"

"Last Saturday."

"After Tessa went missing, then?"

James didn't know what he was getting at. "Tell them to do their fucking jobs and find my wife."

"James, listen," Robert started. "My job here isn't to presume guilt or innocence. My job is to defend you within the confines of the law."

He didn't understand that James didn't do any of it.

Robert made a note in his legal pad and cleared his throat. "So, let's talk real then. You said you don't even know if that was your wife's real name. How do you know she wasn't running a racket on you?"

"A racket?"

"Girl's running from her past. Fake name. Says someone is after her. What if she was working with someone to set you up? And then she took off?"

James pounded his fist again. "What would she get out of setting me up? What does someone get out of Rosita being dead?"

"I don't know those answers, James. I'm just saying, you not knowing about your wife's past isn't going to help you."

James sat silent, and then brought up the message from earlier. "I got a message from someone named Bella Johnson. A reporter. She doesn't believe I did this. Can we get ahead of this?"

"Who? Where is she from?"

James played the message on speakerphone for Robert, and he listened with intensity.

"Okay," Robert said. "One opinion is one opinion, but if it puts another story out there, it can't hurt. I want to be here when she interviews you." Robert looked in his phone's calendar and tapped a few buttons. "Call her back. Find out if she can get here at nine-thirty tomorrow morning."

James called her, and she answered. James explained that his lawyer would be present for the interview, and it was a date for nine-thirty the next morning.

Robert stayed, listening to James and plotting and planning a defense, until almost eleven at night. The next morning, James knew he needed more than just one cup of coffee. He woke at seven-thirty, Candy still sleeping with her back toward him, in Tessa's spot. He turned over and spooned her, the way he usually did with Tessa every morning, and his heart broke in two. Actually, his heart had split in half every day since last Thursday.

"Hey, girl. Let's get you some breakfast."

Candy swiveled onto her back, all four paws in the air, as she usually did when she wanted her belly rubbed. James obliged for a while, longer than he'd planned, then plodded toward the bathroom for a shower. After throwing on a Rangers T-shirt and jogging pants, he went downstairs to the kitchen and started the coffee. His hair was still wet when he prepared Candy's breakfast, mixing her wet dog food with her dry. He was refilling her water bowl when the doorbell rang, and Candy barked at the intrusion. He looked at the clock on the microwave, and it was only eight-thirty. *Terrific*, he thought. *Reporters again.*

He slowly made his way to the door and peeked through the window, trying to remain unseen, and indeed, there was a woman there who spotted him inside and waved. She had long blond hair and wore a casual powder-blue pantsuit with a white collared shirt underneath. Designer sunglasses with too-big frames were perched upon her sculpted nose. She smiled at him and waved maniacally and then, through the glass, spoke.

"Hi, are you James Montgomery? It's me, Bella Johnson. For the interview."

She was early. James undid the two locks and the chain and cracked open the door, making sure she saw him look at his watch, annoyed.

"You're early."

"We said eight-thirty?"

"Nine-thirty."

"Oh." Her smile disappeared, replaced with a self-deprecating expression while she pointed at her head. "Baby brain. I have a six-month-old at home. I mix things up all the time. I'm sorry. I can just sit here on the stoop until you're ready."

She made a move to crouch down on his front steps, but James stopped her.

"It's okay." He opened the door wide. "You can come in and wait." He scanned her again as she stepped into his home, then looked down at his own attire. "I'm not exactly ready yet. And my lawyer Robert isn't here."

"That's okay!" she said, overly cheery, and she entered the foyer as James gestured her into the kitchen. Candy investigated for a minute and barked at the stranger like the good protector she was, and James silenced her. She whined her high-pitched whine and wiggled her butt, but then went back to gobbling her breakfast. Food always won. "Cute dog!" Bella said.

"Thanks. We just adopted her a couple of months ago." His words choked at the "we" and he swallowed it down. "Do you want some coffee? It just brewed."

"Sure! Just a little milk, if that's okay? If you have a nondairy milk, even better, but it's obviously not a deal breaker. Almond milk, oat milk, even that soy milk, although I'd prefer my soy be organic. You should read about what they say about soy nowadays! It was supposed to be a healthy alternative but now it's all GMO this and GMO that. I'm just trying to keep added hormones out of my body while I'm still breastfeeding." She lifted both hands in front of her chest defensively. "TMI! I know. My husband thinks I talk too much. He's always like 'Bella, no one cares about you being a cow right now!' Not that he thinks I'm a cow. It's the breastfeeding, and the fact that I won't shut up about the baby. You know what I mean. Right?"

James pressed his lips together. "Mmm hmm." God, she was a talker. Her husband was right.

She plunked her purse on the table and then pulled out a chair and took a seat, scanning the backyard. "Wow. Beautiful property! Do you get a lot of kids playing in the lake out here? When we lived in Pennsylvania forever ago before my husband got transferred here, there was a lake in the neighborhood. All the kids used to ice skate on it, and I was always like 'Oh my God, they're going to fall in!' and he said I worried too much. He's afraid I'm going to helicopter the baby." James's face was blank, out of sheer shock that she was still talking. "You know, helicopter parents? Always hovering over their kids." She held her arms out and made them spin, then made noises that James didn't understand, her voice like she was imitating someone annoying, which he understood wholeheartedly at that moment. "*Mer Meh Mer*, don't eat sugar, *Meh Meh Mer*, take off your shoes, *Mer Mer Meh*, use the hand sanitizer in your backpack."

These were all too many scenarios, actions, and *too much speech* before he had his first cup of coffee. Plus, why was she so at ease? According to the media, she was alone in a house with a cold-blooded killer.

Maybe it was her defense mechanism. It was also the first time James considered homicide. Anything to get her to shut up for two minutes.

Although he shouldn't joke about that. Not even to himself.

"Can I be so bold to ask for a tour? Maybe see some of Tessa's personal things? It'll be easier for me to connect and then plead for her return. And then I can be totally heartfelt, like, to tell a good story about her if I saw the types of clothes or jewelry she wore, or how she decorated the bedroom or whatever. Girls have that whole intuition thing, you know, it takes one to know one."

James obliged, because he just wanted her to shut up. Candy followed them upstairs, and he quickly walked Bella through the bedroom, and she commented on Tessa's taste when she saw how it was decorated. Even pressed on the mattress to see how Tessa liked to sleep, asking which side of the bed was hers. *Too personal*, James thought.

However, at that point, he'd literally do anything if there was a possibility that Bella would write a touching article that could procure Tessa's safe return. Even killers had to have a human side, right?

He pointed to her side, then he walked out, and she followed. She did a quick head-pop into the other two bedrooms, which were sparsely furnished. Back downstairs, he showed her their wedding photo, and in the corner of the dining room, there were a few pictures that James hadn't yet hung, but Tessa had picked out, so he let Bella see them so she could "vibe out on everything Tessa," as she put it.

It was twenty minutes but felt like twenty years of more baby info dump when Robert showed up early too, *Thank God*. James had already heard all about the baby, the baby's different cries, the baby's nursery of giraffes, the baby being ahead of schedule on her sleep cycle— you name it. He almost couldn't wait to talk about being perceived as a murderer.

Robert was already dressed in his expensive suit and shoes, and James again felt ridiculous for looking like he'd just come from the gym. Robert and Bella exchanged pleasantries, and Robert plunked down the bag of bagels and cream cheese he'd brought. Bella politely refused, probably because GMOs, but James was thankful for something to eat. He offered Robert coffee, and then the three of them sat at the kitchen table, looking at each other, all waiting for someone else to take charge.

"If I advise my client not to answer a question, that's the end of the story," Robert started. "You will not press for further details."

"Right! Okay," Bella said, then dug into her purse and pulled out a small recording device. "I'm going to record this so nothing gets lost in translation. Are we all cool with that?"

"It's preferable," Robert said. "Lost in translation goes both ways."

Bella fumbled with the recorder, a small, slim little thing that James could've hid in the palm of his hand. "Sorry! This is my husband's, and I'm not really sure how to work it. He just got it and of course I had to deal with the sitter this morning and he already left for work, and I couldn't find the directions. The baby needed a change, and I wanted to do that really quick—I like to be a hands-on mom, you know, I don't leave everything to the nanny—and then I had to calm her down before I left. Screaming babies! Anyway, it looks easy." She points to the small buttons on the side. "Play, next, record, delete. Easy. Am I right?"

"Then hit *record*," Robert said with an edge, Bella clearly testing his patience in only two minutes.

"Right. Here we go!" She hit the *record* button and immediately transformed into a reporter. Her voice softened and she talked slowly, enunciating her words. "I'm Bella Johnson from the *Valley Lake Blaze*, and I'm sitting here with accused murderer James Montgomery. There is much speculation in the media about the events that transpired last Thursday night, when his wife Tessa Smyth went missing. She's still missing, but unfortunately, another body was found a few days later, that of his coworker Rosita Morales. James has been accused of her murder. Do you have anything you want to say, Mr. Montgomery?"

Robert nodded at him. Go time.

James first told the story about how he and Tessa met. All the details, excluding names, on Robert's direction. Bella pressed, and Robert cut in with a swift *move on*, with a hand gesture to go with it. James made sure to talk about Tessa, and the things he loved about her—Robert had mentioned earlier to say her name as many times as possible, so whoever had her could connect to the fact that she was a real person. So, he did—spoke of her mystery, her heart, her ability to love James and even their dog, Candy, after what was apparently a rough upbringing. Bella nodded along, even wiping a tear once or twice. He wasn't sure if hers were real or if she was playing concerned reporter, but his tears were real. Talking so intimately and in such detail reminded him of things he'd forgotten—the way she'd always burn eggs but could master a soufflé, how many times she'd made him watch *Legally Blonde*, how she'd liked her wine ice cold. Little things that tugged on his heart daily, but more so now, talking about it. It felt like a eulogy and that terrified him.

He made sure to keep his story about Rosita quick and professional. He didn't want to seem too personal there, since he was also accused in the media of having an affair with her. Jesus, wherever Tessa was being held, he hoped she didn't see those accusations or worse, believe them.

When they wrapped up, Robert handed his card to Bella and said any follow-up would have to be arranged through him.

"Great! I understand. Let me get you my card," Bella said, opening her purse. Then, like a frenetic teenager, she took things out hurriedly, one by one. Makeup bag, phone, pens, wallet—and dumped them on the kitchen table. "Jesus! Where is my card case?" More stuff went flying—tissues, a rogue lipstick, keys. "Son of a—! Of course I forgot it. I probably left it on the bassinet or near the changing table. This is what I get for rushing and trying to be supermom! Going back to work was really hard."

"Right." Robert stood up and extended his hand. "Just email me your info and a copy of this interview at your earliest convenience. I'll walk you to the door."

Candy started to bark again as they walked into the hallway. James was bewildered at Robert playing host, hurriedly ushering her to the door. It slammed shut a minute later. Robert came back into the kitchen, his eyes wide.

"I know. She talks a lot," James said. "That could be good for me, no?"

"No. Not at all. Something bothered me as soon as I got here."

James's heart sunk. "Oh?"

"When I pulled in, I noticed her plates had a Hertz Rent-A-Car holder. I took a picture of the plate."

"Huh." James didn't make the connection. "What does that have to do with anything? Maybe her car is in the shop."

"Fine. I thought that too. But this last scene sealed it for me."

"What scene?"

"Dumping out her bag. All the talk about the baby. But there were no baby wipes, bottles, diaper rash balm— nothing that an obsessed 'supermom' would carry."

"Maybe she separated her work bag from her personal one?"

"Hang on. I'm going to make a quick call. Can I use your office?"

"Sure."

Robert went into the office and closed the door, talking in a hushed voice. James wasn't exactly spying, but he wanted to know what was going on. He could usually read people pretty well and thought that while Bella was a bit of a talker, she seemed personable and genuine.

James was sitting in the living room, petting Candy's head when Robert finished. James turned to him, and Robert's face was white.

"We have a problem, James."

"What's that?"

"There's no one named Bella Johnson working at the *Valley Lake Blaze*." Robert's face was lined with worry. "I know a guy," Robert said. "It might take a few days, but I'll find out who rented that car."

Who the hell did they just talk to?

29

Tessa

After Jupiter's opened back up last month with the redesign, people in town asked Michael who he'd used. I just took another meeting with Frankie at Romano's, a local Italian eatery.

They're a typical "pizza joint" with a few sets of old, rickety wooden tables to the left with the pizza bar on the right. The tables are covered with plastic red-and-white-checked tablecloths which have grease stains embedded in them from years of use. Parmesan in metal tins with tiny spoons sit next to the salt and pepper shakers, and each table has a plastic daisy in a red plastic vase that both look like they were bought on discount from the dollar store. The dining room in the back has six booths, three on each side, with a big round table that can fit ten in the middle. The table has a linen tablecloth, and there are linen napkins under each set of utensils.

Frankie said he wants to modernize the whole space. Keep the old-school Italian look, but also keep up with a clientele that doesn't want to use paper plates and napkins from a metal dispenser on the table. His budget isn't as big as Jupiter's, but I can still make a couple grand. James, of course, is proud of me and wants to have dinner somewhere new tonight to celebrate. He really is perfect, always showcasing even my smallest accomplishments.

Not like when I got an *A* in second or third grade, on a math test I studied really hard for, and I brought it home to my mother, proud. She didn't say a word to me, but instead was happy to use it as a napkin when she drunkenly knocked over her bottle of vodka. I couldn't tell if the red-marker *A* was bleeding into the paper because it was wet, or if my tears made it blurry. Either way, I didn't have much ambition after that. Why bother? Every moment of accomplishment in my life had simply opened the door to disappointment. When Caroline, another girl at school, got straight *A*s, she came in the next day with a tray of fresh baked cupcakes for the whole class, a gift from her mother. All I ever got as a gift were bruises and an occasional hot meal, and by hot, I mean microwaved. Who microwaves ground chuck roast with salt and considers that gourmet? I still gag thinking about it.

But that life is over, and I'm where I'm supposed to be.

James comes home with daffodils, and I place them in a vase with a penny. I read online that placing a penny at the bottom of a vase of water with daffodils or tulips makes them grow up straight and not wilt. Of course, I now use that tip in my business's Instagram.

Maybe I do know what I'm doing, degree or not. James still believes I went to RISD. I have to tell him the truth. About a lot of things. James doesn't lie to me. I decide to tell him at dinner.

We get in the car and he drives to a place at the beach, one we haven't been to before. It's only six o'clock on a Friday, so the real weekenders haven't swarmed yet, and we're seated without a reservation. James orders a bottle of red and holds my hand across the table.

"I'm so proud of you," he says, his smile wide as his face. "You're going to be the most sought-after designer for the whole county soon. Possibly the whole state."

I grin back at him, my cheeks full but not showing any teeth. "Thanks. I actually wanted to talk to you about all of this. About my previous design experience. It's important."

"Oh?" His face shows concern, and he clasps his other hand over mine. "Everything okay?"

I open my mouth to say it. I swear, I was going to. But out of nowhere, a girl comes by our table and throws a glass of water at James's head.

"That's what you get, asshole!"

Asshole. The word reverberates.

The restaurant is still *half* full, and everyone turns to observe. Who is this woman? She's tiny and dark haired, with severe dark eyeliner and heavy eye shadow, maybe even fake eyelashes. She's in a pink sundress with too-high wedges strapped to her feet, making her look like she was going to tip over.

I barely have time to react, and James is wiping his face with a napkin. "Jesus Christ."

The girl looks at me. "So, who the hell are you? You know he has a girlfriend, right?" She turns her anger back to James. "You never even broke up with me. Way to be mature."

My blood thickens. "James, who is this?" Why did she look familiar?

She whips to my direction again. "I'm Joanna; who the hell are you?"

"His wife."

I want to whisper it, but I don't. I say it with agency. James takes that as me being in his corner, which I am most certainly *not* at this very moment, but that's a talk for when we're alone.

"His *what* ?" Joanna is not amused.

James, after taking my napkin and wiping the water left on his face, sticks his left hand in the air, showing his wedding ring.

"Well, this is terrific," she says, then turns to the girl who appears by her side and takes her arm. She's also wearing too much makeup and looks at us disapprovingly. "He's fucking married." Back to James. "Were you always married? Was I your whore on the side?"

"That's enough," James says, then addresses her friend. "Erica, can you take her out of here? She's making a spectacle."

Erica shrugs. "Fine. But she's right. You're an asshole."

They turn and go back to the restaurant's bar to pay the tab, nasty stares lasering into my forehead. Without a word, two busboys come quickly to our table and mop the water on the floor, then wipe down the table with a rag and refill the water. The waiter comes by with two new napkins. He also leaves without a word.

Then, words.

"I'm going to make you pay for this James, you asshole!" Joanna screams from the door on her way out.

Everyone is embarrassed for us. For me.

Faint chitter-chatter comes back to the room slowly. When the stares die down, I direct my attention to James. "Okay. So what the hell was that?"

His face is forlorn, and he grabs my hand, but instinct pulls it away. Quickly.

"Tessa, I'm sorry." He rubs his face, unsure of how to proceed.

"You had a girlfriend when we started dating?" *The other woman.* Now I know why she looks familiar. She was the one in his apartment the night I went back there with Damon. "You told me you broke up when we met. I can't believe you did this. I trusted you."

"Please, it's not like that." My face immediately tells him that he's a liar and not to bother with bullshit. "Okay, it was a little bit like that. Look, me and Joanna were having problems. I was being distant, she lived too far away, it was a whole bunch of things. I wasn't being communicative, and she started following me."

"Right. She was at your apartment the night we met. Said she was leaving you a note. Probably because she still thought you guys were together." I'm trying not to cry. I haven't cried over a man since I met James.

He was never supposed to make me cry.

"Yes. I told her I was going out with friends that night and she texted that she was waiting for me at the house. I told her I'd be out all night and to go home, even though I was almost there. I didn't want to see her. It was over. And yes, it's my fault that I didn't break up with her properly."

"So, you *were* still with her?"

"Tessa, you know I've been with you every single night, since the first time we went out to Jupiter's. But I didn't see her. I swear. I haven't seen her since before I met you." His eyes mist. "I've only wanted you since the moment I laid eyes on you."

"Is that supposed to make me feel better about being the other woman?" My voice elevates and I swear he can see my heart beating through my chest like a cartoon character. "I thought I was done with this. With secrets."

As soon as the words escape my lips, I berate myself for being a hypocrite. How dare I say that to him? I was a treasure trove of lies and secrets. So I soften.

"Look, James, I know I haven't told you much about my past. About—my ex."

He nods. "Do you want to talk about it?"

"I—" I what? I'm a fake, a phony, and worse than you. "I lied too."

He's taken aback, but he can't do much at this point. He's still the one in the doghouse. "Do you want to talk about it?" he asks again.

God, he's going to divorce me. Not that our marriage is a hundred percent legal anyway. I lied about who I am. He has no idea who he's married to.

"My ex. I ran. I left when he was out with clients one night. He's looking for me."

James doesn't flinch, even if he wants to. "How do you know?"

I can't even look him in the eyes and I concentrate on my water glass. "I spoke to someone back at home." Say it, Tessa. "I never really divorced him."

"Fuck." James grabs his own glass of water on the table and downs it in one sip, then wipes the sides of his head with his napkin again. "You're not my wife?"

"I am. But it's a mess. I got the ID. It's a real ID. It has the state seal. It's legit. I just fudged some stuff."

"Fudged?" His voice broke. "How do you fudge a state ID?"

"I have my ways." I stop him right before he says *Who did you fuck to get it?* because I won't forgive him if he says that. "Not like that. Not like what you're thinking."

"I'm not 'thinking' anything." He places his hand on mine. "How bad was it? Who was he?"

238

I can't tell him all the details. He already knows too much. He'll dig.

"He was just an Asshole. One in a line of many. I didn't really have a male role model growing up. Just the alcoholic wife beaters my mom dated. No matter how much I tried to model my life from the movies, it just didn't work out. I'd go for the Edward Lewis, who saw the potential in the girl from the wrong side of the tracks. I ended up with the Mickey Knox character from *Natural Born Killers*. But this last one was a fucking Don Draper. Did everything right, from the outside. On the inside, it was horrendous."

"This is the guy who tattooed you?"

"No. Someone else." I rub my hands over my face. "Look, you got mixed up with a real piece of work. I grew up in backwoods small country. My life sucked."

"Tessa, it's not like that anymore. I love you."

I've heard those words before. Usually before or after I got a right hook.

My tone is hushed. Thank God we're not that close to the next table, but still. "I'm afraid. Of so many things. I couldn't divorce him. He knew everyone and had tabs on me all the time. You know I don't drive, and he loved that. It kept me housebound. He'd send neighbors by to 'check on me' and he'd send things to the house from his office that needed a signature, so he knew I was home. Most of the times it was just a blank piece of paper in a UPS envelope, but he needed to make sure I was there to sign. Called me at home ten times a day. I was a prisoner." I sniffle.

"Why did you put up with that?"

"Because it was still better than the alternative. I went from bad relationship to bad relationship, since I was a kid.

Sure, every guy in my life knocked me around. It's just the way it was for me. It's the only thing I've ever known. My mother's boyfriends were horrible to her, and she just took it. My sisters used to date these pieces of shit too. Even my brothers used to rag on their women. So, with him, that Asshole, I thought it was my ticket out. He at least had a stable job. He wasn't a trucker or bookie or drug dealer, like the rest of my exes."

I pause to gauge his disgust, but he's looking at me with softness in his eyes.

"I didn't graduate from high school. I lied about going to RISD. I was a waitress at a grease pit when I met him. I lived in a shack. I already had a legal state ID with a different Social Security number, something I figured out how to do when I ran from the last foster home. I preferred to work for cash. I did whatever I had to do to get by. And before you ask, no, I was never a prostitute."

He chuckles. "Well, you mentioned the Edward Lewis thing from *Pretty Woman*."

"Hardy har." I clear my throat and go on, quietly. "But yeah. Here's this guy, in a suit, shiny watch, perfect hair, all that stuff. And he took interest in me. Now I know he saw me as a target, but I didn't know that then. I thought he was rescuing me. The happy ending. He wanted to feel better about himself by telling me all the ways he saved me, probably because he was insecure about shooting blanks— thank God he never fathered a child. With me or anyone else. And you know what? I got the house, the dresses, the shoes, but when the violence started, well, I was already used to being hit by others, so yes, I stayed because at least this time he provided for me."

"What was it that made you leave?"

I swallow hard. "He smashed a mug into the side of my face with all his strength. The previous broken bones we were able to better explain away, but I knew he was going to kill me."

James winces. "Jesus. Wasn't that right before Damon—" He doesn't finish the sentence because he doesn't have to.

I nod. "Yes, and then there was you. It all happened so fast. So, so fast. And I know he's looking for me. I'm afraid he's going to find me."

"Look at me, Tessa," James says, and grabs both of my hands. Our eyes meet. "I won't let anything happen to you. I'm going to protect you at any cost."

I know he wants to. James means well, but what could he really do to protect me from my past?

30

James

James waited anxiously for the phone to light up with Robert's number, even though he'd told him it would be a few days before they found out who Bella Johnson really was. He couldn't believe he'd been duped—so desperate to prove his side that he'd fallen prey to a vulture.

Looking online, the articles from real reporters now spread past the city rag and the county news pages. There was statewide coverage in New Jersey. Fake Bella Johnson had been his only hope, because the other articles were savage, and so were the comments.

For his mental health, which was never a problem in the past, he needed to stop reading all the shit that was said online about him.

The doorbell would ring on occasion, and Candy would bark, but James knew better now. If he didn't recognize the person on the stoop immediately, he didn't open the door. He'd been relegated to sitting upstairs in his bedroom with Candy, so she wouldn't get so anxious whenever there was a noise outside. He drew the shades, turned on the TV, pet his dog, and wondered where his wife was. Every time he opened her closet door, he cried. Her perfume smell still clung to some garments that hung, and every time it hit his nose, he'd remember her smile or her crazy hair days, her cooking or her determination. Her side of the sink still had her hair dryer and curling iron and makeup. Like she'd walk in at any second and need a shower and a little grooming. It was what he prayed for.

The cops still had her hairbrush.

James texted Gwen, asking her to come over to sort through her things. Maybe she'd spot something that he couldn't see.

Her reply text was cold.

> Yea, thanks, but no. I believed you last week but now I don't know what to believe anymore. You were screwing around on her, weren't you? Don't contact me or Nick.

He was about to tap back a reply but decided against it. It wouldn't help. It would be seen as aggressive, even if he just wrote *Thanks*.

Then, the damn doorbell rang again. James went into the bathroom and looked out the window facing the front of the house. A cab was parked outside next to the sidewalk. He cautiously walked down the stairs and through the window next to the door, he saw a familiar face. He wasn't sure what the point of the visit was, though, so he only opened the door a sliver.

"Hey," James said. Relief.

"James. You poor thing. Do you mind if we come in?"

Okay, they weren't there to jump down his throat and accuse him of being a killer. It was going to be a good visit.

James opened the door wide and welcomed Hobart and Pearl into his home. Pearl immediately flung her

243

arms around him. "You poor dear. We don't believe what they're saying about you."

Her eyes filled with tears as James shook hands with Hobart, who also came in for a hug.

"We know you wouldn't hurt Tessa," Hobart said.

James led them inside to the kitchen. Hobart had an aluminum tray in his hands, and he placed it on the counter.

"This is some fried chicken and hoppin' John," Pearl said proudly. "I made extra last night to bring today. We know you can't leave and assumed you haven't been eating, but my cooking will have you busting your belt. Sit, sit," Pearl commanded, in James's kitchen. "Where are your dishes?"

"Thanks, Pearl, but you're a guest. Please, let me," James said.

She shook her finger at him. "You best get your butt in that seat next to Hobart."

Sometimes, James forgot that women of her generation were raised to be accommodating. His own mother was the same way—cooking and cleaning, serving and tidying. He didn't want Pearl to feel insulted, so he pointed to the cabinet where the dishes were and put his butt in that seat as she demanded.

"James," Hobart started. "What's going on?"

James told Hobart and Pearl everything, everything that he knew, from beginning to end as Pearl heated up the chicken. He cried again, and so did Hobart and Pearl when James told them about how they met, about Damon.

"This is my fault," Hobart said. "If that bastard Damon took her or did something to her, I'll fix him. I'm the one who took her there that first night."

"You didn't do anything wrong, Hobart," James said. "How were you supposed to know that the bartender was an asshole?" His head swiveled to Pearl, preparing food on the plates. "That smells fantastic. Excuse my ignorance, but what is hoppin' John?"

Pearl clapped. "First timer! This is my momma's momma's momma's recipe. Straight from the old South. I use bacon instead of sausage or fatback, and I use a little vinegar. Just a drop, but it makes a difference." She put a plate in front of both of them, then prepared one for herself and joined them at the table. Before James picked up his fork, Pearl took James's and Hobart's hands and closed her eyes, murmuring, "Lord, thank You for this food. Bless my family and my girls and Mr. James Montgomery, and please hold his dear wife Tessa in Your arms until her safe return." She opened her eyes and nodded. "Go ahead, now."

They stayed for three hours. Hobart was more forthcoming about a few things. James didn't know what Tessa's first few days were like when she got to New Jersey. He assumed she'd always been in the hotel where she was when he met her. He didn't know about the Empire Motel, and what happened there, and how Hobart had to pull a gun too.

As they left, Hobart and Pearl promised to be there for James if he needed anything.

"Thanks for bringing dinner," James said, then rubbed his stomach. "You were right. I didn't know how much I need a home-cooked meal."

"You call us anytime, baby," Pearl said. "Anything you need."

"Thanks. It really means more to me than you know."

After another hug, James closed the door behind them. In a better mood, he should've tried to end the day on a high note. But he didn't. He opened the computer to a new headline:

MURDERED VALLEY LAKE WOMAN ROSITA MORALES SIX WEEKS PREGNANT.

MORE CHARGES PENDING

31

Tessa

James told me he needed to talk to me about something important tonight, so I've had swimming fish in my stomach all day. To be honest, I haven't felt a hundred percent right in a few days anyway. I probably caught a bug from that woman who was openly sneezing all over the produce section at the grocery store last week. Still, there was something in James's voice that was insistent. I know he's been busy this week trying to land a major builder for financing a new town center. It's nearly five-thirty, and my nerves are getting the best of me.

When his car pulls into the garage, Candy starts to bark, as usual. He comes inside and he kisses me hello and smiles, so I assume he's in a good mood and whatever he needs to talk about so desperately is no big deal.

"How was work?" I ask. "Any news yet on the bid for the town center?"

"No, nothing yet. Me and Trey and Rosita have to take them out this Thursday night after work. Hopefully it'll help make the decision. Could be a nice bonus come Christmastime. I'd like to get you a proper diamond." He taps on his own wedding band and smiles. "What's for dinner? You want me to throw something on the grill?"

"I was planning on making tacos." I open the refriger-ator and scan. During these months, James always likes to have hamburgers or hot dogs on tap, just in case he wants to grill. He loves barbecuing and we probably only have another month or so until the weather turns. "We've got some burgers, but we're out of buns. We'll have to make a quick run to town; we can be there and back in ten minutes. Or I can just make the tacos." Or you can just tell me what's bothering you. Either/or.

"Sure, tacos sound good. We can grill Friday. I'll pick up buns on my way home from work."

So accommodating, all the time. "Great." I grab a pan out from under the kitchen island. "So what did you want to talk to me about?"

"Oh. Yeah. Do you want to sit down for a sec?"

Crap. "Sure."

"Hang on. I have to grab something." He runs back into the garage, and I hear trunk open and then slam shut, and he comes back inside with a canvas bag.

"What's that?" I ask.

He places the bag down on the table, and it thuds. "Well, I've been thinking about what we talked about last month. About your ex. About how you think he's after you."

"I don't know if he's still looking for me." I never should've cut contact with Maribel as abruptly as I did. "I think it's better that I just cut ties and move on with my life. Holding on to the past isn't healthy."

"Right. I mean, do you still want me to talk to Evan to have him look into rearranging our... stuff? Making the marriage legal and getting your ID straightened out?"

"Yes, of course, you know I want that. But I'm just afraid once we start that, he'll know where I am. If my name becomes part of public record."

"Well, that's what I wanted to talk to you about." He taps the bag. "Remember I told you I wouldn't let your ex hurt you?"

"Yes."

He places his hand inside the bag and out comes... a gun. A fucking gun. I leap back on my seat, my hands covering my face like I'm watching a ghost jump out from the closet and scare someone in a horror movie.

"Get that away from me!" I scream. Just seeing the barrel of a gun makes my skin crawl. It's the worst type of post-traumatic stress disorder. You have a gun pointed at you when you're young, this is what happens.

"It's okay Tessa. I know how to use it." His hands are on it, and he picks it up.

"Don't point that thing at me!"

"I'm not! I would never. It's not even loaded. Look." He pops the little spinner thing, whatever it's called, out and shows that there are no bullets in it. "See?"

My heart is beating so fast I fear an imminent heart attack.

"James, get that thing out of the house. I don't want that anywhere near me."

He sighs. "I promised to protect you."

"Then get an alarm system. Get cameras." I look at Candy, who is watching our interaction, bewildered, tilting her head back and forth. "Get another dog. A pitbull. I'll take tae kwon do. Just no guns. How did you even get a permit for that?"

His face tells me everything I need to know. He *doesn't* have a permit. It's an *illegal* gun. Street shit, scraped off serial number, probably already used for another murder. And it's in my house.

"How could you?" Tears fall from my eyes, and I don't want to be around him right now. "I'm going for a walk." I stand and head to the door.

"Tessa, wait!" he hollers, but I keep going. The door already slammed behind me.

The air outside is stuffy for mid-September. Indian summer. It's not like I can run away, even though running is the only direction my feet know to go. Instead of walking out of the neighborhood and into town, I turn in the other direction and go to the woods behind the house. The leaves have started to fall and crunch under my foam shoes and between my toes. I whack at twiggy branches as I follow a natural path down to the lake.

I have to step around random kayaks and canoes, leftover from the summer. It's a safe town (as long as Drew isn't here), and no one has a fear of their property being stolen. It's understood between everyone for miles that they can leave their stuff unattended. The lake is a popular fishing spot and there's a small dock that the city maintains, and people usually launch their small boats from it.

When I get to the dock, I remove my flip-flops and sit, my legs dangling from the side. I'm facing west, and the sun is setting, which is beautiful and turns the sky pink in front of me, which makes the smattering of clouds look like cotton candy. My toes don't hit the water, although they threaten to with the few inches of space. I look down and see my reflection.

My horrified expression.

Calm down. You're safe.

It's quiet, and the only sounds are the *bloop-bloop*s of the fish that come to the surface to investigate for algae or tiny minnows to eat. They've likely gotten used to fisherman dropping bread to attract schools of fish to hook for dinner.

James doesn't know about the times I've had guns pulled on me. I've tried to shield him from the past horrors of my life, but if he knew about them, he would've thought twice about bringing a gun into the house. It's a scare tactic to assert power over someone, and I don't want James to be that person in my eyes. Even if he's doing it for me.

I wait for almost an hour, trying to calm down, as the sun sets behind the trees, now making the sky a fiery orange. I've talked myself into not hating James—he really thought he was doing the right thing, and I love him for that—but I still don't want that thing in the house.

Taco Tuesday is ruined, but I've lost my appetite anyway. I think a bath and bed is exactly what I need.

When I walk back into the house, James's face is forlorn, a child scolded. He doesn't speak first, giving me the space that I need.

"I'm going to take a bubble bath upstairs. I'm sorry about dinner, I just don't feel like cooking tonight."

"It's okay," he says. "I'll just run out and grab a slice of pizza. Do you want me to bring any back for you? Or I can grab you one of those salads that you like from there?"

"No, thank you." I'm still polite. "I'm going to bed right after. I'm not hungry. Can you just promise me something? Get rid of it. I don't want it in the house."

"I promise, Tessa. I'll take care of it."

—

After a labored sleep, I wake the next morning cranky and unmotivated to work. I rub my crusty eyes and splash water on my face and brush my teeth. Candy and I head downstairs for our normal routine, where I feed her breakfast and sit outside with my coffee as she explores the small fenced yard. Only this time, I'm too out of sorts to even make coffee, so I watch Candy eat breakfast, and then try to will the queasy feeling away. But it doesn't work, and I have to haul ass inside, barely making it to the bathroom before I throw up bile—I didn't eat the night before so there was nothing to come up.

The worry has made me sick.

I wonder if the gun is still in the house, or if James took it with him. Driving with an illegal weapon. Great idea.

I'm still on the floor of the bathroom spitting stringy saliva when I hear Candy claw at the back door. I flush and rinse my mouth with water, then amble over to the back door to let her in. Still unable to eat or drink, I decide that maybe I need a talk session with Gwen. I text her and ask if she's around, and she said says she's finishing Caleb's breakfast and to come by in a half hour.

I quickly shower and toss on a tank top and denim shorts and tie my hair into a bun at the back of my head. My bangs have gotten longer and annoy the shit out of me, and I attempt to tuck them behind my ears over and over. *Stay*. I say it to myself like I'm talking to Candy. Finally, I just use a bobby pin on each side. I look like R2D2, but who do I have to impress?

The walk over to Gwen only takes a minute or two. Every time I walk up her driveway, I admire the pavers they used, instead of tar and concrete. Even their mailbox has its own paver house built around it, all ornate and detailed. Much better than the stick in the ground that we have, but we spent our discretionary fund opening up the entryway. Maybe next year.

I knock, and Gwen comes to the door, Caleb in her arms, as usual.

"Hey, buddy!" I say to him and smile.

"Hi, Mrs. Teffa," Caleb says. He has problems with his Ss.

"Come on in, T," Gwen says. "Do you want some coffee?"

I don't mean to, but I swallow a small gag and cover my mouth with my hand. The worry from the night before is still there, churning away in my stomach, and until I take care of this issue, I'm afraid I won't be able to keep anything down.

"Oh, jeez, are you okay?" Gwen asks.

"No. Not really. It's why I wanted to come and talk to you."

"Sit down. Let me set Caleb up, hang on."

Gwen is wearing yoga pants and a tank top, basically the only thing I ever see her in, except for the times we go to dinner or for a drink. I see her pushing Caleb in the stroller around the neighborhood—yoga pants and tank. At the grocery store—yoga pants and tank. Weeding the front lawn—yoga pants and a tank. It's her mom outfit. She sets Caleb down at a chair, right next to me, and turns on her iPad in front of him.

"That'll keep him busy," she says. "What's up?"

"Well, last night, I—" I side-eye Caleb, who is looking at me, not the iPad. He presses a button on the screen and some cartoon comes to life. Loudly. "I told James something about my ex—" And, now there's singing. Loudly. Children's voices, in sync. "I told him I was scared of—" Caleb is singing along with them.

I lose focus completely. Gwen is staring at me, her big eyes trained on me with concern, like she's waiting for me to spit it out. Like she can't even hear it.

"I'm sorry, can we go in the other room?" I ask.

"And leave Caleb alone?" She's utterly flabbergasted that someone would suggest leaving a four-year-old boy alone for more than ten seconds. "He'll scream if we leave."

Well, that's great parenting.

"I don't want him to hear what we're about to talk about. It's—sensitive."

"He's not even paying attention." She widens her eyes and waves toward him as he sings along with whatever he's watching. "He loves that show."

"Right, but I can't concentrate with the singing." I chuckle. "I'm not used to kids. I can't tune it out like you do."

She huffs, stands, and walks to the other end of the kitchen, and calls me over. To stand as I talk. "Go ahead. What happened, now?"

"I told James that I was afraid my ex was looking for me."

"Oh. Is he?"

"Last I heard, he was. But that was a couple of months ago. Anyway, we ran into one of James's exes last month and it brought up all these things about my ex, and I told him that I was scared of him. He—he wasn't a good man." I look back at Caleb, still singing, so he can't hear us. "He hit me. It was that type of relationship."

Gwen grabs my arm. "Oh, God. I'm so sorry."

"Yeah, well, I got the hell out of there. It's a whole long thing. Anyway, the reason I'm feeling sick is that we had a fight last night."

"Did James hit you?" Her eyes go from concerned to furious in less time than it takes me to blink.

"No!" I want to clear that up immediately. "He said he wanted to protect me. He got a gun."

"A gun? Are you kidding?" Now she looks at Caleb, likely playing out every scenario of him walking down the block alone, like that would ever happen, and James coming out and pumping her child full of lead. Not that she lets him walk. He's four and she still puts him in a stroller. She reminds me of those people that put their dogs in strollers. "How did he even get a gun?"

"That's the thing. He just 'got one,'" I say, using air quotes.

"Oh, hell no. You need to go to the police."

Overbearing Gwen now wants control of my marriage as well as her toddler. "I can't. I don't want him to go to jail. He thought he was doing the right thing. I don't know. I just hate guns. Like, *hate* them."

"Me too. And I don't want one around Caleb. Oh, God, I can never come over again now. What's he going to do?"

A bit of an overreaction, but sadly, it doesn't shock me. "I told him to get rid of it. By any means possible."

"Good. You think he'll listen?"

"He better!" Just talking about it makes me feel queasy again. Plus, this entire visit has been a waste of time. I don't know what I was expecting to get out of it or why I expected her to take her eyes off that child for an entire minute. "I'm going to go. I think I'm getting a bug. Thanks for the talk."

"Ugh, I think it's going around. Caleb was a little snot machine all morning. I think he's coming down with something too. Hey, if you need anything, let me know."

"Thanks, Gwen."

A quick hug and I'm out the door. My walk turns into a jog and it's all I can do to not vomit all over the front lawn. I'm surprised I make it inside.

32

James

The garage door opened, Candy barked, and James sat up on the couch. He thought quickly about cleaning up but decided he didn't care if the place was a mess. Evan wouldn't care.

Candy ran to Evan as he walked in. He petted her on the head, then looked at his best friend, and his face dropped.

"James, man, I'm sorry. Now they're saying double homicide."

James's whole body ached as he lifted himself up. "This could only be good though, right? Can't they do a DNA test? It's not mine. Can't it help prove I'm not having an affair? It could help clear me. They should be looking for my wife. And when they find her, I'm going to sue these fucks." James was determined.

"On what grounds?"

Evan, always the lawyer. "I don't know. False arrest, once this shit is cleared up."

"Well, technically they had—"

"I don't give a fuck about technically anything. Poor Rosita was pregnant when someone killed her. I wonder if she knew. Oh, God, imagine her last moments."

James didn't want to out anyone, but he was pretty sure he knew who the father of that baby was.

Could Trey be a killer?

No one would believe it at this point. The whole damn state thought James was the killer.

James's cell rang, yet another number he didn't recognize. He grabbed it, and like he was the pitcher at the all-star game in the bottom of the ninth, he whipped it into another wall so hard it left a mark before it shattered on the ground. Candy shot across to the other side of the room in a panic.

Evan's eyes narrowed. "When was the last time you got any real sleep? You look like shit, man. I mean, I get it. But you have to sleep."

"I know, but I can't. I have a missing wife who I can't even look for because I'm fucking locked up here, I'm wrongfully accused of murder, I've got that fake reporter who I let in the house—"

"Whoa. What fake reporter?"

James rubbed the top of his head. His hair was greasy, sticking up in every direction. At this point he'd rather shave it all off than bother dealing with it. Or washing it. "Some lady called yesterday and wanted my side of the story. She came by this morning. Said her name was Bella Johnson, new with the local paper. I gave a whole blubbering interview, but Robert thought there was something off about her because of all the—" He paused, unable to say *baby talk*. "She was just full of shit. No one with that name even works there. I had her here. Even had her tour the house. I don't even know who the fuck she was."

"But Robert's looking into it?"

"Yep."

"Good."

James looked at his cell phone on the floor and picked it up. The screen, of course, was shattered. He was able to make out the remnants of one text message. From Trey.

> You'll have to see Clara Clayton for an exit interview. When this is done.

James laughed, that maniacal laugh that a crazy person on the edge does right before they get their one-way ticket to batshit silly land. Sure, James was now accused of double homicide, but wasn't it funny how Trey covered his ass immediately?

Evan texted Robert, explaining what happened to James's phone and said to give him all the details for the time being. Robert answered—he talked to the DA, and there was new information.

"Well, there's more," Evan said after a long pause while reading a detailed text. "Do you want to hear it?"

"I don't know. Do I?" James asked.

"Robert seems to think this could be good."

"Jesus, there's nothing good about this," James snapped.

"No. Not that." He scrolled through his phone again. "Forensics found out that there was more DNA at the scene. Here. At your house. In addition to Tessa's."

"What does that mean? Proof that someone else took her? That someone else was here?" For the first time in almost a week, James was hopeful. If you could call it that.

"This is where shit is going to get real. If you still claim one hundred percent that you had nothing to do with this—"

"I didn't!" How could he say such a thing?

"I know. But keep claiming your innocence. Because whoever did it left evidence. Amateur mistake." Evan's eyes went wide.

"I want to talk to Robert. Give me your phone."

Evan handed it to James, and in his frustration, he hit an app at the top of the phone. The photo album. And the first picture that popped up was a picture of Tessa. Of Tessa and Evan, together. Smiling.

"What's this?" James turned the phone to his best friend.

"Oh. That." Evan rubbed his beard. "I ran into her at that pizza place she was designing. I was there for lunch. We took a selfie. She didn't tell you?"

James cautiously read his friend's face. "No. She didn't." He looks at the picture again. "This is dated last Thursday. You saw her that day? Before she went missing?"

Evan took the phone from James's hands. "It's my fault. I was supposed to text it to you, but I got sidetracked with a case." He peers at the screen. "I'm sorry you had to see that. Look at that smile. She was always so happy with you."

Tessa wasn't with James when she smiled *that* smile. In fact, he'd detected something glowing about her face in that moment.

Evan tapped a few buttons. "I just texted it to you, so you can have it when you get your phone set up again. But let's focus. Call Robert. Find out what extra DNA was at the scene."

James's head said that Evan was telling the truth. His gut swirled, but it'd been betraying him all week. Focus.

With shaky fingers, James called and heard it straight from Robert's lips—another person's DNA. Another person's blood.

James explained what he did to his cell phone out of frustration, and said that until he got a new one, Evan could be a point of contact, and that he can have full disclosure on what was going on at any time. Evan lived five minutes away, and he wouldn't let the last five minutes of doubt dictate what he knew about his best friend. Evan was the only one James could trust. He hung up, and handed the phone back to Evan.

"They're going to find out the truth, James," Evan said. "We're getting closer."

33

Tessa

Things are still weird with James since I pretty much avoided him yesterday. He gave me my space. I still feel nauseated, like the beginning of the flu is wreaking havoc on me. I get up out of bed with Candy and go downstairs. Right on the counter, there was a little folded up note from James.

> *Tessa—I got rid of the gun. I never want you to feel unsafe. I'll be home as soon as I can tonight. I love you. James*

He's trying, and that's all he's ever done—try to make me feel safe. I instantly forgive him, and I can't wait to see him after his work thing. First, I text him that I don't feel well, just in case he attempts to contact me during the day and I'm napping. I don't want him to think the fight is still going on. It's not.

I put the water in the coffee pot and open the refrigerator to grab the coffee, but as soon as I smell it, my mouth starts to water. Not in the *yum* way, in the oh-my-god-please-make-it-to-the-bathroom-in-time way. I do make it in time and pull my hair back and empty my stomach. Candy sits outside the opening to the bathroom, making sure I'm okay.

I hate being sick. But why, every time I think about or smell coffee—

Holy shit.

What's today's date?

I run to my phone and look at the calendar. Back back back... weeks back. The last time I had my period. It was well over a month ago.

I don't have the flu. I have a case of the babies.

Pushing down the nausea, I stand and run up the stairs, where I have pregnancy tests. Every woman of a certain age does. You know, just in case. I tear open the wrapper and pee on the stick, and pace the bathroom, back and forth, back and forth, which Candy does too, in tandem. It's cute. Ten seconds lasts a year, half a minute lasts a decade, and by the time these two minutes are up, I'm convinced I'll be in assisted living.

I don't even need to look. I know the results.

And I'm correct.

The first time I got this result, I was a teenager. I felt nothing but panic and dread and immediately thought of how to make it go away. The second time, I considered keeping it for a hot second. But with the jobless loser it belonged to, I knew I'd end up just like my mother if I attempted parenthood before I was stable. *I* wanted to be stable. Fuck the guy. *I* needed something concrete.

Third time's the charm.

The only feeling I have now is hope and love and I'm thinking of bottles and mobiles and my belly popping and how cute it's going to be. I want it, I want it so bad, and I finally get to have it. My happy ending.

I have to call James!

No. Tell him in person. If I can make it through the day without hiring a skywriter.

I think of how to tell James, and I'm flabbergasted. What do I say? We've never really talked about it, especially so soon into our marriage. Aside from having to tell him this, I decide I need to come clean to him about everything, not only because it's the right thing to do, but because he deserves it. About my upbringing, my past, Drew. My previous terminated pregnancies. Maybe I need therapy. I always have, I just never had a reason to go through with it. If I'm going to be a mom, I want to be a good one. Not like my mother. I contemplate this for hours. The *how* I tell him is almost as important as the *what* I'm going to tell him.

After a quick shower, I head out to walk into town. The sun is hot like a skillet, and it rejuvenates me as I feel the vitamin D soaking into my skin. When I pass Gwen's house, I want to run in and tell her, but her car isn't in the driveway, and I remember it's Thursday. She has Caleb's art class today. While she's making flowers out of construction paper, I'm, *we're*, walking into town to do some shopping, to figure out a fun way to tell James that he's about to be a dad. My hand hovers over my abdomen. A baby. One that will grow into a toddler, a child. A teenager who I will love, and support, and I'll never give them a reason to run away.

Almost into town, I'm giddy thinking about painting the nursery. First steps, taking off the training wheels, cheering on the soccer or Little League team. There will be Christmas mornings around the tree, family dinners, helping with homework, and college graduations. James and I will be a little old couple, holding hands and still in love as our child dedicates their valedictorian speech to us.

It's everything I've seen in every romantic comedy, rolled into one.

Turning onto Main Street, before I hit the gift shop, there is a local electronics store and I have an idea. I need to hear myself say it first. The bell on the top of the door rings when I open it, and a salesman approaches me before the door even closes.

"Good morning!" He looks at his watch, a digital one that probably beeps on the hour. "I mean, good afternoon!"

He laughs at himself, self-deprecating. He's cheery, nerdy, and adorable. Maybe twenty-one, tall, skinny, glasses. Everything you picture for someone who's trying to sell you stuff you don't need, but you buy it anyway because they sound so knowledgeable, and their passion for doohickeys is unyielding.

"Good afternoon." Then I correct myself. I notice you get better service when you address people by their name instead of assuming they're just workers there to serve you. "Hi, Ralph. My name is Tessa." I extend my hand for a shake, which he returns, sweaty palm and all. "I'm looking for a small recording device?" I say it like a question, holding my thumb and forefinger a few inches apart, indicating that I need one of the tiny, thin ones I see businessmen talking into all the time, likely taking notes for meetings.

"You don't have an iPhone?" He looks at me like I hopped right off the wagon in my prairie dress and bonnet.

"No. I reject technology," I say, with no intention of telling him I use basic burner phones.

"Ah, of course we can help you, Tessa. Follow me."

The store isn't very big, and "follow me" really means take two steps to the left. His arms gesture out in a *tah-dah!* fashion, and I don't know what I'm staring at. On the wall, there are a bunch of different packages, all devices in thick plastic, hanging from chrome hooks.

"Hmm. What do you suggest?" I ask.

"What's the purpose?"

To hear myself say over and over and over that I'm pregnant until I find the way that sounds the best. "Practicing a speech. I need to hear myself say it out loud."

"Of course." He turns his attention to the wall and fingers through a few models and takes one off its hook. "This one has up to eight hours recording time on one single charge. A bargain at two ninety-nine."

Yikes. I don't need eight hours to tell James that I'm pregnant. I don't *think* I do.

"That's a bit above my pay grade," I say. "Anything a little more cost effective?"

"Hmm." His eyes scan up and down, and he grabs another one. Smaller. Thinner. "This one'll get you about four and a half hours on a single charge and automatically uploads it in real time to the cloud. Sort of like the iPhone iCloud, but they call it 'the Moon.'" He points to a little button on the bottom. "See here? That's the delete button. It's a design flaw, too close to the thumb when people hold it and speak into it. Some people delete their speeches before they've had a chance to save them. The cloud feature eliminates that risk." He flips the package over and there's a picture of the moon on the back insert, and he taps it. "Brilliant, right?"

Ralph is so excited that he's educating me, and I know this kid likely works on commission, so I want to give him a sale. "How much?"

"This one is one nineteen. And the Moon subscription is included for a full year. After that, if you want to continue using the service it's only like five bucks a year. A bargain, really."

He's smiling now, and I see that he has braces on his lower teeth.

"Okay. Let's do it."

"Excellent!" He says it too loud and I see someone who's probably his boss, an older man wearing a tie, give a thumbs up. "Let's ring you up."

This time, we both take about ten steps to the right where the register is. The man behind him looks over Ralph's shoulder as he punches buttons on the screen. Ralph is smiling as he fumbles with the opening of the bag and places my new device inside.

"Thanks for the help, Ralph," I say.

"No problem. Thanks for stopping in, and remember us for all of your electric needs!"

"I will." I wink and smile at him, then lightly wave to his boss before I exit the store.

About a block down is the baby store. *The baby store.* Oh my God, I can't believe I'm going in with a purpose. Inside, music is playing in the background, softly—something you'd hear in a movie. "*Hush little baby, don't say a word, momma's gonna buy you a mockingbird.*" It fills me with hope, because I was raised on the likes of Alice Cooper and Tupac, depending on who my mother was screwing at the time.

Another small store, as most of the mom-and-pops on Main Street are, there are only a handful of people inside. A quick scan tells me that the left-hand side has toys for toddlers, the right-hand side has toys for small children under ten, and the back is a bliss world of soft blankets and baby lamb stuffed toys and onesies and mobiles. Tears rush to my eyes.

"Can I help you?" A tall, slim lady approaches me. "Looking for a gift or for yourself?"

"Oh. Hi." Despite my first instinct of wanting to run up Gwen's driveway to spill the news, James needs to be first. "A gift. For a coworker."

"Oh, fantastic. How old is the little one?"

"Brand new. Less than a month," I say, thinking about my bun in the oven.

"All of our infant stuff is back here." She turns and makes a gesture toward the other end of the store. "Let me know if you need help narrowing anything down."

"Will do. Thank you."

I walk to the back of the store when a familiar scent hits me. I must look like a dog, sniffing with my nose in the air, and I realize it's baby lotion. Between fifteen and twenty years of age, a lot of my friends kept their pregnancies, so I've been around babies. And Gwen still treats Caleb like an infant, so I've seen her slathering lotion on his butt before.

I finger through the soft blankets and the kits to make molds of baby handprints and footprints. There's so much to look forward to! Then I see the most perfect present. It's not even for the baby.

It's just a mug. But it says *World's Greatest Dad*.

I snatch it off the shelf and practically run to the front of the store. The same slim lady wraps it in five sheets of blue tissue paper and closes the top with blue ribbon, then places it gently in a small, sturdy brown bag.

Happy with today's bounty, I pass Romano's and decide to stop in and see if the new tablecloths came in yet. To my surprise, Evan is ordering at the counter.

"Hey!" I say excitedly.

He turns and smiles. "Tessa. What are you up to?"

My smile is probably goofy. Should I tell him? I have to tell someone! No, I could never do that to James. He has to be first. "Just passing through. Had to grab a few things." My fingers tighten against the brown bag and I turn it inward, so he doesn't see the logo. I don't want him to know that it's from the baby store.

"I'm just getting a quick slice, I'm in the middle of a nutty case. Hey, let's grab a picture, I'll send it to James. He'd get a kick out of this."

Evan's arm wraps around my shoulder, and I smile—wide. Because I know a secret. I have the new-mother glow.

He takes his pizza to go, and I tell him to come for dinner this weekend and he agrees before he leaves.

After checking on the design progress, I head home in the warm weather, and only then do I realize that I *definitely* have to tell James about my past. We'll need to get a lawyer—I should call Evan, because I'll need to do it right. I'll need to dissolve my marriage to Drew, and I need to make the one with James legal, with my real information. I'm mad at myself as I think about how I've deceived him. He's my child's father. And I need this all done correctly, and soon, because I'll need to get a driver's license. I certainly can't plan to tote a baby around on foot all the time. There will be doctor's appointments. And what if, God forbid, there's an emergency?

I'll be waiting up for James when he gets home from his client shindig tonight, and I'm going to tell him everything.

I welcome the night alone to practice. It used to bother me being left alone, knowing what Drew was doing behind my back. But what was my recourse? Bitching about it and getting a black eye? Or worse, like the time Drew broke one of my ribs when I questioned his where-abouts. While I was on the floor, screaming in searing pain, he told me not to move and he'd be right back, like I could even go anywhere. He'd taken my cell phone and zip-tied my wrists around a load bearing pole in the living room and stormed out. Came back twenty minutes later, and I heard the car still running in the garage.

"Get up," he said, and cut the zip tie. Yanked me by my hair and dragged me to the garage, where his car was smashed on the passenger side. He opened the door and threw me in, not caring that the pain was worse each time I moved. "We're going to the hospital. We were just in an accident. On Northwest Vine Street. The car came out of nowhere, hit us, and took off. It was a white SUV. Do you understand?"

The ache in my midsection blinded me, but I nodded yes, happy to at least be taken somewhere that would pump me full of painkillers and make sure, through an X-ray, that the broken bone didn't pierce any organs, which if I was being honest, I thought might've happened. I wanted to be fixed, and Drew was taking me to be fixed.

At the time, that's all I cared about.

Drew knew everyone, everywhere, and I was sure his hedge fund was laundering money for corporate bigwigs and politicians—he spent entirely too much time in DC. He'd be able to make the trip in less than ninety minutes from where we lived in Delaware. At the very least, he was trading inside information. Too many people kissed his ass.

He was able to cover his tracks too well.

So, nights alone usually left me with fear and paranoia. Now, safe with James, I know he's just doing what he has to do for work, and he'll rush home to see me, his wife, and Candy, his dog. We have such a great life, and I've changed everything about my outlook on the future, and I can't wait to tell him why.

"Come here, Candy," I say, and she ambles toward me, looking up at me with her huge brown eyes, so loving, so trusting. I pet her head and she purrs like a cat again, so cute. "Let's go into the office."

I stand and she follows me as I walk, knowing the routine. The heavy leather chair rolls back on the tile floor, and she plunks herself into the soft bed right next to the desk. I turn on the computer and do research for modernizing Romano's. I'm deep into ideas when I look down at my wedding ring, and I see that it needs a cleaning. In the upstairs bathroom, I have a jewelry cleaner, so I place it in the container and shake it up until it foams, then scrub it with the provided brush. It glows, and it looks perfect. I want it flawless and shiny for when I tell James, so I place it in my jewelry box. I'll put it on right before he gets home and break the news.

I have to practice my speech to James about the pregnancy.

I head back to the kitchen and get the bag with the recording device. After reading the instructions, I connect it to the WiFi and set up the account online. I put the receipt in James's monthly folder, where he stores all his expenses. He'll want this for the end of the year, I'm sure, to write it off as part of my business needs. Which it will be good for, too. I can take ideas in real time as I'm walking through a space. Certainly beats a notepad and pen, or being impersonal by typing notes into a phone the whole time.

I locate the record button, which turns it on and off, and yes, holding it in my hand I see what Ralph at the store meant, how the notes can be erased with the button right next to it. A design flaw indeed.

I push the button and speak.

"James, we made a baby!"

No. I stop the recording but don't erase it. I want to hear how they all sound out loud at once, but even I heard how silly that sounded as the words escaped my mouth. I press the button again.

I try every variation of *James, I'm pregnant*, even once using the term "with child." I roll my eyes at how it all sounds, and I thank God that I came up with this idea first. This is supposed to be a good thing and I'm already dumbing it down. My eyes drift to my flat stomach—there's a baby in there!—and I speak again.

"James, I think I've loved you from the moment I laid eyes on you, and you've made me happier than I've ever been." I pause, choking up, because I want to tell him everything, and it spills out. "I'm so sorry that I lied to you. My Social Security number is fake, and my last name is a variation to say the least. I've been running from my ex-husband, my past, my foster homes, my abuse, my addictions—but I don't want to run anymore. I want to come clean about my lies." Whatever, I can erase it later. "I want to, because I want my life with you to go forward without complications. It has to be this way, because it's not just me and you anymore." Dramatic pause, of course. "James, I'm pregnant. I can't wait for this new step in our lives, and I can't wait to hold our baby. And I want you to know that you've made me the happiest person who's ever walked the earth. You need to know that. I love you, and I'm already counting the seconds toward the amazing future we're going to have together. We're a family."

I play it back, and it sounds heartfelt, not rehearsed. But I continue speaking into it over and over. In some versions, I mention Maribel's help with Drew. In others, I say I want Evan to fix this for me legally. Others still, I say how happy I am that Trey gave him the promotion because the timing was perfect. I even say I'm thankful for Damon, because it led me to him. I go over it a few more times, listening to them all until the doorbell rings, and Candy stirs, lifting her head curiously, but not barking. I look at my watch, only six-thirty, and assume it's Gwen stopping over with Caleb, for one of our talk sessions. I place the device on the counter and head to the foyer. When I open the door, I'm floored at the coincidence of the person on the stoop.

I was just talking about you.

34

James

James was happy to leave the house. Robert secured permission from the courts for James to leave, so long as he went directly to Robert's office. Strange, leaving the house, since James had been quarantined via ankle bracelet for the last few days, but he got in his car and drove a few towns away. It felt good leaving, since the house had been the target for the prying eyes of Valley Lake. He didn't even go to his curb to collect the mail, for fear of having neighbors look at him like someone who committed a double homicide. As far as everyone in town knew, he was a dead man walking, his time of freedom winding down. On his ride, he didn't stop for coffee on the route in the off chance that someone recognized him from his picture online, his *mug shot*, and then the pitchforks would come out.

Plus, with what he was paying Robert, they should offer him coffee on arrival at the very least. Thank god for credit cards. If the truth wasn't cleared up soon, James feared he would have to take out a second mortgage. Which he wouldn't get. Being an industry professional, he knew he didn't have equity in the house to pull money out. Even worse, he had no strings to pull. Was his own bank going to help him? Trey? No way. Trey fired him.

Well, Trey was going to have to answer if James's freedom was on the line.

Robert did say earlier that he thought the charges could be dropped for Rosita's murder. They had nothing except that she was shot with the same caliber gun as the one they took from James's house. There was no proof he'd done anything to Tessa, and the extra DNA was still being analyzed. And the VLPD, that Solomon prick, made his point with James's arrest—his intention was to make James look like a homicidal maniac in case they couldn't find Jane Doe's killer. Or if Tessa turned up somewhere—no, James wouldn't think about that. Tessa was fine. He was going to find her.

Well done, Solomon, you asshole.

It took James about forty minutes to get to Robert's office, in a town that had a little bit more of a city feel than Valley Lake's Main Street. Robert's building was sleek, with a mirrored outside that reflected the bridge connecting the city in the background. Thankfully, the parking was underground. He took the ticket from the machine, happy there was no attendant who would possibly say "Hey, you look familiar, aren't you—" before stopping and shielding themselves from the vicious murderer they'd just come face-to-face with in a parking garage.

He parked far away from the elevator, on purpose, not wanting to run into anyone. He approached the seventh floor where Robert's firm was situated and felt the apprehension as soon as he opened the glass doors. Prying eyes from behind the receptionist's desk cut through him like a saber.

"Hi. I'm here for Robert Brown. James—"

"Yes, James Montgomery."

Her hair was red and cut into a short, straight bob just above her shoulders, and she wore thick black-framed glasses. Her lips were outlined a dark red to match her hair, and they didn't move from their straight line. No matter how many criminals she dealt with daily, James was sure this was her first double homicide in suburbia. *Guilty killer!*

She got up and walked around the desk and curled her finger, indicating he should follow her, so he did. She led him to Robert's office at the end of the hallway, behind another set of glass doors. James could see it was a huge corner office with a great view of the bridge and the water, but what concerned him was Robert's frantic stance. His sleeves were rolled up to his elbow, his usually sleek hair was out of place, and voice was raised at whoever he was talking to on the phone. His head snapped to their direction and he waved James in.

James turned around. "Thank—" Nope, no need for *thank you*, redhead was already gone. *Guilty killer!*

Robert pointed to the empty seat in front of his desk. His face flushed with frustration.

"I don't care!" He slammed the phone down and blew out a puff of air. "We have a problem, James. Rosita's body was missing an earring on her left lobe. A big emerald earring. And they just found it in your house. Your bedroom, to be specific."

What the— "Wait. What? Who? Who's in my house?"

"I got a courtesy call from the DA about executing another search warrant. Your phone is still busted so I couldn't get in touch with you and I knew you were on your way already. There was another anonymous tip, someone claiming to know about your affair with her, just like someone who said they saw you go to her house the night she was murdered."

One hundred percent impossible. Who was framing him? "This is insane, Robert. How are they allowed in my house?"

"I sent Evan over to let them in—you said he could be the point of contact. He's overseeing the whole thing."

James was panic-stricken. How were Rosita's belongings in his house? She was only there once, for his promotion party. And he'd seen her in those earrings after that. She always had those things on.

"Well, you were already arrested for her murder, but this is going to make the charges impossible to drop. Impossible!" He slams both hands down on his desk. "I don't know what we're going to do. I mean, the anonymous tips are all hearsay. But still. This isn't good. They might revoke your bail."

He was going to die in jail. For something he didn't do.

Time for the big guns.

"Look, I'm not accusing him of being a murderer, but I'll bet my last dollar I know who the father of that baby was. I wonder if—"

Like an angel on his shoulder knowing James was innocent, Robert's phone rang, and he lifted a finger to stop James's rant before he answered the phone.

"Robert Brown," he answered as he picked up the phone. "Oh, your timing couldn't be better. What did you find out?" Robert wrote something down on a notepad. "Got it. I have James Montgomery here right now. I'll find out." He slammed the phone down. "That was my guy who was getting information about the rent-a-car. Do you know anyone named Maribel Lopez?"

35

Tessa

When I pull the door back and my eyes adjust, I think they must be betraying me. I'm beyond stunned at the woman standing in front of me. She's tiny and afraid, dressed in all black, with her blond hair tucked inside a baseball cap.

"Maribel?" My voice catches in my throat, full of shock. "Oh my God, what are you doing here? How did you find me?"

"Can I come in?" Her eyes are rimmed red, so I know she's been crying. "Drew is here. He found you. We need to talk."

My carefully cultivated world spins out of orbit in front of me. *Drew is here. He found you.* The words, while spoken aloud, don't register immediately. Yet I nod, surely white as a ghost, and move away from the opening to let her in, and she shuffles past me inside. I stick my head out the door and look left to right to see if she's been followed. Someone—Drew—could be hiding anywhere at the end of the cul-de-sac. Hell, he could be in the bushes right outside the front door and launch an attack. I need to protect her, and myself.

I close the door slowly, quietly, like I'm keeping the whole meeting a secret.

I wish I made more noise and caused a ruckus, one that would inform the neighbors, because after I turn to her, I only remember pain.

Blackout.

When I wake, it's darker, but not proper nighttime so I assume I've only been out an hour. What happened? My head hurts. My hands are tied. How did—

"Welcome back, Tessa."

Maribel is sitting in front of me in the kitchen, a gun in her hand.

At the sight of the gun, my anxiety kicks in and the sweat starts to run down my back. A gun. Wait—a gun? Maribel. She's not on my side. What happened?

"Where's my dog?" Motherly instinct.

"The dog is fine. Locked in the office. I'm not a monster," she says, although that's exactly what she is. "But you're about to find out what I'm really capable of."

Fear hits my insides like a lightning strike, and the woman in front of me no longer looks the way she did the last time I saw her, months ago, when she told me she'd help me put Drew away. Now, she's dressed in monochrome black like a vigilante, pointing the cool steel barrel of the gun toward me.

"I don't understand." I struggle with the ropes. They're loose. "Let me out!"

As I writhe on the ground, she watches with a smile. "Really, Tessa, what are you going to do if you get out of the ropes? I have a fucking gun. You might want to think twice about trying to escape. You aren't in charge anymore. You never were."

"What are you talking about?"

She scratched the side of her head with the tip of the gun and I wonder for a hot second what I'll do if she accidentally blows her brains out right in my kitchen.

"You, Tessa. What's so fucking special about *you*?"

"I don't know what you mean. Why are you doing this? You were helping me!"

"I was never helping you, you pathetic bitch! How thick are you? Drew is mine, and he always will be."

"You can have him!" I shout. "I'm married to someone else! I don't want Drew!"

"Oh, maybe not. But Drew wants you. Hasn't stopped talking about you since the day you left. I had to tell him I was working with you, because I wanted him to know what a whore you really are. Jumped right into bed with this latest one, didn't you? For sure Drew would know I was better suited for him, but no, he wants his perfect life on paper back. The obeying wifey, who cooks his dinner and cleans his clothes and runs his errands and comes to business functions in designer dresses. Me? I'm his plaything on the side—he didn't let me slide into your spot the way I should've after you left. It should've been easy. Help you disappear, and he'd get over you. Didn't. Quite. Work. That. Way." She emphasizes her words.

"No," I say and shake my head. What she's saying doesn't land. "You helped me frame him."

She scoffs. "That's what I wanted you to think. That's why you were able to find the one article—so you could think I was on your side. I was hoping you'd tell me where you were so I could take care of this sooner. I'd never put Drew away. We love each other. And you, you idiot. You had previously told me you were going south, but on the phone, you said you were going out to the shore. Everyone knows that means New Jersey. How stupid are you? You didn't go far enough away. And that's a problem for me."

"Oh Maribel, no." She fell into the same trap I did. "No, he's going to do the same thing to you."

She laughs a hearty laugh. "To me? *Me?* I work at a hedge fund. I have an MBA. I'm not someone to be fucked with. But you? Shit, he told me all about you, you piece of shit. Fucked by foster daddies and shuffling from truck stop to truck stop? He knew what you were. A white trash waitress. A target. Someone who *could* be fucked with. So, he did."

"Don't you see what type of person that makes him?"

She waves the gun, and I wince.

"No, no, no, sweet, stupid Tessa. He acts like that to you, because that's all you deserve. I deserve better. I *command* better."

"I don't understand. I thought the cops had evidence against him?"

"Jesus, you're not listening to me. I never told the cops about the affair. I never put my grandmother's ring in your bedroom or planted a gun in his sock drawer or put the blood in his trunk. Yes, there was one casualty—his job. The firm looked at the original report as a distraction. After the initial brouhaha died down about you being missing, everyone just assumed you left. No biggie, right? Spouses leave all the time." The gun goes to her lips, as if she's deep in thought. "But no, Drew became obsessed with finding you. He's not used to losing. And our little plan stopped working for me. And as fate would have it, when we found you, I decided it was time to annihilate my problem once and for all."

She wasn't lying earlier. Drew knows where I am?

"D-Drew is here?" I know my voice is warbling.

"Our man fell into a bit of a funk with his name attached to a missing wife. Our An*drew* reinvented himself as Andy. Got a new job as CFO for a builder. Since I knew you were at the shore, he researched areas here that needed new shopping centers, so he could spend more time here. And wouldn't you know it, right here in this shit town in New Jersey, he saw you. Your wedding picture to Jason, right on his desk when they were having a meeting earlier this week about getting financing for that town center."

"James. His name is James." *James, my knight in shining armor. Please save me again.*

She rolled her eyes. "Like I give a fuck what his name is. Drew called me, all excited that he found you, and he was looking for a way to bring you back into his life. Our life. *My* life. I can't have that, Tessa. I can't."

"You're not listening, Maribel. I don't want him." My thumb slides under the knot. I can get out. I have to get out.

She shakes her head back and forth wildly. "But he wants you. No one will take him away from me. Not you, and not that other slut at the bank. He fucked her last night, you know. Rosita. Called me and bragged about it too."

For a hot second, I see her humanity, like she almost hears how ridiculous she sounds when she speaks out loud. But then, the wild-eyed beast is back, the one trying to get rid of me permanently. I try to reason with her on a human level. A woman's level.

"Maribel, please. Don't you see what type of man he is? He brags about cheating on you? Like you said, you're smart. You're beautiful. You can do so much better than an asshole like him."

She points the gun at me again. "Don't talk about him that way."

I look away. "It's okay, Maribel. I get it. You're obsessed with him. I was too, which is why I let him do what he did. He's a narcissist. You don't realize you're being manipulated. There's a better life out there. I found one. You can too."

"No. I need you gone." Then she nods, like she just made up the next sentence on the spot. "Yes, I need you gone, and Rosita too. I won't have him leave me for her either."

My eyes are closed, and it hits me. "Rosita? Are you—"

"Of course, she's next!" She waves the gun around in the air again. "You think I'm going to let her come between us?"

"Maribel, you're never going to get away with this."

"Sure I am. I had a great teacher." She taps the side of her head. "Once, someone told me it was a good idea to plant my grandmother's ring in her bedroom to prove an affair." Her eyes are digging into my brain and I know I'm fucked. "Of course, I pretended I did, and that Drew's influence kept it all under wraps, but the truth is, it's a brilliant ploy. I'll kill you and hide your body for a few days. I'll kill Rosita. I'm going to plant this gun in the house." She waves it around again, too casual, like water is going to spout out of the tip, not bullets. "I have my ways to get into your house again—trust me—and I'll plant something of hers in your bedroom. She's a climber. Fucked Drew, told him she's been fucking Trey too. Nice pillow talk, huh? She's a climber and a slut."

That can't be true. Trey loves Aleesha; I've seen them together. "Rosita isn't like that. You don't know her."

"*You* don't know her. Drew asked Rosita to steal your wedding picture from James's office so he could examine it and make sure it was really you. She's doing it tomorrow. She's going to take the thing right off the desk in the morning and give it to Drew later in the day when they have a meeting. She's helping him break you and James up, then she's going to take your husband's job, which she feels she should've gotten anyway. She's a horrible person. Don't defend her."

That's unfortunate, if true. But it doesn't mean she needs to die. "Please, don't hurt Rosita," I beg.

"I can make it look like James and Rosita were having an affair, and that he wanted to get rid of you both. I know where to put your blood, Tessa. I know how to frame James for both murders, so thanks for that. You're smarter than you look."

The plan was brilliant and, unfortunately, mine.

"You don't know what you're doing," I whisper. "Maribel, please. Please don't do this. Don't do it to James. He's a good man. I'll do anything, I'm begging you."

She rises and goes to the living room, just as I'm able to squirm out of the ropes. But it's not soon enough, and she comes back into the kitchen with my favorite pillow. The huge gold memory foam pillow that James and I leaned on together on the L-shaped couch while watching TV in the evenings. The bronze tassels swing as she positions the gun deep into it to muffle the sound.

I squeeze my eyes shut, waiting for the gun to go off.

Goodbye, James. Goodbye, unborn child. I never even got a chance to see his eyes light up when I told him. It's the one card I have left.

"Maribel, I'm pregnant. Please. Please don't."

She twitches and I immediately see the regret in her eyes when the gun goes off, likely by accident. Memory foam is everywhere. I'm on my back, the pain is searing, hot, and my first instinct is to try to rip the bullet out, but I'm no surgeon. I'm going to die. Worse than that, my baby is going to die. I'm sad, hopeless, and desperate.

I'm also enraged. Maternal instinct is real.

The guttural sound that comes out of my mouth stuns me, especially as I leap up and attack a shocked Maribel, who doesn't expect me to be free from the ropes. Before I know it, I'm on top of her, the gun goes flying backward, and my hands are around her throat, my nails digging into her neck. There's so much blood around us, I don't know whether I opened her throat or it's just pouring out of me at an alarming rate. She screams a high-pitched scream, as much as she can muster while I attempt to strangle the murderer out of her. Her arms flail around me, and she reaches out and plunges her finger into my wound.

I don't think the bullet hit anything vital, but it's in my shoulder and it fucking hurts when she presses into it. I falter.

Now she's standing above me, and punches me with all her might. I know how to take a punch, but she sends me backward and my head hits the side of the stone table. She scrambles for the gun and holds it on me.

"Fuck!" she screams, the gun slipping from her grip due to all the blood. "Don't fucking move."

I'm seeing stars anyway, Candy is barking from the office, and Maribel is pacing back and forth. "Fuck. Are you really pregnant?"

My shoulder is bleeding, and with all the torture I've been through in my life, this is the worst. "I am."

Her voice cracks. "Drew is going to kill me." She grabs her phone, yet she's not distracted enough for me to make a move, which is impossible anyway. The pain is like nothing I've ever experienced, and I'll pass out from dizziness if I attempt to stand.

She throws a rag from the kitchen at me. "Put pressure on it." She dials and panic comes out of her mouth when the call connects. "Drew, I need help."

Holy shit, she called that asshole. I only get one side of the conversation.

"I need help... I'm at Tessa's, and baby... baby, I shot her. No, she's alive. She's pregnant... she needs help, who's that guy you know up here?... Okay, I'll bring her... a new one? Where is it? ...No, I'll remember... fine, just fucking tell me where it is... yes, 899 Centaur Parkway... yes..." She looks at me. "I will." She disconnects the call and walks toward me. "Sorry about this. Well, not really."

Her arm goes up, and the gun smacks down on my head.

36

James

"Maribel Lopez? Never heard of her," James said. "Who the hell is Maribel Lopez?"

"That's who rented the car that was at your house. The woman who said her name was Bella Johnson."

"Well, who is she?"

"I have no idea. I'll get my PI on this." Robert sits at his huge mahogany desk and starts tapping into his computer. "This can break the case wide open. Once we find out who she is."

"Tessa never mentioned her either." James begged his brain to remember. Was that one of her sisters? No, he would've remembered that. Would he, though? Did she even tell him about her sisters? Twins. They were twins. Their names? Hell, could've been James and Candy for all he knew. Fuck! Why didn't he know more?

"Is there anything you need me here for right now?" James said, working through the revelation. "Now that I have a name, I want to go home and see if anything like that sticks out in any of her stuff. I want to know who this Maribel is, why she wanted to come to my house and interview me, and why she changed her name and lied. This woman obviously knew Tessa. And Tessa knew her," he said, thinking back to the very first night that

Solomon came. He said Tessa knew the person and let her in, because otherwise Candy would've attacked.

Candy.

She went crazy when he let Bella in the house. James thought she was just being protective over a stranger, but fuck, why did he not trust his judgment? Something was wrong. He knew it. God, he wanted to kick himself. Why did he let that strange woman tour his house?

Fuck! She killed Rosita. She planted the earring during the tour. That's how it got there! She called in the anonymous tip herself. Why would she kill Rosita?

He knew she had to have Tessa. *Why?*

Robert agreed that James should leave, so he did. Raced down to his car, paid the parking fee through the automaton, and sped home. A few times he thought he might get pulled over for speeding but didn't care, although he should've. Murder rap sheet, and all.

When he pulled into his driveway, Evan's car was there.

James was so thankful that, through all of this, he had Evan every step of the way. Friends to the end. Inside, Evan was on the phone, Candy at his feet. His eyebrows rose when James walked in early from his meeting with Robert.

"James, I got here as soon as Robert called me. They found—"

"Evan." James cut him off. "Thanks, man. Thanks for coming so quickly." Bro hug. Pat, pat. Things were looking up. "The fake reporter. Robert just got a call. The woman who rented the car was named Maribel Lopez."

"I know. He texted me," Evan said. "Who the hell is that?"

"I have no idea." James looked around his home, in disarray again from the executed search warrant. "She planted that earring. I know it. I just have to find out how Tessa knew her."

"I'm here. Whatever you need."

And James knew that and was so grateful that his best friend of twenty-five years never faltered. He wished Tessa had someone like him in her life. At any point.

Unless this Maribel was always there, a wolf in sheep's clothing.

Evan left for a meeting, so James and Candy were alone in the house again. James was beside himself when he entered the office. It was in complete disarray, with papers strewn everywhere. He needed to start the cleaning-up process somewhere, and the first thing he grabbed was his monthly expense folder. A receipt fell out, one that he didn't remember.

It was from last Thursday. The day Tessa went missing.

It was for about a hundred and twenty dollars, and it was from the electronics store in town. After a close inspection, James pocketed the receipt and got in the car. Fuck the ankle bracelet—let them come and get him. Speeding down the driveway, the monitor vibrated the second he left his property. He didn't have long. It took him three minutes to get to town, and like God wanted him to solve the mystery, there was a parking spot on Main Street right in front of the electronics store. He parked and ran in, not knowing how much time he had until the cops hauled his ass back to prison for leaving his home.

"Good morning, how can I help you?" the skinny, nerdy kid asked, then looked at him with narrow eyes. "Hey, aren't you—"

"Yes, I'm James Montgomery. Yes, my wife is missing, and yes, they've accused me of murdering my coworker." Nothing like getting the facts out of the way. They both knew exactly who he was. "I found something that can help me, and I need your help finding my wife. And in clearing my name." He didn't have time for pleasantries and small talk.

The kid's eyes shifted nervously, and he took a few slow steps backward and put up his hands defensively. "I—I don't know what you're looking for," he stuttered.

"This." James held up the receipt. "My wife was in here the day she went missing. What did she buy?"

"I'm—I'm s-s-sorry, I can't help you." The kid looked like he was about to shit his pants.

James softened and looked at his name tag. "Look, Ralph. I didn't kill anyone. I have to find her. I think this might help me discover what happened. Please, can you look it up?" James was desperate. "Please? Her name was Tessa. About five-six, dark hair. Beautiful." He said it with tears in his eyes.

"Right. I remember," Ralph said. He pointed to the other end of the store. "She wanted one of those."

James swiveled his head to the wall, and there was a display of recording devices lined up like toy soldiers. He walked over and his eyes scanned top to bottom.

"What are these? Which one? Why?" He asked the questions like Ralph knew Tessa personally.

Ralph moved cautiously, and his index finger shifted over the wall until he found it. "This one. This is what she bought."

James knew it instantly. It was the same device Bella Johnson—Maribel Lopez—used for the interview.

It was Tessa's. James knew it. This Maribel character had Tessa.

"Did she say why she wanted it?"

"No. She asked to record stuff. I remember commenting that she didn't have an iPhone."

James was perplexed. What would Tessa want to record?

"Is there anything else you remember?" James's head swung to the door, looking for the inevitable blinking lights. Ticktock. "Please. I need to find my wife. I think I know who has her. Her life is probably at stake, along with my freedom. And I need to know where she is. What did she record?"

"I don't know." Ralph seemed somewhat on his side now. "But if she set it up, it should be in the Moon."

"The Moon?" Was this kid on crack?

"Yeah, the Moon." He put on his salesman hat, and his voice changed. "This particular device has a design flaw, where the record and delete button are close together. See?" He pointed at it through the plastic, and James remembered Bella/Maribel mentioning the same thing. "So, if she set up the account, it backed up to the Moon. It's the low-rent version of the iPhone iCloud."

Bingo! "You're telling me there could be a recording of what she was doing that day?"

"Yes. If she set up the account online."

His desperation came back tenfold. "Can you please, please find out which one she got from this receipt? Does it have a PIN or anything? How can I access it?"

"You'd have to look on the computer and sign in. It asks for a password when you set it up. It needs to be a combination of capital letters and lowercase letters and numbers and one symbol. Eight digits total."

James was fucked, and he knew it. He'd never be able to figure that out.

And then, Ralph saved him.

"There's a specific number associated with the one she bought. We have to scan the back and they're all different. If you're really innocent, then bring it to the police. They should be able to get a warrant to search it."

"Ralph, I think I love you. Can you please give me that number?"

He looked unsure. "They can come in and get it if they have a warrant."

James's face fell, and tears brimmed his lids. "I don't know how long my wife has, and I'm trying to prove my innocence. Please!"

James watched as Ralph tossed the idea around in his brain like a ping-pong ball, then game, set, match. "Okay. Hang on."

As Ralph wrote down the info, it started. The sirens blared, first low, then louder as they got closer. They were coming for him.

"Ralph, please hurry. They're coming. I need you to show this to them. Please."

A screech stopped the car diagonal in front of the door, and Solomon stepped out and whipped open the door.

"Well, well," Solomon said to James, while dangling handcuffs from his forefinger. "Just the person I wanted to see. Put your arms behind your back, Mr. Montgomery."

James's eyes pleaded with Ralph, and he finally pushed a piece of paper toward him on the counter.

"I don't have time for this, Solomon." James held up the receipt and the slip of paper where Ralph had the device's access number. "I think there's something you should see."

37

Tessa

I don't know how long I've been out, but when I open my eyes, I'm in a strange bedroom. Blue walls, frilly white curtains, ugly paintings you'd see in a cheap hotel, and I'm under a comforter with a blue and white gingham pattern. There's a window to my left—it's evening. Dusk. I can tell the way the light moves into the room. I'm in pain everywhere—my head, my shoulder, my arm—fuck. I'm attached to an IV.

My baby.

"Hello?" My voice is raspy, like I haven't eaten or drunk anything in a week. I may not have. "Is anyone there?"

A light flips on to my right. "Well, hello there, Tessa."

I don't need to look—I recognize the voice and my stomach turns inside out. I press my eyes shut, willing him to go away. It's just a nightmare.

"You gave us quite the scare, darling." Drew stands and walks to the bed, then sits on the edge, too close to me and a tear falls down my cheek. "I've had you sedated for a few days."

"Where am I?" Where's James?

"Shh, shh, my darling." His finger touches my lips, and I know I don't have the strength to bite him. "Don't you worry. You're fine. The baby is fine. You've been very well taken care of." He motions to the machinery in the room. There's a big contraption that's beeping, with squiggly lines of different colors and lots of medical bags attached to wires on hooks. If I didn't know any better, I'd think I was in the hospital.

Oh, God. How does he know about the baby?

Maribel.

"Where's Maribel? She did this."

"I know, I know. She brought you to me because she knew Jack could get here and fix you up. You remember Dr. Kelly, I presume? He removed the bullet. Got you on antibiotics. Kept you asleep to heal."

Jack Kelly is a less-than-scrupulous doctor that Drew knows from Philadelphia, one who will give him medical-grade painkillers if he wants to get high, or, on occasion, if I needed them after a beating. Or if I needed to be stitched up and not have any questions asked. Drew knows someone horrible and immoral from every walk of life.

"I remember Jack" is all I say.

"Jack pulled through and got his ass up here when I told him it was an emergency. Don't worry, you're safe. All the tests were done while you were sleeping."

Up here. I'm still near my house. "What tests? How long was I sleeping?"

"Well, tests on our baby, of course. You remember that's the only thing I *can't* do? But I own you, and now, this baby. Little baby Grant is going to be just fine. I hope it's a girl. You know I always wanted a little girl."

His smile is evil, and horror seeps through my bones as I get a chill, which makes me shiver noticeably, and he pulls that ugly comforter farther up to my neck. If Drew thinks for one second that he's getting his hands on my baby, I—oh God, I'll what? What can I really do? He's kept me housebound and cut off from the world before and he'll do it again.

"Where am I?"

"I said you're safe." This time, the smile is gone, his voice is deeper and he's not messing around. He's not going to let me go.

James. I have to get out of here.

I move, just for comfort reasons, but the pain is everywhere. I try to wiggle my toes to see if I still have feeling in my legs, which I do, but they're like wet spaghetti right now. I can't make a run for it. I don't even know how long it's been since I've moved.

He did say my baby was safe. My baby, with my husband James. My everything. Drew has taken away so much; I won't let him take this too. I need to find out where I am, how long I've been here, where Maribel is, and what his plan is.

So I do the unthinkable. I survive, because that's who I am in my bones. A survivor. I begin flexing the muscles in my legs and rotating my ankles.

I turn to him, and smile.

"Are you going to take me home?"

Now his disgusting hand is on my face, the backs of his fingers touching my cheek. He smiles back.

Then he backhands me. Hard. I let my head flop to the side. He prefers me submissive.

"Take you home? Of course you're coming home with me as soon as we can get you out of this bed. Which, now that you're awake, seems like it could be soon. You were out for five days. I wanted you to heal without complications. Make sure the baby was okay. While I took care of everything else."

"What else? What else did you do for me, baby?"

He's rubbing my leg, and I face him and force a smile again, even with my cheek throbbing. I know exactly where every fingerprint will be and how it will look. I feel the bile crawling up my throat, but I push it back down when he begins to talk.

"Maribel played along for the first few days, pretending she wanted you to heal too. But I know how she gets." He laughs and blows a breath out of his mouth. "Man, she was a jealous one. She was thrilled when you left me. But you're mine. That's what no one understands. I own you." His eyes are wild, possessed. Obsessed with me. "I know what she's capable of, after she killed Rosita a few days ago. Sure, setting up your man for that was par for the course, but she really killed Rosita because I fucked her. Maribel wouldn't be able to stand the fact that you're in my life again. That we're a family. I couldn't take a chance with her around you anymore."

Oh, God. So Maribel did kill Rosita, just like she said she would. Oh no. Is James safe? Where is he?

Instead, I play good wifey. Compliant. "I'm glad you're all mine again. I knew about your affair, and it hurt so much. But you're the man, and you provided for me. Who was I to really say anything?" I gulp. "Where is Maribel now?"

He rubs his hand over the back of his neck. "I put her body in the basement. This is an Airbnb rental just outside of the town where you played house with that James character. She won't hurt you anymore."

He killed Maribel. He's going to drag me back to Delaware and keep me locked away and raise my baby as his own.

No way.

I nod at him. "Thank you for doing that. For killing her, to protect me. I always knew you loved me."

He rushes over to the bed and I involuntarily wince, thinking he's going to punch me again, but instead he pulls the cover off me and forces me to stand. He hugs me, hard, and if I didn't know any better, I'd actually think he cares.

I know better.

The wires from the IV twist and pull on my skin. "Ouch. Careful," I say, and point to it. I'm standing on my own two legs. I can do this. "I'm hungry. Is there food here? Can I make you something?"

After every beating, after every time he patched me up and saved me from himself, I was still expected to cater to him. Today should be no different.

"There's food in the kitchen."

I take a step to make sure I can, and I'm able to. I have to survive. "Can we take this out?" I hold my hand up to him, the one with the needle in it. "You were always gentle with me. Can you do it?"

You son of a bitch.

I hate the feeling of the IV being dragged out, and I get queasy but I remember the big picture. Now is not the time for nausea.

I immediately grab the heavy glass lamp from the nightstand and hit him as hard as I can on the head, shattering it.

He grunts and slams into the wall. Unfortunately, I know I haven't killed him—I've only pissed him off. I have to get away from him.

I run.

38

James

Solomon wasn't amused at James playing detective, invest-igator, cop, judge, and jury better than he did himself. James sat alone in the cold room in the police station, with the cuffs pinched around his wrists. That jerk wouldn't even take them off as he waited for Robert at the Valley Lake Police Department building. And he'd been there for almost two hours.

Still. The fact that he wasn't wearing orange and in county jail already had to mean something, right?

The whole ride back to the station, James begged for his freedom, begged Solomon to listen to him as he tossed out his discoveries about possibly having inform-ation on what happened to Tessa, about Maribel, Bella, the recording device, the Moon. Solomon answered him by lighting a cigarette in the patrol car and then smiling for the cameras as he dragged the murderer inside the police station. The cameras that were likely there because Solomon called them himself. The small-town cop got to have his name displayed everywhere for the past week. James was sure he'd be using this leverage to run for mayor, maybe even something bigger. *Local portly detective catches bad, bad man.*

Jerk-off.

The screech of the door revealed a smiling Robert and a tight-lipped, downtrodden, defeated Solomon entering the room. Prick.

"Well, Mr. Montgomery," Solomon started after throwing some papers on the table, "some new information has come to light."

"I bet," James said under his breath, knowing full well those were the last words Solomon wanted to utter. He wanted his arrest. He wanted his initial accusation to be correct. James glanced at Robert and held his wrists in the air. "Is this legal?" His head whipped to Solomon. "Can you get these fucking cuffs off?"

Solomon smarted at being spoken to in that fashion but strode over and unlocked the handcuffs. James immediately rubbed his wrists, then his face, and looked again at Robert. "What's going on?"

Robert nodded in Solomon's direction. "My guy talked to him. I told him I was there during the interview with Maribel. Ralph from the electronics store gave them the information. They worked with the company. They—they have a recording, James. From last Thursday."

Jae swallowed; his eyes were wide. "And? What was on the recording?"

Robert and Solomon looked at each other, but Solomon took the reins this time. "There's a lead. An address. We're getting a tactical unit together. They're coordinating now, but they should be dispatched in the next fifteen minutes."

James stood. "I'm coming."

"No, Mr. Montgomery, you're not."

James looked at Robert. Pleading.

"Detective Solomon, I do believe you have to let my client go at this time," Robert said.

Solomon resigned, and nodded. "We're going to drop the charges, Mr. Montgomery. You're free to go."

James thanked Robert and Robert gave him a signal with his eyes. James read it as *hurry up and get up and let's go now*. So he did.

Robert walked swiftly to the back door of the station and James had to speed walk to keep up. "Robert, where is she? Is she okay? Is she alive? Who has her?"

Robert put a finger to his lips. "Let's just get you out safely back here. The reporters are out front."

"I don't care about that. I care about Tessa. What's going on?"

Robert pushed on the door and pulled right to the curb was Evan's car. "Get in the front," Robert said. James did as he was asked, and Robert got into the back seat. "I have a transcript of the recording."

"Give it to me," James demanded.

"No. Not yet. I—I don't want you to see it yet."

Tears sprang to James's eyes. It wasn't good news. What was on the recording that Robert didn't want him to hear? "Is she dead? Oh God, is she dead?" He looked at Evan, whose face was as crestfallen as James's felt. "Please, tell me."

Robert took a deep breath. "I don't know, James. I know she was shot—"

"Oh my God!" James exclaimed as pictures of her beautiful, smiling face flashed through his head. Unfortunately, those images were followed by Jane Doe on the table. Cut up, tortured, and shot. Of Rosita shot.

"She might be okay. Maribel took Tessa somewhere—they knew each other. I have the address where she might be. This is where they're sending the tactical unit." He looked at Evan. "It was 899 Centaur Parkway."

Evan plugged it into the navigation and turned to James. "We can beat them there. Ready?"

Robert held up a hand. "I don't want to be disbarred. I can't go. If anyone asks, you saw the address on the papers Solomon threw on the table. Now go."

"Robert, I don't know what to say," Evan said, and they did their little finger-gun secret handshake again. "We'll never be able to thank you enough."

James yanked on Robert's suit jacket and actually hugged the man from the front seat, then turned to a smiling Evan. "It's time."

Robert exited the car, and Evan sped away.

39

Tessa

I open the bedroom door and run.

"You fucking bitch!" Drew screams behind me.

There's a hallway. Stairs.

I almost make it, and then my hair is yanked from behind. I fall to the ground and now I'm being dragged backward as my noodle legs fight for stability against the hardwood floor. He lets go unexpectedly and my head clunks onto the floor. Then he grabs my injured arm and the pain from the bullet wound makes me go limp as he pulls me back into the bedroom.

Drew grunts and lifts a leg, about to stomp on me and I instinctively clutch my abdomen. Don't you dare hurt this baby. I *will* fucking kill you.

He puts his leg down. This asshole really thinks this baby is going to be his.

But he still doesn't give a shit about me, evidenced by how he leans down and punches my face. Twice. Jesus, between Damon's punch and this one may have been the longest I've gone without being hit in two decades, and the pain isn't familiar anymore.

I've grown accustomed to being loved.

I'm on the floor, spitting blood. Weak. Drew puts his hand on his head and paces.

"You just never fucking learn, do you?" he says.

Oh, I've learned a thing or two, you psychotic asshole. Like when I dropped a wine glass and you picked up a shard—and cut me with it, so I would "learn" not to break things.

Thank you for that, darling husband of mine.

The next time he turns to pace away from me, I grab a piece of the shattered lamp and I stab it right into his Achilles.

The sound that emits from his mouth is animalistic and he drops to the ground and grasps his ankle. He's still wailing in pain as I crawl on the rest of the broken glass, cutting freedom into my palms as I head toward the door. I stand as he reaches for me, a last desperate attempt to keep me in his clutches.

I find the stairs and rush down. There's a front door. I open it and I can't believe my eyes.

Two men are running up the lawn. I squint, and I see Evan. And the other is James, shouting my name.

Is this a dream? My bloody arms are outstretched, reaching for him. I scream his name for help, because I'm free.

I'm free.

I'm about to run toward him but seeing James caused me to let my guard down, and I don't hear Drew drum down the stairs behind me. He's bigger and stronger than I am. I should've known it was going to take more than a shard of glass to take him down, and he grabs my hair again. Now I feel the familiar touch of a gun barrel at my temple.

James and Evan stop cold. James's face is twisted.

"Andy?" he says. "Andy, what are you doing to my wife?"

Right. That's what Maribel told me. James doesn't know yet, that the person he was working with is Drew. My abusive ex-husband.

"Get back!" Drew shouts. "I'll shoot her!"

"He's my husband, James," I say. "The one I was running from."

Tears are running down my face as James takes a step closer, and in a flash, the gun is pointed at him instead.

No. Not James. I stop struggling beneath Drew's arm. I'll go with you, Asshole. Just don't hurt James.

James is a mixture of relief and confusion and rage. His hands are up defensively, as are Evan's. James doesn't take his eyes off me.

"It's okay, Tessa. It's over. They know. They're on their way," he says with a nod. "He's not getting away with this."

And then I see the black vans speeding over from a distance, and the best feeling I've ever had washes over me as Drew loosens his grip. He knows he lost.

He lets me go.

I run to James and collapse in his arms. "You saved me," I say. "Again."

He holds my face and it doesn't hurt, and he kisses my lips despite the blood. "I never stopped looking. I told you I'd always protect you."

It's the best movie ending I've ever seen.

Until the gun goes off behind me.

40

James

It was weeks later, on a Monday morning, and James was officially a free man. Exonerated. All charges dropped. Ralph from the electronics store was right. The record button was in an awkward spot, and Tessa forgot to turn it off when Maribel showed up at the house. Maribel then stole the device and erased everything from that evening, but she didn't know about the Moon backup. The entire incident, along with Maribel's explanation on who she was, and what she was going to do to Rosita, was on there. So was the interview she did with James as Bella Johnson. Uploaded to the Moon.

Evidence. The whole thing was open and shut.

Between the recording, Tessa's testimony, Maribel's body in that basement, and Andrew Grant's decision to take his own life by eating the barrel of that gun instead of facing what was coming to him, James was free. So was Tessa. Finally.

Of course, Trey got out unscathed. Rosita's being pregnant was attributed to some boyfriend no one knew of, and James decided not to let the cat out of the bag. There was no reason to hurt Trey's wife, Aleesha. Even Jane Doe was identified in the interim. She was from out of state, and they arrested her boyfriend in connection with her murder.

The paperwork was filed and expedited, and Tessa's current ID was legal. For the next few days, anyway.

"You ready?" he asked her as he finished his coffee from his favorite mug.

World's Greatest Dad.

"Yeah, I think I have everything," she said. "Everything I could find, anyway."

She'd been working hard on the nursery, all grays and yellows—daffodils—with pops of pink and blue. They didn't know the sex of the baby yet and they planned to keep it a surprise.

She stood by the door with a small bag over her shoulder. James washed out the mug at the sink, then set it on the shelf to dry while they were away. His bags were already packed and in the trunk. He hooked Candy up to the leash.

"Come on, girl. You want to go visit Grandma and Grandpa?"

Her butt wiggled, and they closed the door to their home behind them. They were driving down to Florida so James could formally introduce Tessa to his parents. Evan and his parents, and Hobart and Pearl, would follow in a few days.

And they would be the only witnesses on the beach, with the pastor, when she legally became Tessa Montgomery.

Acknowledgments

So many people have lifted me on this journey, so I'm going to gush. The first and most important is Anne Tibbets, my fantastic agent, whose hard work, fierce loyalty, dedication, and friendship have propelled my dreams into a reality. Thank you for taking a chance on me, and by giving me the freedom to write what I want to write without hovering. I feel so lucky every day that you're my agent. I'm crossing my fingers for a long and prosperous career for both of us, together.

Thank you to Luisa Smith, my beyond brilliant editor, for picking this book up, dusting it off, knocking it around, shining it up, and making it great. You've been a dream to work with! I look forward to taking your direction in the future, with a smile. To the rest of the team at Scarlet—thank you to my publishers Charles Perry, Otto Penzler, and Jake Shapiro in publicity for getting this book into the hands of so many wonderful readers. And to the creative team who developed my cover—excellent job!

Barbara Poelle. I still owe you that martini. Okay, three.

Vanessa Lillie, I wouldn't be here without you. You're not only a talented author and go-getter, but you're someone I'll always be proud to call a friend. I'd also like to shout out amazingly talented authors Jennifer Pashley, Danielle Girard, Lynne Constantine, and Wendy Walker.

Thank you for everything you've done for the newbie. And to my additional critique partners and great authors, Mary Keliikoa and Dr. Jessica Payne.

My beautiful and amazing cousins Victoria Overpeck and Nicole Slininger: blood made us family, we made us friends. And special thanks to my good friends Krista Tully Nelson, Wendy Crimmins, and Sue Principato for your encouragement.

Other amazing support has come from Steve Viner, Katerina Ermolin and Crystal Smalls-Wright. Utmost thanks to IG Book Blogger @Ludwigreads—putting me on a list of 2021 anticipated thrillers with bestselling authors I idolize made me feel like I finally made it. Thanks to Marc Bonagura and everyone in his Brookdale Spring '17 Creative Writing class, especially my poodle, Matthew Mazzucca.

Chris Mormando—you keep acting, I'll keep writing. I'm convinced these paths will cross again someday. And I have to mention my cheer section of close friends. Jami Hooker, Tara Feehan, Keri Feeney, Carolyn Skoczek, Meghan Kretz, Diana O'Malley, Connie Hirsch, Morgan Mann, and of course, Tracey Ramponi, who is watching over all of us from heaven. And to my newest friend Lauren Mikucki who became one of my closest... we'll always have Huddy's.

Old friends are the best friends, so special shout out to Suzanne Cohen, Jillian Jaques, Tara Reilly, Jennifer Higgins, Ginny Kotler, Janina Vitenas, Stacey Figueroa, and Gina Bonczek. I've known you all for multiple decades and your continued friendship and support mean the world to me.

Of course, one stands out in particular. My BFF, my ride-or-die since I was four years old. The one who has been there for every single thing in my life, no matter distance or obstacles, the one who always drops everything when I need her: Ann Marie DePaulis, you are the best friend anybody could ever ask for, you always have been, and you will be when we're drinking coffee and eating cheesecake like the Golden Girls we always said we'd be.

The rest of my family—my sister Kristin Homrighausen, my goddaughter Bethany Walter, Angela and Paul Sala, Susan and Gary Claypool, and the best decisions my cousins ever made, Jim Overpeck and Mike Slininger. This is also for my grandparents in heaven, John and Helen Gallo.

My parents, Hank and Geri Sbordone. Where do I start, where do I end? You've both always been there for me with unconditional love and support, encouraging me to live how I wanted to live, and you allowed me to spread my wings to make my own dreams come true. I am where I am because of you.

To my husband and doggie-daddy John: when you say, "I didn't do anything, you did it," it's much more than that. When life threw me a curveball, you swept in and saved the day, giving me the ability and time to make a go of this whole author thing. A lot of people aren't that lucky. I'm among the luckiest to live forever with you. In fifty years, you'll still be the one I run to, the one I belong to, and the one I want for life. I love you (and Cosmo, too!).

And finally, to the readers: Thank you for taking a chance on a debut author. I hope I've entertained you and will continue to do so for years to come.